I0687477

Loveland

by

Andrea Downing

This is a work of fiction. Names, characters, places, and incidents are either the product of the author's imagination or are used fictitiously, and any resemblance to actual persons living or dead, business establishments, events, or locales, is entirely coincidental.

Loveland

COPYRIGHT © 2012 by Andrea Downing

All rights reserved. No part of this book may be used or reproduced in any manner whatsoever without written permission of the author or The Wild Rose Press, Inc. except in the case of brief quotations embodied in critical articles or reviews.
Contact Information: info@thewildrosepress.com

Cover Art by *Debby Taylor*

The Wild Rose Press, Inc.
PO Box 708
Adams Basin, NY 14410-0708
Visit us at www.thewildrosepress.com

Publishing History
First Cactus Rose Edition, 2012
Print ISBN 978-1-61217-323-8
Digital ISBN 978-1-61217-324-5

Published in the United States of America

She sat on a stool and pulled off first one boot, then the other and kicked them aside, then she stood and put her leg on the stool to roll down her stockings one by one. He marveled at her wantonness, her lack of propriety. "Alex, stop," he said gently putting his hand on hers. "Stop. You know..." But he was lost. She took his face in her hands and pulled him to her, kissing him so any resistance he had had was now shattered. His heart beat faster at the sweetness of her mouth, the softness of her tongue, the lack of air as they sought each other. His hands moved over her feeling the outline of her body, knowing its curves, its gentleness, its yielding. "Are you sure?" he asked at last.

"I want you so much, Jesse, I want you so much, I'm not going to wait three years. And if...if anything happens, so what? We'll get married, that'll be it."

"Yes, but Alex, you can't—I mean it'd be a 'shotgun' wedding, it's not how—"

"Ssh," she whispered. She put her finger to his mouth and then turned for him to unhook her gown. He ran his hands gently down her exposed back, feeling each scar, then kissed her neck.

"You have nothing on under..."

"It's how the gown is made. Monsieur Worth builds the undergarments into the gown." Her voice was at barely a whisper, a tremor showing her nerves. She turned and still held the gown up to her, then, looking at Jesse, let it drop to the floor.

Praise for Andrea Downing

"Downing has deftly created not only an adventurous story but she has painted characters who surprise and delight at every turn. A love story, yes, but also an authentic tale of the west in its glory days."

~*Velda Brotherton, author of Stone Heart's Woman*

Dedication

For Cristal, who believes anything is possible.

Acknowledgements

Several people have been particularly encouraging with their kind words. My thanks to Lindi Bilgorri, Sue Meek, Patricia Tober and Dee Thomas for their friendship.

I am grateful to Cindy Davis, my editor, for her patient support—and sense of humor. And to Charles Wachtel for his sage advice.

Finally, I am greatly indebted to my daughter, Cristal Downing, for giving up her vacation time to accompany me on a research trip to the Loveland/Greeley/Fort Collins area and for doing all the driving so I was able to take copious notes and enjoy the scenery. She was also kind enough to go with me to the Pawnee National Grasslands and to visit Cheyenne, WY, so I could stand on the site of the Cheyenne Club, and patient enough to put up with several days of my Country and Western music playing in the car and hotel room. Love you, darlin'.

March 2nd, 1881

The clamor started at ten o'clock when all the men were in their bunks. Piercing the chill night air and hanging in the wind like tattered shrouds on the trees, the screams of twelve-year-old Lady Alexandra Calthorpe were frenzied, wild and uncontrolled.

"Jesse!" Alex cried, hoping her best friend among the punchers might hear. "Jesse!"

"Alexandra, please, please," begged her governess, Madame Helene. She tried to control her own emotions so as to comfort her charge while doing what must be done. "We must go. You've always known we must go!"

"Tom!" Alex screamed for the ranch foreman who had been almost a surrogate father. "Jesse!" she tried once more.

"Alex!" Her uncle's voice was more harsh than he intended, but Oliver Calthorpe had little say in the demands of his brother Frederic, Duke of Faringdon—Lady Alex must now be returned to England.

"Cal!" Alex cried, hoping her other friend might be there. "Jesse!"

The two cowboys rose from their bunks and came out half-dressed, guns in their hands, to find Tom Yost, their foreman, standing by the office ready to stop them.

"What the hell," said Jesse. "What's going on?"

"She's leaving," answered Tom. "They're taking Alex for the midnight train to New York. There's nothing you can do." His voice was flat and cold, but his heart was breaking. He thought back on the four years Lady Alex had spent at the ranch, the four years he had watched her grow and blossom from a shy young girl hardly able to talk with the punchers to someone who embraced life on the ranch, lived it to the fullest.

"What're you talkin' about? She didn't even say good-bye. She can't be leavin'," said Cal, already feeling her loss.

"Calthorpe thought it would be far less painful for her to just go. If she knew in advance, she might have tried to run away."

Jesse took a step to go past Tom but the older man held him back. "It's best this way, Jess. She would have been hysterical for days if she'd had to say good-byes."

"And she's not now?" Anger heated Jesse as he shrugged off Tom's hand. They stood some moments listening to the screams as more of the men came out. "Hell, Tom. How could you? How could *Madame*?"

"I discussed it with Madame. She was in tears too but felt there was no other choice." Tom's voice was so raw Jesse looked at him long and hard only to realize they all felt the same pain.

"Does Annie know?"

"No. I'll have to tell her."

"I can't stand this." Cal started to push past Tom. But the carriage was gone now and there on the steps to the great house was only the faithful maid, Rose, standing there sobbing, left to console.

Part One: 1886

Chapter One

When Jesse Makepeace got to the station on that April morning, the Express from New York had already arrived. The one passenger remaining on the platform was a young woman arguing with the porter.

"Oh, for heaven's sake," she said. "Please don't throw those things about. That's my easel, and it's fairly fragile. Oh, look, please take care!"

She stood there helpless. Well-dressed in a pink wool suit with a hat and gloves, she reminded him of a little bird, fluttering as it learned to fly. He stood fascinated, her delicate beauty enthralling him. And then, hearing the English accent, he remembered why he was there.

"'Scuse me ma'am, would you be lookin' for someone from the Faringdon?"

She turned to him, and a smile like the sun coming up on the best summer day spread across her face. "Hello, Jesse." She got up on tiptoes and gave him a quick peck on the cheek.

His fingers went to his face where she had kissed him. She had her hands resting loosely on his arms and her eyes held his.

"*Alex?*"

She laughed and smiled. "Who did you think it was?"

"You're all growed up!"

"Well, that's what happens to little girls." Her eyes were still locked with his. "Didn't Oliver or Tom

3

tell you to expect me?"

"No, I… Tom said there'd be two European ladies. He didn't say anything else. It's obvious he's played a joke on me! Where's Madame?"

"Oh, Jess," she replied at last letting him go. "She *died*. She just…well, one evening she was fine and the next morning she was just *gone*."

"You came out all alone? On the train?"

"Yes. Look," she said, now taking control, "can we go? We've got two hours to catch up and I'm so anxious to get home and all. Can we just load up and go? We'll talk on the way."

"Look, Lady Alex—"

"It was Alex a minute ago. It's still me, Jess."

It was her—and yet it wasn't. Half-woman, half-child—he was confused by the feelings he had, which he felt were almost obscene. She must be seventeen now, he figured; the five years back in England would have changed her, made her a lady instead of the wild young girl who had ridden in her brother's castoff jodhpurs and her uncle's rolled-up shirts, looking for all the world like some strange child outlaw. Yet he wasn't reluctant to give in. "All right. Alex then. There won't be room for all this. We'll have to send someone back with a wagon for some of it."

"It's all right. We'll take the easel and the paint box, please, and my rifles. The clothes can wait. If we can fit one bag—"

"These are light rifles." He lifted one from its scabbard and hefted the weight of it in his hand.

"Purdys. They're made to order, so they're made for my strength."

"Must cost a bit." When she didn't respond, he continued, "Been doin' a bit of huntin' then, have you?"

"They were a present from my brother David for the shooting season. I think I've used them maybe once, if you must know. But here, well, I thought they might be sensible to bring."

He looked at her, stopped himself from commenting, and loaded the buggy as best he could.

They started out in silence still finding their footing with one another. Jesse was trying desperately to reconcile his bewildered feelings for the girl sitting next to him with the memories of the child who had left over five years ago. "So what happened to Madame Helene?" he asked at long last.

"Oh, goodness. It was awful. I mean, everything was fine, she was her usual self on the voyage over and everything. We had an appointment to meet with Jonathon Sturgis who is the dealer at New York Fine Arts."

"So you're painting now?"

"Yes, it seems to be the one possible way I have of making any money, short of becoming a governess myself, which I think I'd be rather unsuited for, don't you?"

Jesse laughed. "Well, not the Alex I know maybe." He looked across at her as he drove to see if she was all right with his comment. "What do you need money for, anyway, Alex? I thought—"

"You thought I would go from my father to my uncle to my brother to a husband, and everyone would be just fine and dandy, paying for me all my life. Is that it?" She sounded a bit piqued. "I thought you knew me better than that, Jesse."

"I only meant—" He stopped. This was a new Alex and he didn't want to get off on the wrong foot. "So what happened to Madame?"

"We had the meeting—which went well, by the way, thank for you asking," she added acerbically.

"You didn't give me a chance. You're telling me 'bout Madame."

"Yes. Sorry. Sorry," she repeated. "Oh, poor dear Helene. I suppose I'm just wound up after the whole ordeal." She rubbed her forehead and stole a look at him.

"Well, simmer down." He waited a minute, then said, "Go on."

"So after the meeting, we went on to celebrate at Delmonico's, had a lovely dinner, got back to the hotel and went to bed. In the morning I awoke past the time Helene usually came in with my breakfast, so I went in to see what was happening..."

"She was dead?"

"Yes." Alex bit a nail and passed a hand across her forehead. "Then, of course all hell broke loose. The manager called for the British Consul who came along—a pompous little man, absolutely the worst kind of petty administrator—and he in turn insisted I move straight into the Consulate to be "cared for" by his family. I mean, 'cared for' as if I were some sort of invalid or something. He wired Uncle Oliver as my father never answered because...because Helene was actually not supposed to be with me."

"Why ever not? Were you supposed to be traveling on your own all the way from England?"

"Of course not. Don't be ridiculous," she snapped. "Oh, blast, I'm sorry Jess. It's just—"

"For heaven's sake, calm down. You're here now and everything is gonna be all right."

"Yes, you're right. I suppose. Anyway, Oliver wired back to the Consulate and said I could come on, on my own." She stopped for a moment, removed her gloves, bent down and pulled the pin from the back of her hat and took it off, then unbuttoned her shoes.

"What're you doin'?" he asked, puzzled.

"What the hell does it look like I'm doing, Jesse?" She watched him try to hide a smile and look away. She had picked up curse words from David and her rebellious nature had held on to them as a way of being insubordinate to her father. It would no

6

doubt be remarked upon by the punchers who had always been such gentlemen. But they would have to get used to it; she'd had enough of people telling her what to do and how to behave.

She glared at Jesse with impatience before continuing, "Poor Helene. Anyway, after the funeral I insisted on getting the very next train out, which happily was the Express. I had to go through all her things, which was incredibly depressing, and find the tickets and money."

"So you've handled money at last," Jesse tried to lighten things up a bit.

"Well, no, I didn't in the end because meals in the dining car were included, for what they were worth, and I had this hundred dollar note which is all the cash Helene had. Apparently she was counting on our Letters of Introduction all over the bloody place or something. I don't know. Maybe I just didn't find the small cash. Anyway, they took me to the station and I haven't been able to tip anyone which is why the porter was throwing my things about."

"Heck, Alex, you shoulda said. I coulda given him somethin'. Them porters make most of their money from the tips."

"Do they? Oh, well, sorry. How the hell would I know?" She looked at him, taking in the changes in him, how he had filled out, was somehow more manly yet lean with it, muscular. But it was still the same old Jesse, worn leather vest and checked shirt with snaps, straggling sun-bleached hair hanging out the back of his hat. "I see you have a new hat. It suits you. I like it."

He took a breath to stop himself from commenting on her swearing, then said, "Well, you didn't 'spect me to be wearin' the same hat as five year ago, did you?"

"I didn't expect anything. I thought maybe you

had gone. You and Cal and the others. It could have been all changed at the Faringdon."

"No. We're still here, most of us. You mighta written."

"Helene wrote Tom and Annie, didn't she? If I had written, the letters would have been intercepted anyway." She stopped and bit a nail. "You should be married by now. Are you married?"

He looked at her a moment, then turned back to the road. "There ya go, always trying to have me married off."

"But you're what, twenty-seven now? You should be married with a passel of kids runnin' aroun'," she mimicked.

"Well, I ain't. Anyways, I thought it was you who'd be married. I sneaked a peek in Mr. Calthorpe's London papers a while back—"

"The London newspapers?" she panicked.

"Yeah, 'course. You know we get the London papers for Mr. Calthorpe. Bit late of course but they do come." He wondered for a moment about her reaction, then went on. "It was when you had that debutante party."

"Oh," she said with some relief.

"They said you were the Deb of the Season or somemat, and the most beautiful gal in London."

"Oh, what nonsense is that? I tell you. Really!"

"Well, wasn't the whole purpose of that *coming out*, that day-bew, to marry you off to some rich fella or somethin'?"

"Oh...oh, look, Jess." She changed the subject. "I missed this *so* much. The mountains and the columbine on the prairie and the pines and the cattle and the men."

"Well, we all missed you," he said, his voice now gentle.

"Did you? I bet not. I think you're just saying that to please me, aren't you?"

"It were pretty bad when you left. That night. Cal and I were fit to be tied. We could hear ya screamin' and all, but Tom said not to try anythin'. He had his gun out as well."

"It doesn't matter. Really it doesn't. It's all so long ago. Long, long ago." She was quiet a moment then said, "Stop, please? We've got to stop for a moment. I want to drink it all in. Oh, goodness I'm so happy to be back," and at long last she relaxed.

He pulled up the horses and for a time they sat there with Alex taking it in. She still could not get over the crispness, the freshness of the air and the way the sky seemed endless, completely surrounding her. She liked the wind on her face and the sigh of its breath through the distant piñons, its suspiration in the trees as if it, too, had seen something wonderful. And most of all she liked the space, like an unwritten page or an unfilled canvas, which had the promise of creation.

All at once she got down from the buggy before Jesse could get around to help her, and ran down the little hill and twirled around.

Jesse stood watching her for a moment, then said, "You haven't changed, I don't suppose."

"Oh, no! Colorado is in my soul now. I can't believe I'm back!" She walked a few paces more down the hill.

Suddenly his gun went off and she jumped and turned to look at him.

"Hell, Alex," he said, forgetting himself. "You oughta know better'n to walk barefoot in the grass here. You coulda been bit."

Then she spied the prairie rattler lying dead near her feet. She laughed, covering her mouth with her hand as if it were a great joke. "Oh, Jess. I think I belong to you now, don't I?"

She started walking back toward him and he badly wanted to open his arms and embrace her, protect her as he had when she was small. Her wildness wasn't gone, nor her joy and interest in everything around her; he could see that. Now her auburn hair was coming loose and it caught the sun so that streaks of gold glimmered round her face as the wind ruffled her skirts. He caught his breath and didn't answer.

"Isn't there some Indian thing about, well, when someone saves your life, you belong to them? Or is it the other kind of Indian—the Asian one? I forget."

"Alex, I don't think you're ever gonna belong to anyone."

And she laughed and said, "Well, I guess we'll see."

Chapter Two

On the drive down to the main house Alex made him stop again.

In 1876, the ranch had been nothing more than a straggle of buildings. But Oliver Calthorpe could not rest easy until the Faringdon rivaled Moreton Frewen's mansion up in Wyoming with its two stories and grand staircase. Alex had adored her small room with its view out to grasslands and pine, but as the years went by, the second story was added, along with a veranda running right around. French doors had led from the main bedrooms onto this walkway with steps down to what would eventually be mature gardens.

"Oh, for heaven's sake, Jesse, what the hell has Oliver done?"

"Improving things is what he's calling it," was his reply, though he obviously knew exactly what she meant.

The changed house was larger, more imposing, and had been stone clad. Instead of the old wooden terraces, there were now brick paths around the house, and the gardens, of course, had matured and were more formal. Stone painted blackamoors were posted either side of a path for horses to be tied. The house looked totally out of place in its surroundings and she could see a footman now waiting for their arrival. And there were Oliver and Tom.

"Well, here you are," said Oliver helping her down from the buggy. He held her at arms' length. "Looking lovelier than ever. Doesn't she, Tom?"

It was when she was hugged by Tom that Alex

knew she was truly back. She wanted to stay in his embrace, feeling the comfort of home there, but had to pull away so as not to upset Oliver, who had given her a quick kiss on the cheek. But it was to the patient and gentle Tom she looked for assurance. A lithe, well-built man, now in his mid-thirties, he and his wife Annie had been virtual parents to the young girl, constantly concerned about her well-being, and Alex had enjoyed their company far more than her uncle's.

"We've all missed you so, Lady Alex," he said.

"You haven't changed," she replied. And he hadn't, although she noted the gray creeping into Oliver's hair and moustache and thought how much older he looked now.

"Annie's dying to see ya," Tom went on.

"I'm so happy to be here. To be home," she replied. "I'll go to see her first thing in the morning. The children must be grown so."

"Oh, yes."

She studied him a moment to see if there was any sign of what he knew, if Oliver had said, if Helene's letter had arrived, but his face was just the same as always, kind and patient and wanting nothing more than her happiness.

"I'll be at the Homestead first thing tomorrow," she repeated. Then she followed Oliver into the house.

Oliver Calthorpe had not been suited for either the military or the Church, traditional occupations for the second sons of the aristocracy. In 1861, he had left England for the war-beleaguered east coast of the United States and headed to Texas to learn the ranch business. But Texas, too, had seceded from the Union and rather than get drawn into a conflict to which, as an Englishman, he attached no significance nor had the stomach to pursue, he moved north, first up through Kansas and into

Nebraska, finally ending up in Fort Collins in the Territory of Colorado. By now he had had a vision, and although the wars with the Indian nations continued, he knew they could not last. Denied by primogeniture to any slice of England, and with a remittance from his brother, which barely covered his costly tastes, he had decided to build his own empire in Colorado at shareholders' expense. He had returned to England in late 1867 on a double mission—to consult with his brother, the duke, about their sound investment, the ranch he had started between the Thompson and the Cache le Poudre rivers, and to claim the woman he had left behind. He had proven successful at only one of these objectives.

Alex regarded her uncle with mixed feelings as she entered the drawing room, and wondered if she would ever see him in an avuncular role. Her uncle was not an aggressive man, despite a stature and deportment some might have found forbidding, yet she found it difficult to warm to him in any manner, to form the relationship which should have been shaped some years ago.

"Uncle..."

"Alex...it's so wonderful to have you back here. We've missed you so..."

"Have you?" She held her hands together in front of her as if she might wring the words out. "I believe we should clear the air..."

"What's done is done, my dear." He moved toward his whiskey decanters, then stopped and turned back to her. "We've all missed you so," he repeated awkwardly.

"It's nice of you to say that," she replied, speculating on the truth of his words. For a moment she felt she would like a cigarette, it must be nice to have something like that, but of course it would be unheard of for a lady to smoke, shocking for her uncle, and he was no doubt shocked enough. She took a few more steps into the drawing room and looked about. "I would think I was something of an embarrassment to you. I mean there will be letters to the English families, your friends—if they don't already know, they'll all know soon enough."

"Soon enough. We'll ride the storm." His voice had a positive note to it but she wasn't fooled by it.

"I'm sorry—if it helps. I'm sorry if I'm a burden but I can't tell you how happy I was when Father said he was sending me back. I love the ranch...but I might be getting some money together soon so perhaps you will want me to leave, move into one of the boarding houses—"

"Don't be ridiculous!" he snapped, suddenly displaying his true colors, "it would only make matters worse. You'll live here. We'll carry on as normal, act normal. Where do you intend to get this money anyway? You're seventeen years old for goodness sake, a lady—work is unheard of."

"I want to be independent—you'll have to understand that," she said in her most imperious tone. She finally settled into one of the wing chairs by the fire and looked up at him. "Before Helene passed away we went to see a dealer in New York—"

"What kind of a dealer for goodness sake?"

"If you'll let me finish!" She stopped for a second, her eyes blazing up at him before she calmed again. "An art dealer. He took some paintings I had done in Italy while recuperating. He thought they were very good. He said if they sold he would consider giving me my own exhibition, I could have a career as an artist—"

"Stop! Stop right there!" Oliver paced and looked back at her, his eyes wide with his fury. "There will be no career, there will be no money from art, and you will act like a proper young lady henceforth. And when your father requests your return—"

"No! Not any more, Oliver. I won't be going home. My father has hated me since the day I was born. All my life he has punished me for my mother's death. And if you won't have me here because you're too afraid of him firing you as manager and making you leave the Faringdon, then I shall go to live with Tom and Annie—"

"You don't think Tom would lose his job as well? Will you live with that? He has two children."

"Well." She stood up, staring him down, her mouth a firm straight line. "At least I know Tom Yost can get a job anywhere. The question is, can you?"

Oliver stared back at her, then turned and paced the room. "This is not the way I meant to start." His tone was quieter. "This is not what I wanted. I wanted..." His voice trailed off. "I thought I could do something for you, that you would be happy here—"

"You mean you wanted to do something to make it up to my mother. You think that by making me happy you can appease your own guilt?"

Oliver took a deep breath before turning away. "I don't know what you're talking about."

"I think you do. You forget I walked in on a conversation between you and David when he visited all those years ago. It's never been any secret in the family that both you and Papa were in love with her, that he *stole* her from you. Maybe you think if you make things up to me...or maybe there is something else, something even more pressing as a reason to tolerate my presence here?"

"I do not need to tolerate you!" He ran a hand pushing his hair back. "I am happy—very happy—to have you here," he said in a softer voice. "I don't doubt there will be problems, but we'll survive."

Alex went up to him and looked at him long and hard. "We'll survive," she repeated in his quiet tone.

"Well, that says it all, doesn't it, Uncle Oliver? You feel my presence here is something which must be survived." And she walked out.

She would endure living with her uncle as long as it took to become independent, but she would no longer fear her father, would no longer have anything to do with that breed of men who possessed women, who saw her as nothing more than a chattel in the preserved and sealed world of the aristocracy.

She was back in Colorado now, and she was going to be free.

Chapter Three

In the early morning Alex stood at her window to see the men preparing to go out on herd. Pale light filtered through a mist giving her the impression the scene in the distance was behind a sheer curtain; it made her feel for a moment like a voyeur. She could make out Jesse knocking the dust from his hat as he headed back into the rear yard, and the old wrangler Joe who was checking the shoes on one of the horses. There was Garrett, another of the older punchers, who she had always thought had a sadness he carried around with him like a gift he wanted to hand back. Just saddling up was Garrison, their rough string rider, who had loaned her his horsehair lariat to learn how to rope. Reb and Terry seemed to be arguing about something, which wasn't unusual, and then there was Cal Jenks, Jesse's best friend, who had taught her guitar and always called her "Ladilex." Her spirits lifted and she flew down the steps and out to catch them before they rode off.

Dressed in a long black frock coat for riding, with David's most recent pair of cast off jodhpurs hitched up, she saw Jesse come out with Cal, glance her way, and then settle his lanky frame back against the office wall, pull his hat down, and cross his arms.

Alex stopped to fix back strands of hair escaping from her plait. She caught Cal's eye but there was no sense of recognition from him, only a look of bewilderment as he strolled over to Garrison and gave the other puncher a poke in the ribs.

"Hot damn," he mumbled.

Alex stopped and looked the men over. No one said anything for a moment, and then she burst out laughing, guessing neither Jesse nor Tom had let on.

"What's the matter?" she asked. "Do you think I'm part of some great conspiracy against the laws of nature? Have women still not got legs in Colorado?"

There was a moment's silence before Cal said, in a tone almost identical to Jesse's the previous day, *"Ladilex?"*

"You blackguard." She turned to Jesse. "You didn't tell them! Ah, but I see you did tell Joe to put a sidesaddle on old Dainty. Very funny, Jesse. Very funny indeed." She shook hands with her old friends, said hellos to some new punchers, and gave Cal a hug and a prod for not recognizing her.

"You learn to cook, sew and clean yet so's we can get hitched?" he teased. He slowly chewed on some chicle, his dark eyes the only sign he was suppressing a smile.

"Are you proposing, Cal Jenks? If I said yes you'd run so fast we wouldn't see you for dust. Your hat would be the only thing left of you between here and Tennessee."

Cal chewed thoughtfully. "Ah, heck, I reckon I can't leave yet, Ladilex. I ain't never finished the ballad I been writing you. You remember? 'Out on the prairie where the columbine grow...' *One* must always finish *one's* work, ain't that right, Jesse?" He dragged out the word one, trying to mimic Alex's accent.

"I reckon *one* must, Cal," Jesse replied, pushing his hat back.

"You two are as impossible as you ever were, I see. One simply cannot tolerate this!" she jested right back. *"I reckon* I'll have to just ride off!"

Cal laughed. "Aw heck, you sure we speak the same dang language, Ladilex?"

"No, but we can try. So how far have you got with this ballad then, Cal—are you having fun?"

"Fun? Fun? Heck Ladilex, you call that fun? Why tailin' down a steer or ridin' drag 'cross the Llano is a hide more fun than writin' you all a ballad. How many words you all think there is to rhyme with Ladilex? You think of one."

Alex laughed as the other punchers saddled up and moved off, leaving her alone with Cal and Jesse. She turned and loosened the girth on the sidesaddle. "Why don't we just get rid of this damn thing?" she asked the wrangler Joe.

"Because," responded Jesse, "sometimes we do have real ladies who visit and need it. You keep cussin' like that we're gonna have to wash yer mouth out, missy."

"Ha!" was Alex's good-natured reply. She started to take the saddle back into the tack room but Joe went to take it from her. He had soft brown eyes and a long moustache, and smelled of the woody scent of the tobacco he used for rolling.

"Now lemme see if I remember what you said to me first time you arrived? I wasn't to call you Ma'am as in ham 'cause that was what you called the Queen. I had to call you Marm with an R in it. Was that right, Lady Lex?"

"That's right, Joe. But quite honestly I think I'd prefer it if everyone just called me Alex."

"Yeah, well, that'll go down real well with your uncle," put in Jesse. "Like giving him a canteen of water taken downriver of the herd."

Alex giggled as she pulled off the saddle. "Suit yourself, then, *Mr*. Makepeace."

"Lady Lex," Joe said. "You all still don't look like ya can handle a 40 lb. saddle none. Last time we seen ya, we didn't know whether to eat ya or feed ya to the birds. We thought the dang horse was gonna get you in one gulp."

"Well, I may be small, Joe, but I'm pretty tough." And she strode off to get the other saddle.

Jesse continued to lean against the office wall as Cal sauntered over and shouldered up next to him.

"You kept this pretty durn quiet." Cal scraped a line in the dirt with his boot heel. "I mean, it's sorta plain indecent the feelin's I got right now. Sorta like incest or somethin'."

Jesse laughed and waited until Alex came out and saddled up. She gave him a quick smile and a wave before riding off.

It wasn't until he got to the tack room that he knew the reason she hadn't stopped to chat. His saddle was gone and in its place was the lady's sidesaddle.

****

Alex pulled up her horse a distance from the Homestead to watch Annie Yost going about her chores. She recalled how she had instinctively known she could trust Annie and what she thought her to be was most definitely what she was: honest, caring and giving. Annie was a handsome woman, not plain, nor markedly beautiful, but with a kind, open face which invited both confidence and confidences. The foreman's wife had been a surrogate mother to Alex during her earlier stay at the ranch. Now she hugged her and held her, the damp from Alex's tears on her neck, and stopped herself from crying; she stood there in the yard with the girl in her arms.

"I'm sorry." At long last, Alex pulled away. "It's so stupid of me really. I'm here now and I'm so happy."

"Well, you don't seem happy," laughed Annie. "Let me look at you." She held Alex at arm's length while the girl sniffled, searched for a hankie and blew her nose. "My goodness, but you are a beauty. It's as Madame said, that's for sure."

"I suppose Tom told you about Helene?"

"Yes. We were both very sorry to hear. She was a very fine woman." She put her arm around Alex and led her into the house. "Notice any changes?"

"Oh, goodness! Look, a proper staircase up and a whole banister and everything. It's wonderful. And you've opened up the back too. Oh, look!"

The Homestead had been the original ranch house for the Faringdon, or Double F Ranch, as it was sometimes called. When Oliver had decided to move his headquarters to what he considered a more impressive location with trees and nearby pond, he had handed over the well-proportioned log cabin to his foreman. Tom and Annie had made it a home, bringing in hewn pine and leather furniture and the necessities of kitchen stove and ice box. When Alex had first seen the house, she had loved the place immediately and without reserve. There was a stone fireplace, in front of which were some comfortable seats, and a dining table with hewn benches on which to sit. The kitchen area was off to the left and Tom had built cabinets and cupboards either side of the sink and stove. To the right was a door leading to what was once a downstairs bedroom but which, Alex had come to know, was now Tom's study. Built into the roof of the house there was a loft floor, which had been divided into three bedrooms. But what she liked best was the informality, the relaxed hominess of the place; this appealed to Alex immensely.

Tom had obviously made improvements to the Homestead during the past five years. Not only had he made a sturdy stairway up to the bedroom floor, where before there had been just a ladder, but he had knocked through to the rear of the house so Alex could now see through this back door to a large wooden table and a cook-out area, and a swing hanging from a tree down toward his barn.

"Oh, it's wonderful," she said looking out.

"And see." Annie's face beamed. "He's also knocked through to the wash house and privy so we don't have to get our feet wet in winter." They both laughed.

"I can't wait to see the children. They must've grown so."

"They'll be home after school. J.J.'s just coming up to seven now, of course, and Sue Ann, well, she's quite a young lady I guess. Gonna be ten this summer. Alex, can you believe it?"

"No. Time goes so quickly." She sank into a chair.

"Well, yes it does. Look at you—"

"Yes, look at me—one marriage under my belt already." And there it was: spread out between the two of them like a deck of cards waiting for players.

"Oh, Alex. It weren't your fault. What happened...it was a terrible thing for your father to do to you."

"How much do you know? How much does Tom know?"

"Madame wrote. I'll get the letter."

Annie unfolded what Alex could see was a piece of stationery from David's home in Italy. She took it and read:

> "Castello Montegufoni,
> San Gimignano,
> Toscana, Italia
> 2 Novembre, 1885

My dear Monsieur and Madame Yost,

> I regret I have been unable to write for some time to let you know how things fare for us. It has not been good, and my time has been taken with many things concerning Alexandra. I am sure you will forgive me when you learn that which has come to pass.

As you are aware, Alexandra, as the daughter of a Duke, was to make her debut last year, and indeed she did. The parties are endless, I think, but Lady A. was a great success and had much written of her in the papers. One particular young man, the heir to another great lord, a Marquess, seemed completely enraptured by her and paid her great attentions. I don't have to explain to you my young ward was not in the least interested and in addition had been warned by friends this young man was not of suitable character, shall we say?

Despite this, her father decided this was the perfect match for Lady A.—to unite two great families, two huge fortunes and no doubt to get Alexandra out of his house. When she protested, he threatened her that if she did not proceed with this marriage which by now had been arranged, he would disinherit her and throw her out without a sou. Perhaps you cannot understand, from where you are, Alexandra had no option but to proceed. If she refused, the only work she might then find to support herself would be as a governess, and her father would certainly manage to prevent anyone from hiring her. Ladies of such birth have no other decent means of support.

In all this you will want to know where Lord David and I were. Lord David was at his home here in Italia but wrote to his sister to say perhaps it was for the best, once married she could at least carry on as she wished and would be free of her father. As for me, I tried to intervene on her behalf and was summarily dismissed—sent back to Paris leaving Alexandra without any confidante. This was the worst thing for her. But before I left, my darling formed a small plan.

The marriage took place. Alexandra had been given laudanum to calm her nerves but she never took this. She pretended to be resigned and happy, I understand, throughout the whole procedure of the wedding, and the couple left for Paris on their wedding trip.

Alexandra had told me she would never let this man touch her in that way you will comprehend. How she thought this could possibly go on indefinitely, I do not know, but that was her intention. The first night, on the boat train, apparently was not a problem as the groom was far too drunk to think of such matters. Settled into their hotel in Paris, the next night Alexandra managed to slip some of her laudanum into his drink and so another night was passed in this way. The third night was similar; they had been out to dine with his friends, Alexandra returning early on her own.

On the next day, Lord John went off riding in the Bois de Boulogne leaving his bride to her painting. She visited me at this time, not knowing her husband would return early. When he was alone in the hotel suite, he had found the laudanum and when Alexandra came in, he was in a rage. He threw the bottle at her and somehow managed to grab her palette knife to strike her on the face. This is not a sharp implement you may know—it has no point— but the sides of it can cut. Alexandra went to grab the knife thereby cutting her palm and making her hand useless for defense. At this time, his lordship took his riding crop and beat her.

It was the maid who found her later that evening. Lord John was gone and my darling was rushed to the hospital. The only good thing was the maid found my Paris address. I went there as soon as I was told—I will not go into what I found in that dreadful place, what I saw—but I wired Lord David immediately. He came for us both and so here we are in Italia where hopefully Alexandra can make a full recovery.

I am so sorry I do not write better news for you. This has been a most trying time for us all and I hope to have better news next time.

Your friend,
Helene Champrigand"

Alex put the letter back into the envelope. "Does anyone else know?"

"No. Not from us."

"David wrote to Father that the marriage must be annulled. He told him it had never been consummated, and if an annulment was not arranged Father would never see him again. Of course," she looked across at Annie, "David now has his own money from the Italian estate and he knew he could apply this pressure to Papa who holds title and inheritance and the whole question of family and aristocracy above all else. I recuperated whilst arguments—letters—went back and forth. In the end, just so as to appear to still have the upper hand, and to get me out of sight as this was now a colossal scandal, Papa wrote he would arrange the annulment forthwith on one condition: that I returned to Colorado."

She stopped and smiled at Annie to see if she

understood. "You see, I had never let on how much I loved this place because I knew...I *knew* if I did, I would never see it again. And Papa thought he was punishing me by separating me from David and sending me here. Funny, isn't it?"

"Oh, Alex," Annie reached for her hand, "this has all been so terrible for you."

"Yes. But look at the results," she added with a smile.

****

Sue Ann babbled on while Alex lay back on the floor, a stockinged foot waving about as she listened to the two children. Just home from school, they sat by Alex pulling strands of her auburn hair out, Medusa-like, in snaking lengths which J.J. carefully arranged.

"Tell me again how you became a lady." Sue Ann wore a dreamy expression. "You should be a princess. Why aren't you a princess?"

Alex laughed. "Princesses are the daughters of kings and queens, sweetheart. I am the daughter of a duke so I get called Lady and my brother gets one of my father's lesser titles, which in his case is Lord David, Earl of Lavenbrook. The previous duke was my father's uncle and if he had had a son, the title would have passed to the son but since he didn't, my father inherited it and I was a born a lady. Poor old Uncle Oliver is just plain Mister because he wasn't the son of a duke." She stopped for a minute. "Did you follow any of that?"

Annie looked over at the three of them, content with her extended family.

J.J. was impatient with the girls, however. "Can you read this to us? Miz Dawson reads it but—"

"Oh, stop, you silly." Sue Ann grabbed the book away. "No one wants to hear your silly old book."

"Sue Ann," Annie reprimanded her. "You've been droning on to Lady Alex, now let J.J. have a chance!"

"Sorry, Mama."

Alex took the book and looked at it. "*Little Lord Fauntleroy* by Frances Hodgson Burnett. What the h— I mean," she said getting the eye from Annie, "whatever is this about?"

Sue Ann moved up alongside her and continued pulling lengths of Alex's hair out in a fan about her head.

"If you read it," J.J. said sensibly, "you'll find out. I'm up to here I think," he pointed to somewhere on page seven.

Alex sighed. "All right then. I'll read for a bit. But I'll have to go soon."

"No, no, stay for dinner," begged Sue Ann.

"Yes, stay Alex," Annie said.

"I can't really. I shouldn't. Oliver will be expecting me and anyway we don't eat until eight up at the house so— Ow!"

"Sorry," J.J. said, letting go of some of her hair he had pulled. "Are you going to read?"

Lying back, Alex rested her right foot on her left knee and held the book above her face. "'He told him he might live as he pleased, and die where he pleased, that he should be cut off from his family forever and that he need never expect help from his father as long as he lived'... Lucky him," she commented, not hearing the others come in.

"'The Captain was very sad when he read the letter; he was very fond of England...' Well, the dang fool had never been to Colorado, that's for certain." She slammed down the book.

"You recognize that foot, Jess?" a familiar voice said.

"Can't say I do, Cal. A might too small to carry a proper person I'da thought."

Alex sat up and stared at the two of them over the top of the sofa. They had to stop themselves from laughing when they saw her hair messed up so much, but she thought she had the last laugh. "Have a good ride today, Mr. Makepeace?" She started to pull on her boots.

"I had a good ride, Ma'am. Found the leg thing on the sidesaddle is a dang good place to hang a rope."

"You didn't." She stomped into her boots and tried to see out the door.

Tom came. "Two extra for dinner, Annie, Or is it three?" he added when he saw Alex.

"Two. I'm off," She gave the children a hug each.

"Yeah, you remember, Tom." There was a hint of amusement in Jesse's voice. "She lives on a ranch but she don't..."

"EAT BEEF!" the three men said in unison.

Tom shook with laughter. "We having beef?" he asked his wife.

"We are. But we're having chocolate cake too." Annie looked at Alex with a questioning brow.

"Now, here's the thing," put in Cal, chewing his gum pensively. "Ladilex don't eat beef but she can sure put away enough chocolate cake to fill a man for winter. How d'you do that? How d'you do that and stay so dang small, is what I wanna know?"

"Magic, pure magic, Cal." Alex turned back to Annie. "Dinner is very tempting despite the company of your other guests but I really must go. It wouldn't be fair to leave poor old Uncle Oliver on just my second night back." She turned back to the men. "And I better not find any sidesaddle on my mount, Jesse Makepeace."

"No, Ma'am. Sidesaddle's moving on to Garrett tomorrow I think. What do you say, Cal?"

Alex laughed. "And Tom...I really do need another horse. Dainty is ready for pasture."

"Well, you'll have to see Garrison. He's in charge of the remuda."

"Oh, she can ride Brandy for now," offered Jesse, thinking he'd do just about anything to see her smile.

"Really? Really?" she repeated. "Isn't he your cutting horse?"

"Naw, got a new cuttin' horse. I jus' keep Brandy in my string in case one of the others is lame. But I do want my saddle back. Been ridin' with some old—"

"You mean..." She put her hand to her mouth. "You really didn't find it? I told Joe—"

"Oh, yeah, Joe. Joe thought it was a great joke. You don't really think he told me where the dang thing was?"

Alex stared at him for a moment. She began to say something but suddenly was overcome with such happiness at being with her friends again she had to stop to hold back tears and looked away.

"Speaking of magic," Jesse went on, "circus is comin'. Me and Cal thought you might want to—"

"Yes! Yes please," she cut him off as she headed for the door and yanked it open. "Bye everyone." She started to hurry out. "I'll see you at Church, Jess."

"What the heck happened there?" puzzled Tom as he watched her mount up.

"Uh-oh," said Cal. He looked at Jesse who was watching Alex ride away. "Uh-oh."

Chapter Four

It was so good to be home, it was so good to be back. For the most part Alex was able to put things behind her. She loved being there, loved all the men, the way they talked, the way they moved, the way they smelled of leather and fresh air, their clothes, their manners and etiquette. They were more gentlemen than any lord she had ever met, kinder, gentler and better mannered than any aristocrat from London. Maybe it was a matter of feeling safe around them, of feeling protected; she didn't know, wasn't sure, but with Annie and Tom to see every day, she was certainly happier now than she had been in a long time.

Yet church on Sunday was not a pleasant prospect. Oliver regularly used the church gathering as an occasion, stepping down from his buggy and smoothing the creases from his suit before helping Alex out. He would make sure to see as many friends as possible between the carriage and the church door, and give a nod to the two hands who often joined him on Sundays: Jesse Makepeace and Garrett Landry. Jesse had been brought up in Texas in a strict but loving household; having been taken under Tom Yost's wing when he came north, Jess' good manners and steady upbringing had not deserted him. Garrett, on the other hand, went as if it were a trial he had to attend with himself as the accused. As for Oliver, his motives were purely social; there was a lot of news to be had on a Sunday, business deals to be made and invitations and engagements to be proffered or accepted. And there was Alex to show off, watch the gentry make little curtsies or bows to his niece, the daughter of the Duke of Faringdon.

But not now.

With letters from home reaching the British ranchers, along with newspaper clippings from London, Alex was fairly certain of what to expect. Oliver was, of course, an indication of the English community's attitude toward what had transpired. As far as her uncle was concerned, Alex had reneged on her marital vows and he was charged with the task of picking up the pieces.

****

Jesse and Garrett followed them on horseback to the English Church, but Jesse came round to help Alex down from the buggy. Her face was glum; she looked up at him as if she wanted to say something but then turned and went on to Oliver, who stood there waiting. He hesitated before giving her his arm and walking on.

This Sunday, there seemed to be more folks than usual outside the church. "Is this a welcomin' committee?" Jesse whispered to Garrett. Garrett looked around, then stopped behind Alex and Oliver. She turned to look back at them, distinctly nervous as Oliver started to talk with friends.

Low voices spoke in whispers behind Jesse. Two of the smartly dressed ranchers' sons snickered, "...certainly like to get my pecker into that one."

"You'd risk it?" said the other. "I heard she poisoned her husband. Tried to kill the poor sod."

"Oh, yes, but I'd teach her a trick or ...Ow! Darn fool, watch where you're going."

"Oh, I am so sorry," Jesse declared with mock sincerity, having taken a step backward on to the fellow's foot with his heeled boot. "I do beg your pardon."

"How could she show her face?" an elderly

woman said to her friend. "Why, it's a perfect disgrace, a girl like that. Divorced!"

"Oh, I don't think she's divorced, Ethel. Not yet anyway. Divorces back home take forever. They have to go through Parliament."

It went on until at last they got to their seats. Jesse listened to it all with growing tension; whatever else she might be, Alex was still part of the Faringdon family and they all looked after one another. He slipped into their pew from the far side and moved up next to Alex, her face set like stone, looking straight ahead, and he saw she had been crying. Jesse reached into his pocket and extended his hand and offered her a clean handkerchief.

Alex looked at his hand, then up at him. Little lines had appeared at the sides of his eyes, a deep sprinkle of freckles on his tanned face, and a small cut where he'd nicked himself shaving. She remembered the time he had lifted her up when she was eight because she had seen a child at the train station hold out its arms to its father and Alex had done the same to Jesse, and when he had picked her up she had been tongue-tied and spellbound by him, enthralled by his cornflower blue eyes and long lashes and the shaggy hair she had loved to play with at the back of his neck. She had thought he was the most beautiful person she had ever seen. Now, sitting next to him, she noticed the "parentheses" around his mouth as he smiled at her, and a small mole at the end of his sideburns. But just his being there and being the same Jesse she had always known made the tears come faster and she took the proffered hanky and discreetly dabbed her eyes, then looked forward again.

There was nothing more between them. She sat silently during the hymns, listening to Jesse's light tenor, while on her other side her uncle's deep baritone was prominent but off-key. After the service

Oliver fairly rushed Alex to the rig and Garrett and Jesse went on, as always, to the Yost's for lunch.

****

Jesse's need to know the truth about Alex—whether she was or was not married—was painful. If he had felt he had let her down when she was whisked away five years ago, then his need to protect her now surprised even him. He burst in to the Homestead.

"Is Alex married?"

Tom was reading at the table but at a glance from Annie, he put down the paper. "Children go outside until lunch, please."

"Mama, is Lady Alex married?" Sue Ann wanted to know.

"No, she isn't," Annie replied. "Now do what your father asks, please."

Jesse's unease was mounting as the four adults watched the children bang the back door behind them. He said, "Sorry. Sorry, Tom I wasn't thinkin'."

"No, you weren't." Tom waited a minute. "What happened?"

Jesse slumped at the table while Garrett leaned against the mantel.

"It were pretty durn awful at the church for her," said Garrett. "Folk ignorin' her or being right rude. Rumors flyin' 'bout."

"They said she'd been married and is getting a divorce. Is that right? Said she tried to poison her husband." Jesse's eyes searched Tom's face for an answer.

"Oh, what nonsense!" Annie whipped the cloth down and took a seat at the table. "Tell them, Tom."

"It's not our place, Annie. If we start gossiping, we're no better'n them."

"But we know the truth," she said in some exasperation.

Jesse looked from one to the other. "Which is?"

Tom hesitated, then said, "Why don't you ask Alex what the truth is, Jess? If you think it's your business, if you think this makes a difference as to who she is, or how good a person she is, or whatever it is she is to you personally, if you think you have a *right* to know, why don't you ask her? Why the heck are you askin' me?"

Jesse sat with his chin in his hand for a while taking in what Tom had said. He couldn't say he had a right to know, it wasn't necessarily his business, and it wasn't going to change who she was or what she was to him—which he hadn't even figured out as yet. He was ten years older than she, had sat with her on his lap, watched her grow up. His confusion was palpable.

Annie broke the silence. "Here is what you should know. Here is what they should all know, Tom, for goodness sake. Alex was forced to marry some lord or other—against her will. She tried to prevent his advances by putting laudanum in his drink. He found out and the marriage has been annulled. Not divorced, *annulled*. That's about it. That's what happened. That's what you should know."

****

Back in 1876, when Jesse and the other men of the Double F Ranch had been told Mr. Calthorpe's young niece was coming to stay, their reaction had been puzzlement. Jesse had wondered what a young girl would do on a ranch in the wilds of Colorado; others had felt a tinge of annoyance at this intrusion into their everyday routines while still others thought back on the families they had left behind. The bafflement most of them had felt was also touched with curiosity. It had been years for many since they had lived amongst a family, and the idea of a young child around the ranch needed some accommodation in their organized and solitary lives.

Alex had won them over, however; enchanted by her huge green eyes and the rosebud mouth that seemed to fill her delicate oval face, amazed at the quiet yet concise little voice which asked them endless questions and demanded they repeat their time-worn stories, there hadn't been a single man at the Double F who hadn't become a better father or uncle to her than the two men who held those titles.

But after the episode at the church, Alex knew full well that all the men would eventually hear what had befallen her in the five years since she left for England. She decided to keep to herself the next few days, riding out, sketching, starting a painting of the men on their horses with the herd, clouds of dust, lariats swung out. She didn't want their pity and she didn't want them to feel awkward around her so she avoided them for the most part. She didn't talk to them much and they in turn respected her silences, watched from a distance to see she was all right. She had no idea who knew what, or what had been said, or how anyone had reacted to whatever they had been told, and she cared even less now. The painting consumed her. This was what she wanted more than anything now; this was her ticket to being free.

On an afternoon toward the end of the week she rode up to the chuck wagon to refill her canteen from the water butt. A man she didn't recognize lay spread-eagle on the ground, facedown, with a group of the other punchers around him. Cal sidled up to her, tin mug of coffee in hand, and tried to block her view.

"What's up?" she asked, furrowing her brow.

"Oh, just a bit of fun," he answered a bit too nonchalantly.

"Doesn't look like fun for the man on the ground." She looked at Cal questioningly, but he avoided her eyes and took another sip of coffee. Cal had always been her good friend—the one who listened and never lost his temper, the one who would without reservation take her side, see her point of view. "What's happening, Cal?" She tried to push past. "And don't tell me not to worry my pretty little head."

"Oh, heck Ladilex, you leave them alone now, ya hear?" he said with some embarrassment. "Just a bit of good ol' frontier justice."

"Frontier justice, huh?" She stood there smoldering. "How's that for frontier justice," and she flung some water in his face before she picked up Brandy's reins and rode off.

It was called "chapping" she learned later from Annie, where the victim had his backside smacked with the leather of his own chaps. Annie didn't say why the man was being chastised in this manner but Alex inferred it had something to do with herself. At least her old friends were protecting her honor, and then she felt sorry about what she'd done to Cal.

One evening some days later Alex got involved in finishing up a painting, and it was past dark when she finally arrived back at the corral. The men's voices drifted out to her before she could see them all, their horses were saddled and torches were just now being lit.

"What's going on?" she asked Oliver, who stood there, hands on his hips, watching her dismount. She approached him somewhat hesitantly for their relationship wasn't any easier than it had been when she was younger. She regarded him neither warmly nor yet unhappily, but perhaps warily at times. He had said little to her regarding her annulled marriage and less about the local reaction to it.

"Where the hell have you been? Do you know we were just starting out to search for you? Do you have any idea of the time?" His anger was resonant.

"Search for me? Whatever for?"

"I was worried. It's late. You can't go gallivanting about the countryside here as you wish. You could have been hurt. You could be laying hurt somewhere, attacked by a bear or mountain lion, thrown from your horse. Anything could have happened to you."

"You're joking, aren't you? I have my rifle here." She pulled the gun from its scabbard.

"I think you owe Tom and the men an apology," Oliver fumed. "I think you owe us all an apology."

Alex looked long and hard at Oliver; he seemed to understand her less now than he had five years ago. She turned to Tom. "I apologize, Tom, to you and the men that Oliver thought it necessary to send you all out looking for me when you obviously have much better things to do with your time. Not to mention you all are probably tired and hungry after a day's work and really didn't need this nonsense!"

Oliver was furious. "That's not what I meant," he snarled between his teeth. "I want an apology this minute, young lady."

"I just gave you one. I'm not a child any more, Oliver."

"But you are a young lady and should bloody well behave like one!"

"I am late and I have apologized. I didn't know I had to go reporting in every five minutes as to my whereabouts."

"No one is asking you to report in every five minutes. We are asking for the common courtesy of letting us know where you'll be."

"How many hundreds of square miles is this spread? How many millions of acres do our cattle roam? Common courtesy? Well, my goodness." She loosened the cinch on her saddle.

"I'm waiting!" Oliver's voice was harsh and sharp.

"You can wait 'til hell freezes over. I've given my apology."

Cal raised an eyebrow, but Jesse she couldn't read. He stood there with his thumbs in his belt, head down. Tom and the others just watched the whole scene unfold in an embarrassed silence.

"You owe the men an apology," Oliver repeated. "This minute. Or you can go back to your father!"

"My father?" Alex snickered. "My father?" she said, coming to boiling point. "Now therein lies the rub, as I believe Shakespeare would say. Just who the hell is he, Oliver? You tell me and I'll give you a better apology. Or maybe it will be you giving me an apology—that's to be decided yet I think. My father? You can rot in hell."

"Go to your room this minute!" His voice was low and threatening.

"Like hell I will!" She retightened the cinch on her saddle and before he could stop her she rode out.

By the time Oliver gave the order to go after her, Alex was out of sight. Jesse agreed with Tom that they would split up, Tom going to the Homestead to see if Alex had taken refuge with Annie. Knowing she had no provisions with her, no bedroll, and only her paints in the saddlebags, Jesse figured she would head to one of the line camps perhaps. It was near the road to Boyd he and Cal found her, sitting on her saddle blanket looking up at the stars.

Breathing somewhat resigned sighs of relief, they squatted on either side of her.

"Remember stopping the buggy here once, Jess, when you had to take me home from church? You showed me Horsetooth Rock somewhere over there marking Fort Collins." Alex pointed into the darkness. "And we watched the antelope running, and the quail in the cottonwood down by the lake. I always loved Boyd, listening to the water lapping and the hum of the crickets and grasshoppers, and the cattle always seemed so contented here, grazing right up to the lake shore. Remember?"

"Yeah," said Jesse quietly. "You were like a little porcelain doll."

She turned to look at him.

Cal cleared his throat. "Stars are pretty good tonight," he said sitting himself down. He looked over at Alex, seeing the woman trying to struggle out of the child she had been.

"Did we ever teach you how to tell time by the stars?" Jesse settled down on the blanket by her other side. "Or are you carryin' a fancy watch that don't seem to work real well?" he quipped.

"You did try to teach me once I think, but I wasn't a particularly good student as I recall. Something about the North Star and the Big Dipper?"

"Ursa Major," Cal pointed out. The three of them lay back, heads together on the blanket.

"There's an eagle's nest high up in that tree," Alex said. "I can just about see it by the moonlight."

"An eyrie. Hey, she's right." Jesse sat up again and put his hat back on. The proximity to Alex stirred feelings in him he couldn't quite deal with as yet.

They watched the sky for a time in silence. The grass was wet and Alex shivered with the cold in her thin jacket.

"Gonna have to get some better duds 'n that," Cal said.

"Yes, I'm making a list before I go into town."

"Ain't you brought suitable clothes?" Jesse asked. "You knew where you were headed."

"Suitable, yes, for the grand salons of Europe. For the English Hunt Season perhaps, but not, perhaps, for a Colorado ranch. Who's getting supplies next week?"

"My job," said Jesse. "I leave for Loveland at six Monday mornin'. No waitin' 'round neither for spoilt young ladies who can't tell time."

She smacked him on the leg. "I am not spoiled!" She pulled up some buffalo grass and then said, "Call for me at 5.45. I'll be ready."

"If'n Mr. Calthorpe lets you out of the house again," added Cal.

"Yeah. Well. Time to take you prisoner." Jesse got to his feet and extended his hand.

"Very funny."

Alex took Jesse's gloved hand, entwining her fingers with his. Jesse held them there a moment longer than might be necessary. Cal sighed and brushed himself off, then helped Alex onto her horse.

****

Oliver was waiting for them in his office. He thanked the men peremptorily, saw them out, then returned to Alex with a face like thunder.

"Don't you ever embarrass me like that again!"

She looked at him, then without saying anything turned on her heel to go.

"No, wait!" His tone was more conciliatory. He stood until she had turned back to him, then sighed. "Without Madame Helene it's very difficult...it's very difficult to know how to treat you—"

"Try treating me like an adult, why don't you?"

"I am. I have only your best interests at heart, you must know—"

"Are you my father?" Her tone was blunt.

He stood still and stared at her for a long moment, a moment in which she stared right back at him. "No. Why would you think that?"

"I told you before—a conversation I overheard years ago, dates I've put together, things said to me. I'm not an idiot, Oliver. I'm asking you, are you my father?"

"And I've just answered no." He took a few steps,

then turned. "Nothing would make me more proud than to be your father. But I am not. I loved your mother very much; she was everything to me. I could never look at another woman after her. I would have done anything—and did do everything I could for her. But I am not your father." He waited a while and tried to find words to both comfort her and yet put the matter to rest. "She was the most beautiful woman I'd ever seen. She was everything a man could wish for. But I couldn't compete with my brother and we both knew that. He could give her everything. I could give her nothing."

"But you did return to England in 1867. You were there for some months. Did you, or did you not have an affair with my mother?"

"It wasn't what you think."

"David walked in on you. He knows what he saw."

"No, no he doesn't. It wasn't anything like that." There was a note of desperation in Oliver's voice.

"What was it then? What was it like?"

"Alexandra. Please. It's all a very long time ago and I swear to you—I am not your father."

They stood staring at each other before Alex turned to go. "I'll change for dinner." She went toward the hall.

"Wait. Please." She stopped again and turned. "I know it's been difficult for you. I understand what you've been through—"

"Do you? Do you really?" Sarcasm etched her voice. She thought of how he'd avoided the subject of her marriage since her arrival, how he had almost acted as if the scandal were all her fault. She felt all he worried about was the dent it had put in his social life.

"No. Maybe not. But I am certainly on your side, Alex, whether you believe it or not."

"My side? What is my side, Oliver?"

"I think we can weather this if we stick together. I have my own problems as well."

"Your problems? And what are they, may I ask? Can't get your Havanas as quickly as you'd like? Your tailor cut your suits a bit too narrow? What are your problems?" She watched as he closed the door.

"Ranch problems. You live here now but you don't seem to be aware of how we've had to cut back this year. Beef prices plummeted in '85. A lot of the ranches folded. Frewen is gone, the Herberts, others. The Cheyenne Club is practically empty—"

"Oh, dear. My, that's a pity!" Her tone was caustic.

He chose to ignore this and continued, "There's so much cattle being raised now, it's overproduction. Tom and I will have to decide whether to hold the cattle over the winter to see if prices improve next year—"

"And if they don't?" she asked with real concern.

"If they don't, I don't know. I sold some shares onto Tom Yost and I think he, in turn, sold a couple to one of the hands..." His voice trailed off.

"Jesse Makepeace?" she guessed.

"Possibly. It wasn't any of my business. Some of the ranchers are moving shares into their daughters' and wives' names in case of bankruptcy—so the creditors can't get their hands on them."

"Well, have no fear! Papa would never do that! Are you afraid I'll be a major shareholder, Oliver, because I can allay any fears you may have on that account right here and now!"

"Don't be ridiculous. I could lose everything."

She looked at him, then turned to go but stopped at the door. The account books were open on his desk and she made a mental note to try to see them at some stage. "I know one thing. You can't do better than Tom Yost for foreman. If anyone can weather the storm, it's Tom."

42

Chapter Five

The arguments were not over.

Late Saturday night, when the men were just back from letting off steam in Loveland, Oliver's carriage pulled up in front of the house and Alex, in evening dress, got out. Her voice was at fever pitch and she shook with rage.

"Don't you ever, ever do that to me again! How could you? How could you? The most boring people, the most boring evening I've ever had the misfortune to spend, and that nasty little trumped up fool of a man, Henderson, all over me-it was disgusting."

"Lower. Your. Voice," snarled Oliver. "Or you can go to your room right now!"

"Go to my room? Go to my room? Gladly! I'd have been thoroughly happy—no, ecstatic!—to have spent the entire evening in my room, if you must know, rather than spend it with those insipid little mealy-mouthed damn fools. Go to my room? With pleasure, sir!" She marched up the path to the house.

Jesse was with the men listening at the corral while unsaddling their horses, and he could just make out her form. Alex had grown into a real beauty, like some goddess or something, he couldn't put it into words. She was something beyond anything he had ever known, and yet it was Alex, li'l Ladilex, as Cal called her, standing there with her sumptuous hair wound into coils back off her face, pearls woven in, and wearing a shimmering evening dress. Where was the child he had known?

"We have friends," Oliver was saying. "One must

associate with one's friends. We're a community. We must all stick together."

"I'll tell you what, Uncle Oliver." Alex turned back and jabbed the air with the fan in her hand. "You stick with them. You associate with them. You invite them to tea and dinner and have them bore you stiff. Me, I'd rather associate with the punchers any day of the week. I'd prefer having a two-minute conversation with any one of our men rather than sit through an evening of listening to that moronic Henderson woman talk about her English china, and her crystal imported from Ireland, and her tablecloths from Malta and godonlyknows what else! As if all of their petty bourgeois accoutrements would impress me!"

"I'm telling you now, Alexandra, if you don't behave—"

"If I don't behave? If I don't behave? What will happen that hasn't already happened to me, Uncle Oliver, you tell me that!" And she marched into the house.

They had to reach an arrangement, a compromise: they both knew that. Despite what she had said about leaving for a boarding house, Alex really wanted to live at the ranch, she loved it there; it was the only place she had ever felt was home, a safe haven from the world. She adored the Yosts, loved the punchers and had good friends among the men. Oliver had too many other matters to occupy him now than to have to keep dealing with his headstrong niece. Alex realized a bargain would be made.

They struck a deal. Alex would have free run of the ranch as long as she told someone exactly what her plans were. If her plans changed, she had to let someone know so, hopefully, they would always have a general idea as to where she had gone. In return, she promised Oliver to attend social occasions, but no more than two a month, other than Church, and including hostessing dinners at the ranch—and she would act pleasant and ladylike throughout. She could wear her pants outfits on the ranch with the addition—at Oliver's request—of a sidearm for protection, but not in town unless there was good reason.

So when Jesse came to call for her at 5.45 on the Monday morning, a much happier Alex rushed down the steps. Rose, contented to be serving Her Ladyship once again, dashed after her, handed Jesse two sacks packed with meals for the trip, and caught Alex to give her a hairbrush. Seconds later Rose re-appeared just in time to shout Alex wasn't wearing any shoes and what was she thinking? Jesse took the shoes, handed Alex into the wagon, threw the shoes in after her, and they took off.

Loveland was the preferred town for shopping and entertainment. Built in David Barnes' wheat field around a train station when the line was put through between Denver and Fort Collins— eventually going on to Cheyenne—it was friendlier and more welcoming to the cow punchers than the more developed Greeley to the east of the ranch. Greeley was a dry town which would make any working man avoid it, and it had fencing around the town perimeters in order to keep the cows out, an idea which never sat very well with the punchers.

Jesse and Alex entered the store as Sheriff Amos Dunn said, "Yeah, I hear the Darcy Brothers are running wild over by Evans' place."

"Well, would you look at that?" exclaimed the shopkeeper, Mr. Bender, a rotund balding man with eyeglasses perched on his nose. "Could that possibly be little Lady Alex? Aren't you all growed up."

Alex smiled politely and gave Mrs. Bender a hug. "It's so nice to be back."

"Well, it's just lovely to see you, dear," Mrs.

Bender responded with a squeeze.

Sheriff Dunn tipped his hat to Alex. "Better get back to work. Nice to see you again, Lady Alex. Welcome home," he said as he left the shop and the bell tinkled behind him.

Alex stood there awkwardly for a moment. The shop had not changed one iota; there were the barrels of flour and grains, the large tins of coffee and other beans, the jars of preserves and the canned goods. She eyed the gun racks and the bolts of cloth, the stacks of men's work wear and the produce from local farms that made tempting displays. Realizing word was probably out as to, not only her return, but her recent past, she stood with Jesse for an awkward moment then excused herself to go to the bank. "You might want to have a look at my list," she told Mrs. Bender, handing it to her. "I'll be back as soon as I can."

The bank was a musty affair with teller's grilles along the right hand wall and the manager's office at the far back. A young woman sat at a desk in front of the door to the office. Working conscientiously, her head bowed over some papers, she was attired in a plain work skirt and white shirtwaist, yet Alex knew men would find her blonde hair and clean features appealing.

"May I help you?" She smiled up at Alex.

The woman's name was engraved on a plaque on her desk: Miss Nancy Roderick. For a moment, Alex forgot why she had come. Something bothered her, something she couldn't remember. Finally, she stuttered out she would like to see the manager.

"May I ask what your business is with him?" She was still smiling at Alex patiently.

"I-I'm Alexandra Calthorpe. From the Double F. I want to open a bank account please."

"Oh, Miss Calthorpe." The woman stood and faced Alex. "Mr. Calthorpe's niece, isn't it? I'll see if

Mr. Conway can see you."

Nancy Roderick went through the door with a brief tap on the glass. Alex couldn't be bothered to correct her about her title, but stood there patiently until Nancy came back out, an elderly man following on her heels.

"Lady Alexandra, isn't it?" The man extended his hand. "Herbert Conway. Come in, come in."

Conway showed Alex into his office and directed her to a chair in front of his desk. "I understand you wish to open an account with us? That's fine." He searched for something in one of his desk drawers. "If we could just fill out this form," he went on, handing her the sheet he had pulled out.

The paper was quite simple: name, address, birth date, opening funds, occupation. "My opening funds, I guess you'd call them, are going to be wired into the account from New York." At least that is what Jonathon Sturgis had told her if the paintings ever sold.

"Oh, that's fine." Mr. Conway pushed a pen and ink toward her. "How is your uncle these days?" he asked, sitting back in his chair.

"Very well, thank you," mumbled Alex as she filled in the form. She handed it back to him.

"Now, let's see." Conway pushed some glasses up on his nose. "Uh-huh, uh-huh. Oh, dear. No, this won't do." He put the paper down and looked at a startled Alex. "I'm afraid, my dear, a young lady must be at least eighteen to open an account with us."

"Eighteen? That's ridiculous," she stated, her hackles rising. "I'll be eighteen at the end of August; it's only another few months."

"And we will welcome you back then. With open arms. But for now, I'm afraid the only way you can open an account is with a letter of permission from your guardian or a male counter-signatory over the age of twenty-one. Did you bring a letter from your uncle?"

"No. I mean, if I had known I would have but—"

"Well, no problem. You just run along and come back with one and you can open—"

"But I want to open the account now. Today." She stopped and stared at Conway. "Can it be any male over the age of twenty-one? Does he have to be related?"

"No, but of course you don't want to go just asking anyone out on the street there." Conway's voice had a note of alarm.

"No, no." Alex jumped up as if she'd been stung. "I'll be right back. Don't go away!"

She ran into the shop in such a frenzy they all turned to look at her in surprise.

"What the…" Jesse started to say as she grabbed him, pulling him toward the door.

"Sorry! Sorry everyone, we'll be right back," and she pulled him out onto the street. "You have to help. They won't let me open an account because I'm not yet eighteen so I need a male counter-signatory, if you please, *male* over the age of twenty-one to open the blasted account. Jesse, please, I have to do this—"

"Hang on, hang on." He put his hands up to calm her down. "What about your uncle?"

"No! No, I want to do this today because if I get any money from the paintings I have to have a bank account number for Jonathon Sturgis to wire me the money."

"Well…" He took a few paces. "I ain't sure, Alex. What'll your uncle say if he finds out I—"

"Oh, bother my uncle! He'll never know and I doubt he'd care one way or the other. Really. Please, Jesse…"

"All right, well, I ain't making any promises. I'll go and talk with Mr. Conway and see what he says."

When she saw Miss Roderick stand to greet "Mr. Makepeace," straightening her skirt and giving him a smile, Alex at last remembered where she had seen the woman. Nancy Roderick had been Jesse's lady friend at July 4th parties. The knowledge brought to Alex the memory of watching them dancing at those parties, Jesse laughing and smiling down at the woman he held in his arms. Jealousy stirred in her. She tried to understand this feeling but couldn't cope with it and brushed it aside.

The two were shown into the office again where Conway laid another paper in front of Jesse. "It's important for you to understand, Mr. Makepeace, if Lady Alexandra here is overdrawn, the responsibility will rest with you."

"I won't be overdrawn," Alex assured them. "I'm trying to save money, not spend it!"

Jesse looked at her with some amusement. Mrs. Bender had read Alex's shopping list and Jesse wondered if Alex knew how it added up. "It'll be fine," he confirmed.

Jesse filled out his form and Mr. Conway explained how Alex would get a bankbook to show her deposits and withdrawals but every time she withdrew any money it had to be counter-signed by Jesse and stamped by the teller. She grinned from ear to ear when they handed her the book and showed her the account number written at the top with her name, and she barely skipped all the way back to the shop.

"Jesse's in love with Nancy, Jesse's in love with Nancy," she teased.

Jesse stopped dead and turned to her, hands on hips. "Alex," he said shaking his head. "I don't want to hear that one more time. I'm tellin' you now. She's a fine woman but I ain't seen Miss Roderick for years 'ceptin' at the bank. Now, don't you go startin' no rumors, ya hear?"

Seeing how serious and annoyed he was, she knew to stop. Yet she couldn't help saying, "Yes, *Mr. Makepeace!*" Inside her, however, there was an amount of relief.

"All right now, so you wanted ten cotton bandanas," Mrs. Bender said. "Any particular color, dear?"

"Oh, no, any old thing will do."

"What do you need ten for, Alex?" Jesse asked.

She looked at him and wrinkled her nose. "Well, they get dirty really quickly, Jesse. How often do you change yours?" She waited for an answer but he only rubbed his head. "Anyway," she went on, "I'll probably wipe my brushes on them."

"Eight pair of denim pants? Are these for *you?*" Mrs. Bender inquired in a tone that showed some disapproval. "Now, dear, you know they don't make no pants for women, don't you?" She looked at Alex over the top of her half-rim glasses.

"Well I suppose a boy's size would do. Have you got those new ones from Mr. Levi Strauss with the watch pocket out the front?"

"We do, but we'll have to see if we have a boy's size that fits. They're seven dollars each. Is that all right?" Mrs. Bender shook her head but didn't voice the censure she would have liked to. She was there to sell things, not to tell folk what they should or should not buy.

"I suppose."

"Here." Mrs. Bender pulled out a pair from a stack. "Go try these on behind the curtain there in the storeroom."

Alex tried on denim pants and boys' shirts and asked Jesse to find a gun for her on her uncle's orders, while Mr. Bender pointed out cartridge belts that would go around Alex's waist at least twice.

"I can't wear that." She grimaced. "They'd make me look like some Mexican bandito from the Wanted posters."

Jesse laughed and Mr. Bender said, "I think I can cut the belt down and move the buckle if you don't mind waiting?"

"Boots?" Alex went on.

"Oh, dear, no." Mrs. Bender shook her head. "I doubt...well, let me do an outline of your foot and take the instep measurement and we can see if we can order some in for you."

While Alex was removing her button-up shoes, a young woman entered the shop. It was Sara Beth, the Bender's daughter. Alex had never had warm feelings for this girl, who in turn had never seemed to have a nice thing to say to her; she was pert and pretty and blond with a retroussé nose which Alex thought, somewhat unkindly, made her look a bit like a pig.

Sara Beth closed her parasol and smiled at Alex. "Why, what have we here? Lady Alex, as I live and breathe. How nice to see you again."

Alex nodded hello as Sara Beth went to the counter and got her apron back on, then fetched down a stack of newspapers.

"Oh, yes, Jesse," Mrs. Bender said as she did the outline of Alex's foot. "You mustn't forget the *London Times* for Mr. C."

"No, for sure," Sara Beth smirked. "Such interesting news."

In that instant, Alex knew. Her blood ran cold as she pulled her shoes back on but Sara Beth was already reading out loud.

"'Lady Alexandra Elizabeth Maria Calthorpe—my, but don't we have a lot of names—daughter of Frederic, Duke of Faringdon, was today found innocent of the attempted murder of her former husband, John, Lord—'"

"That's enough!" snapped Mr. Bender coming out from the storeroom. "Leave it alone now, Sara

Beth, leave the poor child be."

Jesse put a hand on Alex's shoulder, but she moved to the counter to face Sara Beth. "I'll have all of them. I'll buy the lot," she said.

"Oh, but I'm afraid they're all spoken for. These are special order; the *gentry* want their news from England."

"It's all right, Lady Alex," Mrs. Bender said soothingly. "We can tell them these didn't come in. We'll destroy them if you like. We only ever get a Friday edition and some issues never reach us anyways."

"No, I'll pay for them. I'll take them all. Put them on my bill. Please. Really." She stood there watching as Sara Beth gave her a last nasty look and went upstairs.

"Now, let's see. I won't charge you for the boots until I find out if I can get them. Have to send to Denver for those. Same with the paints you asked for, though I have the linseed and turps here for you. That's one dollar each for those. Ten bandanas at fifty cents apiece is five dollars, eight pair of denim pants at seven dollars each is fifty-six dollars, and eight shirts did you say? At four dollars each, that's thirty-two. The Colt's ten, the belt two and the box of ammunition is two." She added up. "That's one hundred and nine dollars. Shall I put that on the Faringdon account, dear?"

"You forgot the papers, Mrs. Bender."

"Oh, really dear, it'll be—"

"I insist," Alex said quietly. "I need them. For papier maché. Really."

Mrs. Bender looked at her a moment, then wrote down, "Eight imported newspapers at one dollar fifty each is twelve dollars so that makes a grand total of one hundred twenty-one dollars."

"Right. I only have a hundred dollar note."

"Bill," corrected Jesse. "It's a hundred dollar *bill*,

Alex."

"So I'll have to leave off, let me see—" Alex took out the crumpled bill from her reticule.

"Well don't you want to put it on the ranch account?" Mrs. Bender asked again.

"No. It's mine. Can we take something off, please? A pair of pants and a shirt perhaps?"

"Well that leaves you with one hundred ten dollars."

Jesse slapped a ten-dollar bill on the counter.

"No. I was going to get a hat as well, Jess."

"I thought you hated hats!"

"Yes, silly frou-frou ones with bows and ribbons. I need a Stetson for riding—even if it will put a line on my face."

He sighed. "Alex. Just put the purchases on account like ever'one else and when your money comes in—"

"Can you please take off another pair of pants and I'll owe Jesse three dollars."

Hope's Hats was on a side street. Jesse and Alex walked there in silence, Jesse nodding briefly to people he knew. He opened the door for Alex, trying to read her face, but there was only a small frown to show anything amiss. The bell jangled as they went in and Mr. Hope stepped out from behind a curtain.

"Ah, Mr. Makepeace. How nice to see you again." Mr. Hope rubbed his hands together in expectation. "And I see you've brought along a young lady to give her opinion."

"Actually, Mr. Hope, we're looking for a hat for the young lady."

"Well, you know we don't sell ladies' hats." The man waved his arm at the displays. "I suggest you go on over to Hannah Tuggy's—"

"This young lady would like a Stetson, Mr. Hope."

Hope was astounded. "I-I'm not sure what you

mean, Mr. Makepeace."

"Seems clear enough, Mr. Hope. Lady Alex wishes to buy a Stetson. You have boys sizes right over there as I recall. Can we take a look?"

Hope looked at Jesse as if he were stark raving mad but said nothing as the two went to the hat stands holding several smaller-sized Stetsons. Alex immediately tried on a black one. She looked at herself in the mirror and then smiled up at Jess but he shook his head, so she put it back.

"How much are they?" she whispered.

"Don't worry. We'll settle up later."

"You keep saying that. What if the money never comes in? What if I never sell a painting in my life?"

"Oh, ye of li'l faith. They'll sell."

Alex stared at him.

There had been an evening when, at age nine, Alex wanted to lasso the corral post and Jesse had helped her with that accomplishment—she wouldn't give up until she had succeeded. He wouldn't let her give up on the painting either. He took a light fawn colored hat sporting a beautiful silver band with a feather medallion at the front, and put it on her head, then adjusted it slightly forward. Her smile was magical. "That's the one," he said.

They walked to the counter to pay. "Twenty-five dollars," Mr. Hope said rather smugly.

At first, Jesse thought the man was overcharging because it was for Alex. But Hope continued, "Silver hat band is fifteen. Handmade. Solid silver."

"How many boys can afford this, Mr. Hope?" Alex reached across and removed the hat band. "I'll owe you ten more dollars," she told Jesse.

"I like the band—"

"I love the band. But I can't afford it. I'm not a rich rancher's son," she added with some irony. "And don't start telling me..." She put her hand out for the money, which he gave her, and she put it on the counter ready to walk out.

The door jangled again. "Out, out!" shouted Hope at the two men who had come in. Their dark features and mode of dress announced they were Mexicans. "We don't serve your kind in this shop!"

"Your kind!" Alex said in disbelief, her face reddening. "Exactly what kind is that, Mr. Hope?"

"Mexicans! Thieves!"

Her eyes flashed and Jesse sighed. She turned to the men. "*Que es lo que usted quiere?*"

"*Esta bien, Señorita, vamos a irnos. No queremos problemas.*" The door closed behind them.

Alex turned to Jesse. He knew what she was thinking; he read her like a book. "Take the hat, Alex," he said in a low voice so Hope wouldn't hear. "We jus' won't come back again."

****

"What happened to the old Indian who used to be outside the shop?" Alex asked, making conversation as they rode back to the ranch. She was eating from the lunch bag and occasionally feeding Jesse a bit.

"What old Indian?" Jesse slid a glance at her and shook the reins a bit.

"You know, the one who used to be squatting outside, begging. The one with the bracelet I always wanted. The turquoise and silver cuff. You remember? I really had my eye on that. I thought if he sold it he would have money to eat."

"No idea. Long gone," Jesse replied absentmindedly.

Alex turned away and sighed. She let the silence stretch for a bit before feeding him another bit of chicken. "You didn't ask," she said at last. "How much do you know?"

He thought of pretending he did not understand what she meant, but looking at her, he knew her need to tell was greater than his need to hear it all. "You don't have to tell me," he replied. "I know you were married and it's been annulled. I know you didn't try to kill 'im, Alex. I know you gave him laudanum to—"

"You said once we were best friends. Friends share everything."

There had been a day, which now seemed so long ago, when he had been telling her how he had come up from Texas, aged fourteen, on a cattle drive, riding drag all the way, eating dust 'til his lungs were choked with it, and how he missed his family, missed watching his baby brother round the house while his mama did her chores. He had explained how his father had died in the War Between the States when he was six and he had become the man of the family, but they were too poor and there were too many mouths to feed at home so he left. Alex, aged eleven at the time, with tears in her eyes, asked who his best friend was, and he had replied jokingly, "Well, you are, of course," trying to get her to smile again. They were different people then, so much younger, and neither knew what lay ahead.

"Friends don't pry," he finally answered. "If you want to tell me more…it's up to you."

Alex looked straight ahead. He wondered if she felt spurned, rejected.

"It's not that I don't care," he said as if he had read her thoughts. "I do care, Alex. It's just…it's none of my business. Unless you make it so, of course."

"I want you to know," she said at last. "I want someone who knows me…" Her voice trailed off. Of course that wasn't it. Annie and Tom already knew, but Jess was different. Jesse would protect her in a different way, defend her somehow. She needed him to know.

"When we were in Paris…on the fateful wedding

trip, we dined out with his friends—I think it was the second evening. It was a friend of his from school and his mistress who he had installed in her own apartments in Paris. She had been—well, like me I suppose—a fairly well-bred woman, maybe not an aristocrat's daughter or what-have-you, but nonetheless well-bred. She had fallen in love with a soldier, given herself to him, and he deserted her. So there she was, a courtesan, if you like. Bound to live forevermore on the generosity of a series of benefactors until her beauty or her luck ran out. I'm telling you this because that evening I looked my alternative fate in the face. It could have been me, had I not consented to this marriage, such as it was.

"But the other side of that evening was the insult to me my husband perpetrated. The only way I can explain it is, if you took me into Miss Bea's and asked me to have dinner with one of the soiled doves." She looked at Jess for a moment to try to read his face but he gave no reaction. He understood perfectly. "You know me well enough that I would have nothing against the poor woman per se. My sympathy was with her completely. But the insult to my honor was…well, it was stupendous to say the least. One's husband simply does not take one out to dine with a-a fallen woman.

"I had to leave early. I complained of a headache. John did not even see me back to the hotel." She stopped for a while as Jesse continued to look ahead. "That was the kind of man he was, Jess. He was a drunkard, a bounder we call them in England, or a blackguard, a gambler, a womanizer. That was the man my dear father wished me to be married to for the rest of my life."

There was a long silence until Jesse said, "You're free now, Alex. You're here."

"Yes. I'm back in Colorado. And all's right with the world," she quoted with some amusement as she fed him a piece of apple somewhat distractedly. "But sometimes I wonder, I wonder why men do as they do to women and why women put up with it. I'm not sure what I'll do if those damn paintings don't sell, Jesse. I really don't."

Jesse headed the wagon down the fork in the road to the Homestead to drop off some supplies for Annie and Tom. Several horses were hitched out front.

"What's goin' on?" Jesse asked, coming in the door with Alex close behind. She went past the men to give Annie a hug and stood there with her in the kitchen area.

"Hayden's been shot," Tom said, referring to one of the men who had been at the Line Camp called Cattail. He was sitting at the head of the table, the punchers around him. "Charging after rustlers up on the north range."

"Sheriff says the Darcy Brothers are out and about," Jesse told him. "Was it them?"

"Prob'ly. Some of our men have already gone after them but if the sheriff's aware, then I should think they'll soon be joined by a posse." He looked across at Annie who was visibly relieved.

Alex picked up a metal implement on the worktop by the sink and started to turn it around in her hands. It had a strange, sharp blade shaped like a crescent moon and she turned it this way and that, trying to figure out what it did. After a time, the room had gone dead quiet. Alex looked up: all eyes were on her. "What? What now?" Her questioning gaze searched all the men. "What's the matter?"

"Heck, woman, you are about the most dang helpless..." Garrison started but he saw Annie shake her head. "Ain'tcha never seen a dang can opener before?"

"No," said Alex with a giggle, "when would I ever have used a can opener, Garrison? Tell me that."

"Lordy, lord," said Reb from a corner. "Woman rides like the wind, carries a rifle, can even throw a lariat if'n she's a mind, but put 'er in a kitch'n..."

Alex looked over at Tom who was quietly laughing. "Ah, well, you jus' have to love 'er, useless as she is."

"Oh, Tom," reprimanded Annie. "She's not useless at all." She took a can of tomatoes sitting there and showed Alex how to use the opener.

Jesse watched her for a moment. "After the circus on Sa'day, Alex, I think the next thing you better make sure you learn to use is that new Colt."

Chapter Six

Brandy was limping.

"Whadya do to my dang horse?" Jesse reined in beside Alex as they got into town.

"Prob'ly only a stone, Jess. We'll take him over to Vernon's and let him have a look," Cal mediated.

"Yes, if we can find any place to tie up. Look at it!" Alex grimaced.

Loveland was busy. Not only was the circus here, but it was Saturday shopping for most people in from the outlying farms and ranches. The place was swarming.

"Behind Miss Bea's. No one ever ties up there." Cal exchanged a questioning look with Jesse who nodded and they walked the horses round the back of the main street. There they found free space on the hitching rail behind the saloon.

Jesse heaved a sigh as he dismounted. "You two wait here. I'll walk Brandy over to the Liv'ry and see what's happenin'." He ran his hand down Brandy's leg to the fetlock. "Damn," he mumbled, "looks like a scrape. All right," he said looking up again. "Be right back."

Cal leaned back against the rail and watched Alex watching Jesse walk away. Almost as tall as Jesse, but dark, he wore his Stetson pushed well forward to shade his eyes. He was never really clean-shaven, but neither did he have a beard, a fact that had fascinated Alex when she was little as she could never figure out how he maintained that stubble.

She looked back at him. "So?" She smiled.

"So..." he responded quietly. Whatever he was

thinking, he wasn't letting Alex know.

Alex crossed her arms, still smiling over at Cal. She was comfortable with her friend, always had been, but his occasional inscrutability both amused and infuriated her. She turned back as Jesse came toward them on the boardwalk, a bag of candies in his hand. Just then, one of the soiled doves slipped out the back door of the saloon, a cigarette between her stained fingers, blouse sliding off one shoulder.

"Those for me, Jesse dear?" she crooned.

Jesse stopped in his tracks. He looked across at Alex and then at Cal, both of who turned and stood by to see what Jesse would do.

Cal chewed his gum, then said, "Mabel, you got a smoke there. I don't think you need them candies as well."

The girl flicked ash in Cal's direction, then turned back to Jesse. She swayed her hips a bit before giving Jesse a slow smile. "See you real soon, darlin'," she purred, just loud enough for Alex to hear, before turning to go inside.

Alex sauntered over to where Jesse still stood transfixed, the bag in his hand. Their eyes met as she nodded her head slightly and lifted the bag from him. "Those fer me, darlin'?" she said.

****

"So when does it start? I can't see anything!"

"Well it hasn't started yet so 'course ya can't see nothin', dummy," said Cal.

"But I won't be able to see!"

"Wanna sit on my lap?" Jesse asked mildly.

Alex looked around to see whom she knew in the audience. Just about everyone, by name at least, was her answer. "I think there're enough rumors about me for the moment, thanks."

"You worried what people might say, Ladilex? That ain't like you. I thought you were above that sorta thing now. Beyond reproach."

Alex snorted. "I don't care what people might say but I don't have to give them fodder for gossip either, Cal." She craned her neck to see over the man in front.

Cal tapped him on the shoulder. "You mind removin' your hat, sir, so's our lady friend here can see?"

The man looked at Cal then over at Alex and nodded politely before removing his hat. Then he faced front and put it right back on.

"Look here," started in Jesse tapping the man on the shoulder again. "We jus' asked you real polite-like to—"

"Jesse! Leave it...it's fine. I can see well enough." Alex sat back and crossed her arms before stealing a glance at Jesse. He was biting his lip, suppressing his anger. "You haven't changed," she muttered over at him. "Not one bit."

They watched intently as the acrobats and jugglers performed, laughed at the ridiculous things the clowns did, thrilled at the balancing acts and got nervous when the lion tamer came out. The crack of the whip and roar of the beast sent Alex covering her eyes and cowering into Jesse, but she sat up again to see the trick riders. Jesse and Cal exchanged looks over the top of her head.

"Hey, Alex, maybe you should try that instead of ropin'. Be right entertainin' watchin' you do that 'round the corral."

"Yeah," joined in Cal. "I wanna see 'er stand on 'er saddle tippy-toe-like and then do a headstand like that."

"Go on. Have your fun, you two. You're only jealous because you know I can outride either of you any day of the week."

"Ohhh," the two men said together.

"Whoa, now, sweetheart," Jesse went on. "Them's fightin' words."

"Any day, Jesse Makepeace, any day!" Alex affirmed. "I know more about horses than the two of you put together. Put together," she repeated when she saw Cal's smirk.

At the end of the show, they filed down the midway with everyone else, past all the sideshows. "Can we go see the snake pit?" Alex wanted to know.

"Heck no," answered Jesse, "there're enough dang snakes in Colorado without paying good money to see them."

"Well, can we see the bearded lady then?"

Cal laughed. "Here," he said, sticking his chin out toward Alex, "ya can feel my face again. That's just as good, ain't it?"

"Come on," said Jesse suddenly pulling Alex's hand. "I'm gonna win you a doll with throwing them balls."

The three of them got in line for Jesse to have a turn throwing balls at wooden faces. As disappointed customers drifted away, Jesse reached in his pocket for his nickel and slapped it on the counter. The roustabout slid it into his pile and turned to set up the wooden faces once more before handing Jesse the three balls.

Jesse felt the heft of the ball in his palm before pulling his arm back and throwing it. Bang! Down went the first one. He turned and gave Alex a smug smile before pulling back and slamming out the second. Bang! Cal stopped chewing in expectation and Alex gripped her hands together as if in prayer. Jesse's arm pulled back and released the third ball, hitting the face squarely.

But it didn't go down.

"That shot was good," said Jesse staring the man down.

"No sirree, the little man has got to go down for it to be good."

"I think you all better think 'bout that some."

Cal leaned on the counter with his hand noticeably on his six-shooter.

"Now looka here. I don't want no trouble from you all. You lost fair and square—"

"The hell I did."

"Jess, I don't really want a doll anyway," Alex conciliated. "I've rather outgrown dolls, haven't I?"

"Well, I sure as heck want my nickel back," he responded still staring at the man.

There was a moment in which Cal made a small movement with his right arm before the man slipped the nickel back across the counter and Jesse pocketed it, his eyes steadily on the roustabout.

"Just for friendly relations, sir," the man said as the three walked off.

"Ah, good ol' Jess," sighed Cal. "Black and white, right and wrong…"

"I didn't see you holdin' back from the matter none."

"Well, heck, Jess, I know you better'n you know yerself. I don't hold back none for my friends." They walked on a bit. "You have no gray areas, Jess. Couldn't be the shot were jus' not strong enough to get the wooden face down?"

"Nope."

"Don't spoil it!" Alex turned and gave Jesse a push. "Don't spoil it by being moody! I've just had one of the best days of my life and—"

"Come 'ere." Cal crouched. "I'm gonna give you a piggy back ride back to the horses."

The diversion worked. Alex held her stomach with laughing so hard and Jesse laughed too. "Gosh durnit, Cal, if that offer ain't plain indecent I don't know what is." But he was still laughing.

"Yes, I think I'm past my piggy back days. Past my doll days, if I ever had them. My piggy back and my sit in lap days are gone now." She threw up her hands as if in disgust.

They passed the saloon and Alex looked over the top of the swinging doors. Cal laughed now but Jesse said, "For goodness sake Alex, what the heck are you thinkin'?"

"What? It's only music and drinkin', ain't it Ladilex?" defended Cal.

"Hmmm. I don't know. But it seems like there's some really good music being played in there. Everyone seems to be having a very good time. Why can't women go in? Why shouldn't women be allowed to go? I mean, you know-*ordinary* women." She fluttered her eyelashes in all innocence.

There was a momentary silence before the two men burst out laughing.

"All right, all right. Have your fun," Alex moaned as they approached the two horses. "But one day women will have equal rights and—"

"Aw, heck, Ladilex. You ain't gonna be one of them suffrage women now, are you? We always thought you were one of us anyways. What you wanna go spoilin' a good thing for?"

Alex laughed again. "Well, now we have a problem," she pointed out as they reached the horses. "Two horses, three people." She turned to look from one to the other.

Cal made the decision for them. "You ride with Jess. Brimstone don't take to strangers kindly and he's only half-broke."

Jesse extended his hand and pulled Alex up behind him. They took to the road at a gentle lope as the town started to empty out. Alex wrapped her arms around Jesse's waist, resting more or less on his gun belt. She didn't give a second thought to holding him like this until, moving back some while adjusting her seat, her hands slipped onto his stomach for a moment. She suddenly felt as if she had swallowed a gallon of ice water and froze. The sheer firmness of his body, the taut muscles, the solid, rock hard strength she felt astounded her.

She had the greatest urge to run her hands over him, to feel that strength, to know those muscles and to finally rest her head against him. She faced straight into his back, looking at the way his shaggy hair fell over his shirt collar just peeking out of his leather vest. The knot of his bandana was just visible under his hair and Alex had a further urge to lift his hat, push his hair aside and untie the neckerchief so she could kiss his neck. Oh, lord, what was she thinking?

She adjusted her hands back onto Jesse's gun belt hoping he hadn't noticed her moving them. Then the thought struck her as to where her hands actually were—within inches of... She turned her head to the side as if one of the men could see her blush. She looked out toward the ranch, trying to dispel those thoughts but as they approached the western range, Alex spotted a cloud of thick dust in the distance.

"What's that?" she asked.

Jesse looked where she was pointing and Cal saw it at the same moment. "Holy— It's a stampede!" Jesse pulled up his bandana. He spurred his horse into a gallop and followed Cal toward the herd. The thundering Longhorns were coming straight at them, noise and dust enveloping them, and no other puncher had managed to get to point yet; the cows were following their leader and headed down the dry draw. Alex gripped Jesse more tightly and bent her knees in to grip the horse's flanks as best she could.

Cal raised his six-shooter and fired several shots in an attempt to scare the herd into turning, but the noise was such and the distance so great that the shots were barely audible. It was hard for Alex to see anything through the dust. Her eyes stung and her mouth tasted as if she had eaten mud pies. She leaned further into Jesse.

Jesse signaled to Cal and the two men split off to the sides of the bunching cattle and turned their horses to get back at the front. With Alex still hanging on, Jesse fired his gun and turned his horse toward Cal, and the two men finally got the herd into a mill. Confused and with no leader, the cows at last crowded in on themselves, stopped their run, and settled. The three riders sat gasping for air amid the settling dust.

"Jeez," said Reb riding up. "I thought we was surely headed into the Rockies to stop them cows." He stopped to catch his breath. "Shit," he said totally forgetting himself, "you did all that with Lady Lex on your rear?"

Jesse's hand felt for Alex's arms about his waist as he turned back to look at her. Bedraggled and dirty, blinking the filth from her eyes, with her hair loose from its plait and her face streaked with mud, she had the widest grin on her face he'd ever seen.

"Can we do that again sometime?" she smirked.

There was no way to hide what had happened. When Alex appeared at the house, Oliver was livid.

"You rode into a stampede!" he thundered.

"Jesse knew what he was doing, Uncle Oliver; there was never any danger—"

"Never any danger? Are you out of your mind? That was not some canter through Hyde Park, Alex. You could have been killed. One man on a horse in a stampede is dangerous enough, but sitting two—"

"Are you saying I'm not a good enough rider to hang on to the back of someone? Oh, for goodness sake." She turned on her heel and started to leave.

"If you had fallen...You could have been crushed in the melee. You could have been shot by a stray bullet. Anything could have happened. Have you no sense at all?"

She stared at him, her lips pursed in anger. "No

sense? I had the sense to hang on. Jesse had to do what he did or your cows would've been in Estes Park! He did his job, and he did it damn well I have to say, and he had every consideration for my having to be there," she lied.

"Every consideration? Just what consideration did he give you? He should have set you down, should have left you somewhere."

"And then what? If the herd had changed direction I could be standing there with no cover, no place to go! Everyone knows cows panic more when they see a person on foot. I was far safer on the back of his horse!"

"He's fired!" Oliver shouted. "I gave you permission to go to the circus with two of my hands—permission against my better judgment I might add—and what happens? You nearly lose your life."

"I did not lose my life! I didn't even come close to losing anything. I am perfectly fine. And," she strode up to Oliver and took several deep breaths, "if you fire that man, I swear you'll be sorry!"

"Are you threatening me?" Oliver growled.

Alex paced the length of the drawing room while Oliver watched, his eyes blazing. Wilson, the butler, knocked but as he entered Oliver waved him out and the door shut again.

"I've looked at the ranch accounts, Uncle Oliver. I've seen the accounts—"

"You what?" he said, his voice lower, hoarse.

"I've seen. I know. You won't fire Jesse."

Chapter Seven

Jesse and Alex agreed after the stampede that the shooting lesson had to be postponed. In the early evening on Monday, when the men changed shifts, Alex waited at the corral and watched the punchers come in from the herd. She had her new Colt in a holster on her belt, the cartridge loops had been filled, and she wore her new hat, Levi denims, and a bandana around her neck.

"Oh, I haveta see this," said Cal riding in. "Will ya look at this, boys?"

"Heck, Lady, you look jus' like someone I used to know," quipped Jesse dismounting. "Mangy little thing, she was, 'bout so high," he said, showing her height at age eight. "Y'all see this, boys?"

Alex stood there patiently letting them have their fun.

"I dunno," Garrison joined in. "Used to have a lady lived here a' times. Y'all remember that, don't ya Reb?"

"A lady? Lemme see now." Reb looked at the sky for inspiration. "A lady? Can't say I do, Gar—"

They stopped as a buggy came up the road toward the ranch headquarters. It halted where the drive split, one way to the main house, the other to the corrals and outbuildings, before it proceeded on toward them. A man jumped down, carrying a notepad. He was in his shirtsleeves, cap pushed back on his head.

Garrison moved up to speak to him, but the man had spotted Alex's long hair and pushed past. "Alexandra Calthorpe? Lady Alexandra Calthorpe?"

he shouted to her.

Alex didn't reply. Jesse and Cal moved in front of her.

"I wonder if I might have a few words? Interview you for the *Loveland Reporter*? Can I interview you 'bout—"

"She doesn't give interviews." Jesse's voice was low and menacing as the others surrounded the man.

Garrison's hand rested on the man's shoulder. "Looks like you best be goin', mister. We're none too keen on folks' nosin' into our bus'ness here."

"Lady Alexandra, it's about your marr—"

Garrison's hand clamped around the man's mouth. Cal moved forward to grab him by the legs, while the others helped pick him up and throw him back into his buggy. Cal jumped on the running board to turn the horse in the right direction, smacked the reins and hopped down, just about giving the man time to grab hold and go on his way.

Alex stood there with her mouth open. She didn't know whether to laugh or cry, when yet another stranger rode up. This time he was distinctly less threatening.

The young boy stayed mounted and looked from one face to the other, somewhat perplexed. "Y'all know a Lady Alexandra Calthorpe?"

"Oh, heck, what now?" said Cal. "What's this for?"

"Gotta telegram for Lady Alex."

Alex gasped. "Jesse, you take it." She cowered back against the office wall. Jesse took the telegram and found a coin to give the boy.

"Should I wait for an answer?" the boy wanted to know.

Jesse held out the telegram to Alex but she shook her head. "You read it," she said barely above a whisper. "They're only ever bad news."

Jesse pulled his knife from a sheath in his boot and slit open the envelope. He read the telegram to himself, a smile slowly spreading across his face. He handed it over to her:

Exhibition great success STOP All paintings sold STOP Please advise account for funds STOP Request fifteen paintings for solo exhibit October STOP Letter follows STOP Jonathon Sturgis.

"I did it," she said softly, half in amazement. "I bloody well did it."

Tears streamed down. Jesse moved to take the corner of her bandana and wipe her face.

"Never used a bandana for that before," Cal noted.

The other men laughed and moved to get their saddles off at last and go in to supper. "Whadja do this time, Ladilex?"

"Sold my paintings, Cal." Alex sniffed back more tears, then thought better of it and found her hanky to blow her nose. She looked up at the two men, from one to the other. "SO? Y'all gonna teach me how to use this a-here Colt," she mimicked. "I reckon it's time."

They rode a short distance from the corrals, to a copse of juniper away from the main ranch. Alex hung on to the back of Jesse for there was no point in saddling up for this short ride, and she knew the men would want to get in for the evening. She held him once more about the waist and felt again the tautness of Jesse's muscles, the strength of his body; a desire to know the rest of that body, to hold him, jolted through her.

As they dismounted, she watched the way he moved. He tied up the horse and strode over to set up the old tin cans which were lying about, while Cal settled back on a large rock and shaded his eyes with his hat.

Alex caught Cal trying to suppress a smile as his

eyes darted away from her and back to Jesse. She wondered for a moment if he found it funny that she wanted to learn to shoot the Colt, yet he knew she must protect herself. Inscrutable as always, she thought.

"Now listen to me, and I want ya to listen real good, Alex. Ya hear?" Jesse said.

Alex nodded in reply, a serious expression on her face.

"First off, you never draw unless you mean to shoot. If you're facin' a man, you look him in the eye so's he knows you mean bus'ness. This ain't no toy, nor no paintbrush neither, you understand?" He waited for her to nod again. "Secondly, don't you go puttin' no cartridge under the hammer. I know it's a six-shooter but if you keep it loaded, you keep only five in. You hear?"

"Why ever not?"

"'Cause if you fall from yer horse or trip while you're afoot or anything else like that, you don't want to go shootin' yerself in the leg, that's why. You keep a cartridge under the hammer, it's bound to happen sooner or later, you hear?"

"I hear."

"All right." He loaded the gun, showed her how to hold it and aim and fire, either by pulling the trigger or by fanning back the hammer. Jesse shot down the six cans, then handed her the empty gun to feel the weight of it while he set them up once more. "Now you load it. All six."

Cal sat up to watch, a smile breaking through. "Be easier for you with holding the trigger and fanning the hammer, I reckon," he put in. "You may find repeatedly pulling the trigger a bit heavy."

Alex raised an eyebrow at him, waited for Jess to clear away from the cans behind her, and fired—bang, bang, bang, bang, bang, bang!

There was silence except for Cal's laughter as he

smacked the earth next to him. Jesse started back toward the horses.

"What? What's the matter?" asked Alex, going after him. "I did what you said, didn't I? I shot all the cans down."

Jesse turned on her, angry. "You want to make a dang fool of someone, find someone else for a change, lady. Next time ya want—"

"What are you talking about?" she asked, perplexed. "How did I make a fool of you—of anyone?"

"You knew dang well how to shoot that thing!"

"You knew I had two rifles. I told you I could shoot. There was no secret about it. It's not that different. I had just never used a revolver, that's all. You wouldn't want me using it for the first time when it was necessary, would you?"

Jesse started to walk away.

"Oh, I am sorry, Jesse dear," Alex simpered in a mocking voice. "I done plumb forgot I'm supposed to be a li'l ol' helpless thing."

The words went unanswered. Jesse mounted and rode off. Alex turned to Cal who sat there, an amused look on his face. "Will you tell me please what's wrong with him? Really! Do you really all just want to subjugate women?"

"You wanna know what's wrong with him?" Cal shook his head in disparaging response. "He's in love with ya, ya dang fool." He stood up. Alex was silent. "No one wants to—what was it?—subja-what? Whatever it is." He smacked his gloved hands together to get the dust off. "Gee, Ladilex, for such an intelligent woman, you sure are dumb."

Alex continued staring at him. "I just got back. He hasn't seen me for five years and suddenly he's in love with me? How can he be in love with me, for goodness sake? Bloody hell," she said forgetting herself completely, and denying to herself what had

73

been staring her right in the face. "It's Jess we're talking about—you know, the sensible one. The solid one. Sturdy. Dependable. Sensible." She looked about as if the answer were to be had from the trees. "Albeit hotheaded," she added as an afterthought almost under her breath.

Cal sighed. "Heck, Ladilex. Don't ya know nothin'?"

"Well, apparently not. Certainly not about men, I should say."

"Well, ya've spent ya life, or a durned good part of it, with 30 or 40 men on a ranch."

"I know! And I love you all, every last one of you, b-but…"

"Yeah," said Cal. "Trouble is, there's a difference 'tween lovin' like y'all are sayin' and bein' in love. And we're all 'in love' with you. Or at least half of us."

Alex's eyes widened at Cal as if she were seeing him for the first time. He always seemed so comfortable with himself, so sure, so centered in a way Jesse never was. With Jesse she always sensed a small frisson of tension beneath the surface, the possibility that the sturdiness and dependability were difficult for him to maintain though he always would because it was the right thing to do. She said, "Well, I certainly hope you're not in love with me, Cal. I need you as a friend—badly. Who wants to go messing up relationships with the intricacies of love, for heaven's sake?"

"Nah, I'm too smart for love, Ladilex." He bent and pulled up some grass, playing with it in his hands for a moment. "Anyways, I could never be there for ya the way y'all need. I like driftin' too much. Been down in Texas much of the time you been away. Bet y'all didn't know that." He let the grass fly off on the wind. "Jess'll always be there for ya. Like ya say, he's dependable."

74

Alex stopped to listen to the wind soughing through the trees, and adjusted her hat back on her head. She didn't know what she felt, had never been accustomed to analyzing what she felt, other than a strong desire for independence which was in direct contradiction to being in love. Being in love meant being possessed. Or had Annie been right when she once said that if you were in love with someone you would feel differently? You would want to be with them. Did she want to be with Jess—for the rest of her life?

"He can't deal with ya bein' so, I don't know…so dang wonderful I guess," Cal said.

"Wonderful? Because I can shoot? I was twelve when Jesse last saw me, Cal. He's not in love with me. Come on," she said at last, "give me a ride back."

****

The noise of the men having dinner in the chuck house didn't hide the particular tap of Cal's boots as he came out from the stables. After seventeen years of riding together, of covering each other's backs, of practically being blood brothers, Jesse knew that peculiar saunter anywhere—and it was headed for him. The door to the bunkhouse whined open at Cal's push just as one of Jesse's boots met the far wall.

"Nice shot; gonna try the other?"

"Very funny." Jesse lay back on his cot, his long legs dangling off the end, his hands cradling his head.

"Wanna eat or wanna talk?" Cal offered.

"Neither, if you don't mind." His leg swung for a moment before he turned his head. "You know, I still find it hard to believe it's the same person?"

Cal leaned comfortably against the next row of bunk beds and looked down at his friend. "It's the same person, Jess, only older. She been married once already." He ran his hand through his hair before sitting down. "You know she doesn't need to be hurt. You know that." Jesse blinked in acknowledgement. "I...I sure love Alex but not the way you love her, Jess. I love havin' her 'bout the place, lookin' at her so dang pretty and fine, hearin' her laugh and I love joshin' about with her. But I'm never gonna make her no husband and I watch the way you two look at each other and...you know, I don't know what gets into you sometimes? You got that temper on you- what the hell are you so mad about anyways?"

Jesse took a deep breath before sitting up and ducking out of the bunks. He stood and stretched. "I don't know. Maybe I'm mad because I reckon I can't have Alex. We're from two different worlds. I can be her friend—everyone's fine with that—but anything more? Calthorpe'll be paying me off and sending me on my way he smells any—"

"Oh, Calthorpe. Calthorpe's so busy building his dang empire here he doesn't see what's going on under his nose. Hell, Tom runs the ranch and we all know that." He thought a moment. "Are you looking for excuses? Or are you just plumb scared?" His eyes met Jesse's for a moment before the other man turned away and went to pick up his boot. "Well, hell, Jess, we're all scared of women. At least Alex...you say you're from two different worlds and, yeah, in a lot of ways she's very much the product of her upbringin' and all, but I can't imagine no other English lady dressing like Alex was kitted out today. You gotta get a hold on that temper and you gotta let her know how you feel."

"Is that your advice?" Jesse stood with his hands on his hips looking over at his best friend. It always surprised him how sensible Cal could be when you got right down to it.

"Yeah, that's my advice. That and we better eat before we starve."

Chapter Eight

The thought bothered Alex—that Jesse might be in love with her, that if she couldn't return his feelings she would hurt him, ruin their friendship. The next afternoon she rode off to see Annie.

"Cal says Jesse's in love with me. How can he be in love with me, Annie? He hardly knows me."

"What do you mean, he hardly knows you? He's known you since you were eight."

"Yes, but that's a very long time ago. I mean, I only just got back. He doesn't know me as an adult—Jesse, of all people! He's always been my best friend, he and Cal. And he's always been fairly sensible—if a little temperamental. How could he just decide, like that, he's in love?"

"Well, what do you feel?"

"That's what I feel. He's always been my best friend of the punchers. He's always been there, protecting me from things, helping me, sorting things out for me. I wouldn't want to be without him. But in love?"

"Maybe you should ask yourself how you would feel if he married someone else. What do you think 'I wouldn't want to be without him' means?"

Alex considered this a moment, pushing the truth, shoving the possible pain, aside. "I-I came back expecting he was married. Obviously, Uncle's letters never mentioned the men and there was no word from you because of Helene's mail being intercepted. I mean, I was married so I just sort of assumed that since he's older..."

"What did you feel?" Annie asked.

Alex looked at her. "Deserted. I guess I felt alone and deserted. But then I felt that anyway after, you know, the whole business. I just wanted to get away from it all. I think I'm too numb still to feel anything really."

"You won't find a better man than Jesse Makepeace, Alex."

"Yes, but that's not the point. I don't want to be in love with him because there's not a better man. I have no intention of marrying. I want my freedom, not…well, you know…"

"Freedom gives you choice, Alex. Having faith in him is a choice, hoping things go right is a choice, love is a choice. You think I'm tied to the house and kids and have no freedom? Is that it?"

"But you're happy. It's what makes you happy, and you make Tom happy. I can see that. But I would just make Jesse miserable."

"Oh, hogwash. You don't know what you want, Alex. I think you've been too hurt, had too many traumas in your young life to have cleared your head enough to know what you really want. You think on it. You think about life here without Jesse." She stopped for a moment to look at her young friend standing there biting her nails. "Maybe because you didn't have two parents who loved each other, who showed you what love really is."

"I had Helene," Alex argued. "And I had David."

"Yes, and you have Tom and me. But maybe you're just not able to recognize your feelings."

Alex paced a bit. She knew the older woman was trying to help her, trying to find the right words to ease her through the emotional tangle of growing up.

Finally Annie went on, "Jesse's such a good man, Alex. He'd make you so happy."

"But is that right? For me to love him because he's a good man and my best friend. And for him to love me because maybe there's no one else."

"First off, who should be your best friend but your husband? And secondly, there's plenty else. Women are throwing themselves at Jesse Makepeace, don't you kid yourself."

"Sara Beth for goodness sake?"

"Yes, and I tell you Jesse wouldn't touch Sara Beth with a forty foot lariat. She's been after him since they were in school together here. He used to come back and tell us how she was following him about and he couldn't shake her. But then there's Nancy Roderick—"

"All right, so what about Nancy Roderick?" Alex remembered the exchange at the bank and what Jesse had said afterward.

"That's quite another story. They were seeing each other for a while but Jesse pulled out, decided Nancy wasn't for him and told her so straight."

"Because she's independent and has a position in the bank?"

"Because he loves this ranch, and is a born rancher and she works in a bank and has no interest in this life!"

Alex thought about this for a while. "But I paint!"

"Yes, you paint now. But you love this ranch as much as he does."

"Our backgrounds are different!"

"And? You keep saying you want to stay here, you want your own money so you can stay here and not worry about what your father says."

"That's not a reason to marry Jesse. Anyway, I can't marry until I'm twenty-one, and by then he'll be thirty-one."

"Are you worried about the age difference?"

"No, of course not."

Annie looked at Alex long and hard. "It seems to me young lady you're trying to convince yourself you're not in love with him."

"No, Annie, I'm not. I'm not convinced I am in love with him. And I'm scared. What if we had a-a relationship, a romance, and it didn't work out? What then? I'll have lost both my best friend and my...my...whatever. Beau?"

Annie scoffed. "You won't lose him. Jesse Makepeace is not the kind of man to just walk away and leave someone."

"But if he was hurt? If we just couldn't face each other as friends anymore?" Alex stopped and paced a bit. "What if, whatever it is I feel for him, whatever I feel that is deeper than just a friendship, turns out to be a young girl's infatuation? I'm hardly out of one trauma and now we're talking about a-a relationship." Her voice trailed off and she chewed a nail. She looked up at Annie. "I wonder if Jesse just liked looking after the little girl, protecting her, and he thinks I'm that same little girl who needs protection?"

"Alex, sweetheart. You are that same little girl who needs protection. You're strong in so many ways but in so many others..."

Alex sank into the chair by the fireplace, got up again and paced, still biting her nails. "Anyway," she went on with some derision, "he's angry at me now because I could use the bloody six-shooter and he thought he was showing me how. I hurt his pride."

Annie laughed and went back to drying dishes. "I doubt that was the reason, Alex. He probably just thought how talented you were, doing that, and couldn't cope with what he felt so he stormed off."

Alex stopped and looked at her friend. "How do you know so much about men, Annie?"

Annie glanced out the window. The children were riding in from school and she put the cloth down to get their meal ready. "Oh, Alex," she said, "I guess it's just experience."

****

On herd at night, circling around at a measured pace and singing softly to settle the cows, Jesse heard one of the other punchers whistling in the distance, and the soft lowing of the cattle in response. It was a clear evening, highlighted by a full moon, with shooting stars dashing through the heavens like travelers hurrying home. Nighthawking gave him time to think, and he remembered the feel of her arms about him, the perfume of her skin when he got close, the way her hair caught the light, and the depth of the green of her eyes. He thought about the way she smiled, as if she kept a special smile only for him, as if they shared a secret, as if they didn't need their voices for each other.

"Y'all got that high school thing, didn't ya?" Reb rode up and broke into Jesse's reveries. "You read that Shakespeare fella? Ain't there lotsa kings an' queens and that in them books?"

"Plays, Reb. They're plays by Shakespeare." Jesse leaned forward in his saddle and rested his hands on the horn.

"So, why do you reckon Lady Lex come back here like that? What's she doin' here anyways, comin' back?"

"First off, Reb, I don't reckon somethin' writ in the fifteen hundreds is any dang clue to the mind of Lady Alex. Second," he added somewhat defensively, "what's your dang problem with her bein' here? Havin' a woman 'round makes it sort of more homey, don't you think? More civilized."

"Hell, I came west to escape *civilized*." Reb spurred his horse into the darkness.

Jesse laughed.

When they met up again on the next circle round Reb said, "We got them dang nightriders and barn burnings and shootin's now with all them new homesteaders movin' in. Seems never-ending to me.

Statehood was the worse dang thing ever happened to this place. Farms springin' up all over the dang place. Sheepherders, for chrissake, ruinin' our grass."

"Double F still controls the open range between the Cache and the Thompson," Jesse reminded him.

Reb snorted in response and went on round again. He wasn't happy unless he had something to complain about.

When they completed their next round Jesse asked, "Don't you wonder what it's like over there, where she comes from?"

"Hell no, Jesse. You read too many of them damn books. You passed that diploma thing, didn't you?"

"I just said so, Reb." Jesse didn't answer too forcefully as he knew he was in for some criticism.

"Way I heared it, Miz Dawson wanted you all to go on to that new university down at Boulder."

"Yup." Jesse waited a moment for Reb to continue. "But—"

"But nothin', Jesse. Way you read, you shoulda been a doctor or a lawyer or somemat."

"I didn't want to be a dang doctor or lawyer, Reb. I don't wanna be stuffed inside all day." His voice was getting heated. "You got that?"

"Yeah, I got that. Thing is, way I see it, you're lookin' moony ever' time Lady Lex walks by and you ain't nothin' but a two-bit cowpuncher. You been a doctor or a lawyer, you mighta stood a chance. You got that?"

"Yeah, I got that," Jesse mumbled under his breath as Reb rode off again. "I got that good and clear."

****

Jonathon Sturgis' letter finally arrived. It contained a clipping from *The New York Times* reviewing the mixed exhibition in which Alex's paintings had been shown. Aside from his request for her to have ready some fifteen works for a solo exhibition in New York in October, which he would like her to attend, he also wished to pay a visit to the ranch at some stage to see how she was doing. It was all good news, and the review was particularly glowing. Alex read it out to her uncle during afternoon tea in the drawing room.

Oliver didn't look up but ruffled his newspaper before reaching for his cup. "I'm off to Cheyenne on Sunday directly after church. Business, don't you know? Perhaps you can go on to the Yosts for luncheon?"

Jesse drove her, of course. There was silence for a while, then he said, "Sorry about the other day. I was a dang fool, wasn't I?"

"No." Alex tried to stop herself from smiling. "I mean, I can paint, I have a good eye, so I should be able to shoot fairly well, shouldn't I?" She let it go at that and rushed on to tell him her news. "I heard from Jonathon, from the gallery in New York. I mean, his letter arrived."

"Oh, yeah?"

Alex sat looking at her hands, happily comforted by the fact Jesse showed some interest. "He repeated his request for fifteen paintings for a solo exhibition, and is coming out in the summer." She tried to keep the excitement from her voice.

Jesse turned and looked at her. "Well, you've really done it, haven't you? I mean, you're going to be a success, Alex." He hesitated before looking ahead again. "You gonna move there, to New York I mean?"

"Oh, heavens, no! Why would I do that?" She hoped he understood what she was saying.

They pulled up in front of the Homestead, and she handed him her bankbook. "What's this for?" he asked.

Alex's eyes lit up. "I need you to sign for the money I owe you so I can go into town and take it out. I can repay you now."

"Been wired already?"

"Yes. Five hundred dollars. Is that a lot? Can I live for a while on that?"

"Five hundred dollars!" he exclaimed in disbelief. "Are you sure? My lord, that's a fortune! It's 'bout what I make in ten months."

"Is it?" Alex felt embarrassed. "Well, I won't have more than two exhibitions a year and, of course, those New York people, you know— They show women's shawls in the Godey's magazine for five hundred dollars and ladies' purses at a hundred and fifty so I expect those people don't mind paying for paintings they like." She sat quietly while he came round to help her down but she hesitated before taking his hand. "Are you angry?"

"No, why would I be angry? I'm really happy for you. It's what you want, isn't it?"

****

With the children gathered around, Annie read the review out loud: "'However, the biggest surprise of the exhibition has to be the works by Lady Alexandra Calthorpe. Just seventeen, and previously known on these shores for her own most remarkable beauty—'"

"Oh, for heaven's sake," interrupted Alex, "What utter nonsense!"

"'Her immense talent comes as a complete surprise. The five paintings here presented were conceived at her brother's estate in Italy, and show a depth of ability from one so young that can only astound. Peasants working in the fields, Romanys in their wagons—'"

"What's a Romany?" Sue Ann wanted to know.

"They're gypsies, darling," Alex replied.

"Are they like Indians?" J.J. demanded.

"Not really. They're...how can I explain? They're people who don't like to live in one place and they travel and live in wagons."

"Indians don't like to live in one place. They traveled across the plains."

"Yes, J.J., but these are Europeans. They're mostly from Romania I think, and they travel around Europe."

"Can I continue?" Annie looked at the two of them. "'Women hanging laundry from the towers of San...San...' How do you pronounce this?"

"San Jim-in-yano," Alex told her.

"'San Gimignano, all come alive as if they would hold a conversation with you in the very next instant. Without any professional schooling in her art, Lady Alexandra has harnessed her talent with precociousness well beyond her years. We will wait to see such perspicacity does not burn itself out early but rather gets channeled into an ever-burgeoning mastery. The exhibition continues at...'"

Jesse looked across the table at her, but it was Garrett who, crossing his arms, said quietly, "Well, maybe not so useless afta all, Lady Lex."

Alex tried to guide the conversation away from herself and her painting. The Darcy Brothers came up, but Tom nixed that because of the children being present and so it went on to spring round-up, which was shortly to get underway.

"Oh, so you'll all be off for weeks and weeks. It's going to be quiet here, that's for sure."

"You've got fifteen paintings to finish by October," Jesse pointed out.

"Well, you all are my subject matter. I shall have to follow you for a bit to get my drawings done. Can I rope too?"

"You cannot." Tom's face was grave and he had a steely glint in his eye.

"Why?" Alex was taken aback by his serious

tone.

"Because," Jesse explained on Tom's behalf, "you're not good enough, Alex. You all know you're not good enough and we can't be watchin' you all the time. 'Sides which you're sure as heck to forefoot one of 'em, and then we'll have trouble."

"Where's your faith in me? Anyway, what's forefooting or whatever it was?"

"It's when you rope only one foot on a calf and he breaks his leg," explained Garrett.

"Oh. Oh dear. I see what you mean," Alex conceded.

Sue Ann looked from Jesse to Alex and back again.

"Anyway, Alex, what do you want to be paintin' us for?" Jesse said. "Think you'd have enough to paint without followin' us aroun'."

Alex looked at him, her mouth open. "Just what is your problem? You are what I paint. You are the most interesting people around. It's what I do, paint people, paint cowpunchers. Just what is your objection? Bloody hell—"

"Now, now," interrupted Tom.

"Sorry. It's difficult enough with the damn wind blowing up dust as I work all day—"

"Alex!" Annie reprimanded.

"Sorry!" She gathered up dishes from the table.

"Whoa, we are touchy today," said Jesse.

"I am not touchy. Certainly not touchy as some!"

"What's that supposed to mean?"

"You know what that means, Jesse Makepeace. If there's touchiness around here, it sure as hell—"

"Alex," admonished Tom again.

Jesse and Alex looked at each other across the room as Sue Ann said, "Jesse, you gonna marry Lady Alex?"

There was a momentary silence before Alex burst out laughing, then covered her mouth with a hand. "Oh, no, darling," she said still laughing, "Jesse knows me far too well for that. He'd never dare."

Then she thought of what Cal had said and turned to avoid looking at Jesse's face.

Chapter Nine

A gunmetal gray sky lowered over the ranch lands with frequent flashes of lightning in the distance, but it wasn't the threatening weather that got Alex's attention. Shouts from the men and the ensuing ruckus drew her to the window. There in the corral was the most magnificent stallion, black with a white blaze and four white pasterns. Joe and Garrison had their lariats about his neck, trying to hold the horse as he reared on his hind legs and strained on the ropes.

Alex ran out, half-dressed, her shirt hanging loose and her boots hardly pulled on. "Stop it!" she screamed. "Stop it, Joe, this minute!"

Alex got up to the corral, the men turning to look at her. "I mean it! Stop it. Take the damn ropes off him."

Jesse came beside her. "Alex, it's a bronco, he's got to be blindfolded and saddled. We haven't time for fancy training. He's got to be saddled and rid. You've seen us break horses before..."

"Not this one! Not this one!" she cried.

"Any horse, Alex. They're all mustangs." But before he knew what was happening, she pulled his gun from its holster and pointed it at Joe, then Garrison. "Take the damn ropes off! Garrison! I mean it! Get the bloody rope off him or I'll shoot, I swear!"

A silence descended on the men like dust settling after a storm. The horse continued its terrified neighing as he strained on the ropes, his eyes wild with terror. Everyone stared at Alex, and

Jesse breathed hard but didn't move, sizing up whether he could take the gun back without her shooting someone. Garrison and Joe still held the ropes, both men looking back at her.

"I mean it," she repeated hoarsely, "get the ropes off!"

Her hand shook, more with anger than fear, as first Joe, then Garrison, got up close to remove the lariats, then backed out of the corral and over the fence. Alex turned the gun over, emptied the chambers, and pushed the gun and cartridges at Jesse, practically throwing them at him before climbing the fence and going into the corral. There was stillness from the men as she stood there, just eyeing the horse, her hands open out to him, as he pranced and bucked and loped about his confined space. Nobody moved; the men were transfixed by the small figure of Alex just standing still, facing down that stallion, murmuring softly to him.

The stallion spun 'round and made a dash toward Alex, stopping short just feet from her. She still did not move, staring him down, keeping her eyes always on his, totally fearless in aspect if not always in heart. She stood so motionless for the most part, it was almost a surprise to find she had moved along the rails, always keeping her face to the horse, her hands open. The men remained mesmerized by her and her soft sing-song words, forgetting their work until Tom rode up and started to shout and had to be shushed by Garrison; then he, too, got down and watched.

Alex eventually made her way around to Joe, who was standing up on the rails at the stable side of the corrals. Still keeping her eyes to the stallion, she said in a very low voice, "I'm sorry, Joe. Truly. I-I never should have done that, but I didn't know what else to do. I'm sorry." Alex sensed Joe was somehow more amused by the whole thing rather than angry.

He tugged on his moustache and in his smoky voice he said, "'S all right, Lady Lex, you jus' keep on doin' whatever it is yer doin'. Maybe there's somemat init fer us all to learn."

"Do you think…" She stopped for a minute while the horse came around again, pawing the earth angrily. "Do you think you might find some sugar cubes or apples for me?"

Joe went off and Alex became aware of the low voices of Jesse and Tom. Still she concentrated completely on the horse, continuing to stand there in the damp heat of the day with her shirt hanging out over her denims, her hair loose and her English paddock boots barely pulled on. Joe returned and spoke quietly to tell her he was there, and she moved back, facing forward, to take the cubes in her hand, which she extended behind her, quickly shoving all but one into a pocket.

The horse eyed her with interest now. He galloped toward her again and reared up at the last moment. Tom made a movement to stop it but Garrison stayed him. "She knows what she's doin', boss. I hate to admit it, but I think she does."

Alex's hand went out with a single cube on it. The stallion's suspicion was almost comical; the men watched as he shook his head first one way, then the other, before proceeding very hesitantly toward Alex and making a final dash to snatch the sugar off her hand and get away with it.

Tom's patience ran out and he told the men to get back to work. Garrison was the last to go, hanging over the corral gate for a last look and a word with Joe who, as wrangler at the stables, stayed on. It gave Alex a chance to apologize to Garrison quietly, an apology he accepted with a small admonishment.

"I think you'll find it's Jess who's angry as all

get-out. But that's 'tween you and him," he advised before riding off.

And so it was. When the men returned that evening, Alex was still there, in the corral with the stallion, who was a much calmer being. The horse followed her now as she walked backward, until she managed to slip out of the corral to get him a feedbag while his back was turned.

"She been at it all day?" Garrison asked Joe as he pulled off his tack.

"Hasn't stopped to eat nary a thing. Fed the durn horse some, but only took some water for herself."

"Has she sacked him out yet?" Garrison asked.

"Yeah, she done that a bit." Joe found his makings and rolled a cigarette. "But she ain't topped him off. Seems to be taking the slow route, I reckon."

"Huh!" grunted Garrison. "It's fine if you have time to take the rough edges off. I thought she wanted an outlaw. Surely don't seem like it. Dang cayuse'll be sweet as pie the time she seems to be spending."

The two men looked over at Jesse who was leading his own horse into the stable, anger etched in every muscle of his face. Joe nodded toward the chuck house and they followed the others in to leave Alex alone when Jesse came out.

She was starting back to the main house when Jesse grabbed her arm and turned her around. "You ever do that again," he said in a voice she had never heard, intense in its anger, rage just below its surface, "I swear to God, Alex, I'll...I'll take you over my knee and give you a lickin' once and for all."

"How dare you!" She shook him off. "How dare you talk to me like that! How dare you! Who the hell do you think you are?"

Jesse jabbed his finger at her to emphasize he meant what he was saying. "Who do I think I am?"

he snarled back. "Who do I think I am? You ever, ever take a gun off me again and point it at someone, you'll find out who the hell I think I am. You know that coulda gone off? You know you coulda killed someone? I told you—out there yonder—I told you, you never point that thing at anyone less'n you mean bus'ness."

"I did bloody well mean business! They were destroying that horse. Furthermore, I knew, and you knew, and they both knew, there wasn't a shot under the hammer. You taught me that, didn't you? So there was no chance of an accident!"

"That don't matter none. You coulda pulled the hammer back twice. Way you was, you were nothin' better'n a loose cannon, Alex. You ever do a thing like that again—"

"You'll what?" She shook with her rage as tears pooled against her will. "I apologized to them both and they accepted my apologies. It's none of your concern—"

"None of my concern! You pulled my gun! You ever do that again— Don't you walk away when I'm talkin' to you!"

She turned back to him after a few steps. "You'll what? You'll what, Jesse? What will you do? I want to hear it! Say it again. What will you do?" And she stood there in the evening darkness, facing him down, wearing him out like she'd faced down the stallion.

****

Alex expected Tom to sit her down and give her a good talking-to, but the reprimand never came. She thought perhaps he would discuss the matter with Oliver, but then she figured Tom would know all too well that would be useless. With the situation left at the status quo, Alex reprised the events in her mind. She knew she had been wrong to pull Jesse's gun but having apologized to Garrison and Joe, she had no inclination to apologize to anyone else—especially not Jesse.

Over the next couple of weeks, Alex went down to the corral to train the horse before the men went out, and she was still there when they got back. The men got bits of news from Joe: how she had found an old jacemo and tried that on the horse, how she was now using a hackamore to ride him about the corral, how they had gone out bareback and he was now in bridle and what type bits she had tried, how she had him on a lunge. "Heck," Garrison told them, "she's spent so much time on that dang horse, it's a wonder she can't just sorta communicate with 'im and tell 'im where she wants to go without a dang bridle!"

They wanted to know had she named him yet and were pleased to hear she had named him Open Range but was calling him Ranger for short. It suited, they felt.

Only Jesse didn't apparently take an interest. Only Jesse went straight out and came straight in without a glance.

One evening after dinner, Alex approached Oliver with her latest idea. "I'm going to have to wear my pants into town for a while," she began.

He snapped shut the ledger he'd been studying but it was obvious he had more important things on his mind than Alex's latest request. "Oh?" he said with little real interest.

"I'm going to Miss Bea's to start a series of paintings of the saloon girls. I hope you won't mind," she added somewhat archly.

"No, no, go right ahead."

"Maybe I'll strip naked and join them," she said as she left the room.

The next day she rode into town dressed in what Rose now referred to as her cow-girl's outfit, stopping first at the Benders' to see if there was any news regarding her boots ("No, dear, I'm afraid I've had to write to our other supplier in Texas...") and then marching boldly through the swinging doors which had held such interest for her in the past. She was prepared for stares, obscenities and rude comments, and outright rejection, but kept going and stayed good-natured throughout.

"What'll it be?" said the barman coming over to her. "No, don't tell me, sarsaparilla!" The whole room laughed.

"No, thank you. I'd like to speak to Miss Bea, please."

The barman put on a dainty English accent. "Who shall I say is calling, Madame?" More laughs.

Alex gave him her most winning smile. "Lady Alexandra Calthorpe, if you please."

He looked at her for a moment in disbelief. "Listen kid, Bea ain't seein' nobody today. Bea's real busy, you get what I mean?" He leered across the bar.

"Well, I can wait," came her smiley reply.

"What's going on, Barney?" bellowed a husky voice from the stairs.

Alex looked up to see what she thought was the most magnificent figure of a woman suitable for portrait she had ever seen. Tall and broad and heavy-set with heavily rouged cheeks, ash darkening her eyes, more feathers than a rooster's tail, there stood the famous Miss Bea, red satin and black lace barely covering her décolleté.

"Miss Bea?" Alex marched around to the bottom of the steps. "I'm Alexandra Calthorpe. And I'd like to paint your portrait."

Chapter Ten

It was, first and foremost, a business deal. Miss Bea told Alex the girls' time was money and at first expected her to pay for the time they would have to pose.

"You can't paint 'em while they're workin'. No man is gonna want that, you understand. So what're you gonna pay me for their time, then?"

"I'm going to pay you in a painting which I shall do—"

"Hell, lady, I don't want no painting. What in tarnation am I gonna do with a painting?"

"A painting of you," Alex went on regardless. "A nude for above the bar. My paintings sell for a great deal of money in New York and I shall take your painting to New York with me in October—"

"I thought you jus' said it was fer above the bar?"

"And you will be famous. I shall take it and bring it back. It will be just for show. You will be famous," she repeated.

Bea stared up at her from behind a great desk in her office. She never offered Alex a chair. Indeed, there wasn't one—only a huge brass bed at the other side of the room, disheveled now but with lacey pillows thrown about the crumpled sheets. Alex glanced at it, then back to Bea.

"My paintings sell for over a hundred dollars apiece," she told her. This was true, because as she had learned, before Jonathon took his commission, they had sold for two hundred dollars each, most of them. "The one I plan to do of you, being large enough to be seen above the bar, would be worth far more. How much do your girls make an hour?"

Bea looked at her, deliberating. "For a mere wisp of a girl you sure know how to talk your way out of a box." She waited a moment before going on. "All right then. You do the painting of me first, then you can choose two girls for two more paintings. You can take the damn nude to New York and make me famous but I want it back here, you understand?"

"Indeed."

"And you don't go botherin' the girls when they got better things to do, you know what I mean?"

"Yes, ma'am."

"Most of all, you don't go namin' names or tellin' tales when you get outa here. Men don't like their wives a-knowin' where they been, you understand? If I see a fall off in business, out ya go."

"It's round-up. There won't be a fall-off in business. It's your slow season," Alex stated, as if she knew what she was talking about.

"Been doin' your homework, ain't ya?" Miss Bea showed her to the door. "Come to think of it, I think it would be best if you was to come up these back steps from the alley. Men see y'all out front, they might get the wrong idea!"

****

Annie was completely horrified of course but Alex really liked Bea, liked her company, her raw humor, her earthiness and, more to the point, loved painting her. The woman was completely immodest, brazen and bawdy, a complete novelty to Alex who came from a world where her maidservant Rose, who dressed her and looked after her in every conceivable way, would close her eyes to hold open a towel as Alex stepped from her bath.

"Bea, you can't keep moving. Every time you move I have to readjust the damn cloth, or your breasts and your you-know-what start showing."

"I thought that was the durn reason to be nude—that folk wanted to see them parts. What's the durn purpose of coverin' 'em up? I ain't here to be modest, Lady A."

"That much I have certainly ascertained," replied Alex getting back to her oils. "But the cover is virtually transparent and the beauty is in your shape and form, not in every damn hair in your...your private area."

Bea roared. "My private area? My goodness but we are pretty durn delicate, ain't we?" She sized up Alex while the girl continued to paint. "You ever been with a man, sweetheart?"

"Of course I've been with a man. I live on a bloody ranch, don't I?"

"No, I mean, *been* with a man. You know, had him make love to you 'n' all."

"Certainly not," said Alex primly, still concentrating on what she was doing. "Why ever would I want to do that?"

"I suppose you all are intendin' to keep yerself for marriage, huh?"

"Keep myself? I have no intention of marrying at all." Alex realized here, at least, was one person who had not heard the gossip of her recent past.

"You all gonna be a spinster? I don't think so, not by the look of ya." She bolted upright all of a sudden. "Wait a minute now. What about you—"

"Bea! You've moved again! What did I tell you?" She came over to push Bea back into position and adjust the cover.

"Heck, ain't Jesse Makepeace been courtin' you?"

Alex stood stock still. She looked at Bea as if she'd been shot, blinked, then went back to her easel where the huge canvas at least partially hid her from view. "I have no idea what you're talking about. Jesse—"

"Ha! The hell you don't! If you don't know it, there're sure some Faringdon boys who know it." She played with the corner of the cover for a moment. "May says he ain't been in for quite some time now." She laid back thinking, but Alex was busy mixing paints. "Says he used to be a dang good lover, too, when he came in, but you know, when they get sweet on someone..."

"I really don't wish to hear about this," Alex retorted, keeping herself busy. Suddenly she was forced to think about Jesse with another woman, Jesse whoring, Jesse doing what men did. The incident the day of the circus with the soiled dove had never bothered her; it had been funny if anything, yet hearing it now so plainly put by Bea, she was stunned. Confused, she put her brush down for a moment, then took it back up. One standard for men, another for women, she thought to herself. Fine, let a man get experience, but I won't be a virginal spinster, that's for sure. "In any case," she added at long last, "there is nothing at all between me and Jesse Makepeace. In fact, if the truth be known, we are not even on speaking terms at the moment."

"Oh, hon, a lovers' quarrel? Hell, I can tell you how to fix that one up right quick."

"Really, Bea. Can we change the subject, please?"

"Well, you listen to me, you're gonna have to do it one day cause you sure as heck don't wanna go dyin' no virgin, and when you do, you wanna be well prepared. Do you know what to expect?"

"My brother has given me some information on the matter, yes." Alex kept painting.

"Your brother? Your brother! Oh, for Pete's sake, Lady A. What in hell does your brother know 'bout it 'ceptin' how to push it in. I'm talkin' 'bout bein' on the receivin' end, darlin'." There was quiet for a while as she twisted the cover through ringed fingers and lay back again. "You know how to kiss?"

****

"Faringdon Ranch,
Colorado, USA!
3 June 1886

Darling David,

I was so glad to hear you have a new love and that things are proceeding well in that area, but of course not so happy to hear you might now not be coming over this summer. That truly would be a huge disappointment. I understand back East they have those new telephones where you can actually talk to someone a distance from you, via wires and things. Wouldn't that be lovely to be able to pick up this telephone and speak to you whenever I liked, although I suppose it will never be able to go from America to England because of the sea. Never mind—it was just an idea.

Oh, David please come visit. I need a bit of "bucking up." I think that is the expression. Have had a terrific row with Jesse—my best friend amongst the punchers, whom I am sure you remember from your visit in '78—so we are now not on speaking terms. I guess it will be a long, hard day until we are. And Oliver is completely off in a world of his own, things bloody awful on the ranch front—don't tell Papa though. I'm sure you won't anyway, but please be sure not to slip as I fear he will have Uncle O. dismissed and then I would have to leave too, I suppose. By the way, sorry to hear about Papa's illness, though Lord only knows why I should be sorry, but there we are.

Row with Jesse was due to something very awful I did, being spoilt young lady I am, and something equally awful he said to me. I actually pulled his gun and threatened two of the men with it, but the point is, I did apologise to them both later and that was accepted, but it seems Mr. Makepeace wanted to thrash me and you can imagine how that went down with yours truly. Ah, well...

The painting is going remarkably well. I have just about completed the chef d'oeuvre—a huge nude of the local madam for above her saloon bar. These have been the most informative sittings of my life. David, those cozy little chats you and I had were not particularly informative really, now were they? Surely you could have given me a bit more information. With Miss Bea, as she is called, although I was a captive audience I can truly say I was an attentive student. In any event, Miss Bea has given me a lesson every woman should have and even if I never do marry, I am now a mine of information. Do you really stick your tongue in someone's mouth when you kiss? I think I have to try to sort out the whore-only items on my list from the real lovers' or "fun" in bed things. Miss Bea, by the way, assures me it is fun in bed, but then she would think that, wouldn't she?

David, I am so happy here I can't tell you. Annie and Tom and the children continue to be my surrogate family and they are such wonderful people (though you will have guessed I cannot discuss the above with Annie—can't really imagine Annie and Tom in bed at all, for goodness sake) I don't know where I would be without them. Poor Tom is looking somewhat harried and worried these days. I'm sure he thinks Oliver a fool and if the ranch pulls through it will certainly be thanks to Tom. As for the men, I love them all (except maybe Jesse, who is being so mean), truly I do. Do you know how they risk their lives every single moment of every day? Riding broncs or outlaws after winter lay-offs, going into the herd to rope or cut, dragging calves to the branding fire. Then there's trailing cattle to the rail head, or riding to circle in the herd, or crossing the river, or working out in a lightning storm or blizzard or, most especially, riding out a stampede. Plus there's danger every time they have to dispute a cut or brand markings with a Rep, every time they sit down to a game of cards—I suppose if they all got rid of their guns some of this might not be so dangerous, but there you go, they need the damned things for the snakes and bears and wolves at least (and aren't those also threats to their life and limb?) and so life is very dangerous here, Darling. It's so exciting!

Your loving sister,
Alex xxxxxxxxxxxxxx
****

Pulling up the wagon, Alex watched the men from a distance. Now in the midst of spring roundup and branding, there was an air of a social occasion as the Reps from other ranches came by to cut their stray cows and calves from the herd. While the punchers were busy with little spare time, Tom had asked her to bring back supplies from town and deliver them to the campsite at Washburn's

Crossing. It had been a long drive and Ranger was tied to the back of the wagon, not liking it at all.

The smell of the burning cowhide was fierce and Alex wondered how the men stood that work all day, yet they never seemed to mind. It fascinated her how they worked together, one man roping the head, another the legs, then a third tailin' down' the calf for a fourth to brand. Alex found this all wonderful; to her, these men were gods with their wide brimmed hats and bandanas, their high-heeled boots with the jingling spurs she loved to hear on the wooden walkways around the headquarters, and their rawhide leggings over the striped or checked pants they favored wearing. With none of the pretenses or condescension that characterized the men she had heretofore encountered, she thought of them as one huge family, a family she had never known. And she wanted to be like them—just like them. Strong. Self-reliant. Free.

The men had stopped for lunch when Alex got there, and watched her as she jumped down to get Ranger untied from the back of the wagon and hobbled, off on his own.

"Four boxes of Sapolio, twenty cans of Eagle Brand," counted off the cook, "ten sacks of Arbuckles'. I asked Boss for a dozen. What happened?"

"Don't look at me, Cookie," answered Alex as she came back from hobbling the horse. "Tom gave me the list. If the punchers didn't drink so much coffee…"

"We have to drink coffee, Lady Lex," said Terry passing her with a plate of food in hand. "If'n we didn't, we'd all be fallin' asleep in the saddle. Now you wouldn't want that, would ya?"

Alex looked across to Ranger where one of the Reps she didn't know was looking him over. "I should leave him, if I were you," she called. "He's not in a very good mood today."

"One helluva cayuse, sonny," answered the man. He came back to the wagon, grabbed a plate and went over to sit with Cal and a group of the others.

Terry snickered.

"Who you calling sonny, Mister?" Alex stood by Cal, hands on hips. The Faringdon outfit all burst out laughing.

"Well, I never," said the Rep, completely taken aback. "It's a-a goshdurn woman!"

Alex shrugged and smiled.

"Hey, wanna try one of these?" Cal held out his fork and tin plate with some unrecognizable food on it.

"What is it?" Alex peered down at the mess.

"Prairie oysters," he said.

"Prairie oysters? I don't like oysters of any kind," she replied scrunching her nose.

"Builds ya up. Good fer you. It'll put hair on yer chest."

"Such as it is," Reb mumbled.

"Hey!" Cal gave him a hard kick with his boot.

"Sorry, Lady Lex." Reb looked up at her with a half-smile on his face. "I don't suppose you kin help it none, bein' half-formed an' all."

"Hey!" Cal gave him another kick. "You know better'n to talk like that."

"Oh, hell, it's just fun."

Jesse turned sharply from his place further along, almost joining Cal in reprimanding Reb. For a split second his eyes met Alex's as she looked away and he turned back to the men near him. Anger colored his face, but was it anger at Reb, anger at her, or anger at himself for threatening her? Alex wondered if he would ever get past those feelings and find the words to apologize to her.

"She seems to be big enough to be wearin' that six-shooter," one of the new men noted. "You know how to use that thing, sweetheart?"

Cal laughed and looked up at Alex. "You all call her sweetheart one more time, you may find out. Then it'll be your prairie oysters we all are eatin'."

Alex sat down next to him, quickly looking again at Jesse further along with the other men. Cal followed her eyes. "You ought to say hello, you know."

"Hello."

"You know what I mean. Who's gonna be the bigger man here, huh? You tell me that?"

"I was just called sonny so it isn't me." She started to stand up. "Are those what I think they are?"

"What do you think they are?" Cal grinned up at her.

She stood for a moment trying to think of something clever to say but it wouldn't come. She felt Jesse's anger from where she stood. "Better get back," she said at last. "I'm working over at Miss Bea's."

She did a little sashay and left them all to muse on that one for a while.

****

It was Garrison who spotted the riderless horse and called the men out on a search party, but Garrett who saw what looked like a bundle of clothes out near the old Cherokee Trail.

Chapter Eleven

"Lord A'mighty, Lady Lex." Garrett jumped from his horse, leaving the animal ground tied. "Why didn't ya get a shot off?"

Alex managed to roll on to her right side and push herself up as he approached, but she hugged her left side in pain, rocking back and forth. "You want me to start a stampede?"

Garrett fired two shots into the air. "Ain't gonna be no stampede round here. Beeves are way out. Anyways, you had us all scared to hell."

Garrison rode up leading a somewhat reluctant Ranger. Cal and a couple of others were behind him, then Jesse rode in at a gallop. He swung off before his horse was reined in.

"Is Ranger all right? He put his foot in a hole," Alex told Garrison.

"Lord, is that all you think 'bout?" He looked over at Jesse as if the other was in charge, but Jesse hung back now that he saw Alex was still among the living.

"I've dislocated my shoulder. It hurts like hell. Someone will have to push it back in place, please." The men shifted uneasily. "It's happened before. You just push it back in. Please!" She looked around. "Cal?"

"Well, heck sweetheart, I ain't no doctor."

"I am not going to sit here waiting for eight hours while someone rides into bloody Greeley." She swayed slightly and looked up again.

"I've done it once before on ol' Laney," Garrison said, "but that was a time ago and I don't think…well, you know, you're sorta on the delicate side, Lady Lex."

She tried to turn to look up at him. "Just do it, please!" she said with gritted teeth. "I'm sure women's and men's shoulders are not all that different."

Garrison hesitated. "Well, I sorta need to actu'lly feel the shoulder. What I mean is, you know…"

"Fine! Someone take my shirt off, please." She looked up.

Cal said, "All right, I think we gonna just leave the two of them together." He looked over at Jesse, but Jess started to walk off back to his horse.

"Well, hang on just a cotton pickin' minute," Garrison spit out. "Y'all can't just leave me here with her."

"Does anyone here realize I am sitting here in pain? Does anyone really care?" She held in the tears, thinking about her back, what it looked like, what she had on underneath her shirt. "Can you just bloody well do something, please?"

"Jess, you know her best," Garrison said. "You take off her shirt."

"I think she'd prefer Garrett to do it. Garrett is oldest here." Jesse's voice was quiet and steady but behind it Alex heard the edge.

"And then I need someone to brace her—less'n she faints an' all."

"Oh, for heaven's sake—I'm not going to bloody well faint!"

"All right." Cal took charge at last. "The rest of you get back to work. It doesn't take more'n four men to help one small gal."

Garrett squatted down in front of Alex and, rather tentatively, unbuttoned her shirt. He nodded up to Cal who removed his gloves, stuffed them in his belt and took careful hold of Alex's shirt collar to try to slip the shirt back.

"Ow!" He stopped. "Look," she continued, "I think it's best to help me get my right arm out of the sleeve, pull the shirt around and then you can slip the other sleeve forward off my left arm."

Cal knelt behind her and gave Jesse a questioningly glance. Jesse didn't move. Garrett eased the right sleeve forward a bit so Cal could help Alex slide her arm out, and then he gently pulled the shirt across to the left side, exposing her back.

He stopped. The only sounds were the horses cropping grass and the rustle of the leaves in the wind. Alex watched as Garrett looked from one face to the next questioning. Jesse walked off toward a stand of cottonwood, his back to the rest of them, his hands on his hips.

"What?" Garrett started, but Cal shook his head.

Alex realized her chemise did not cover everything.

Garrison sank down next to her. "Lady Lex? You have to tell us who done this to ya," he said quietly. "No one can get away with somethin' like that."

She turned and looked at him for a moment. "If you're looking for frontier justice, my friend, I'm afraid you're a bit too late."

"If'n it's your uncle..."

"Oh, don't be a bloody fool, Gar. You think I'd be staying on at the ranch if my uncle was beating me like that? I'd think you knew me better than that. Anyway, you can see they're old scars."

"Alex?" Cal started.

She turned her head sharply and looked at him. It was strange to see Cal so serious, to the point where he actually called her by her first name. She smiled briefly. "Can we get on with this please? Really. I'm afraid you'd have to cross that other continental divide called the Atlantic Ocean to avenge my honor on this one, boys. And quite honestly, I'm not even sure my ex-husband is worth the lead."

Cal took a deep breath. He looked over to where Jesse still stood with his back to them before he proceeded to slip the shirt off. Garrison changed places with Garrett and moved to the front to take Alex's left arm across her stomach bent at an angle while Cal pushed gently forward on her back and then Garrison rotated the arm until the shoulder clicked into place.

"Well, thank you." Alex shuffled back into her shirt.

"Heck, Lady Lex, you're supposed to bind that up and take it easy or somethin'."

She didn't answer. Jesse looked back at her now as she got up and came toward him, tears streaking down her face.

"Don't you do that to me, Jesse." She punched him with her small weak fists, grimacing with her own pain. "Don't you do that! Don't you dare feel sorry for me. Don't you dare!"

Jesse stood there taking it. He stared at her as she beat his chest, and he said nothing, his face tight against his own tears for her. He waited for her to stop and continued standing there, the others looking on as Alex came marching back, bent to pick up her hat, gathered Ranger's reins and rode off.

****

As the round-up wound down, the Reps took their stock back to their outfits, and soon the men were back at headquarters or at the camps. Alex knew word had more or less got out and found the punchers were gentler now around her, had a sort of quiet respect for her, and she hated it. She tried to bully them a bit to show them she was still the same girl, jolly them into joshing with her as they had before. It was slow work. At the same time, she yearned to see Jesse, to speak with him, to try to get life back to the way it was before the argument at the corral, and before he saw the scars. The opportunity didn't present itself. She would see him from a distance some days, riding with the herd, sitting his horse with that peculiar grace he had, throwing his lariat out with an ease that reminded her of people on a dock waving their hankies in farewell. Hoping to just be near him, she slid into one of the corrals one evening to practice her roping.

The light was failing and the birds were settling with their evening calls. Somewhere in the pasture a horse nickered. She sensed Jesse was there, watching, but she never turned as he stood at the fence. She heard him climb over and ease up behind her. He took the coiled rope from her in his left hand and slid his right hand over hers on the swing end, almost forcing her backward into his arms.

She thought of paintings and statues she had seen, imagining his naked arms now, how the muscles would form them into long oblique curves, how he probably had soft downy fair hair on his forearms, how his muscle would slightly bulge as he bent his arm. His voice was soft in her ear, and she could feel his breath on her neck like a whispered secret.

"Gentle-like, right to left, right to left to widen the noose, keep your eye on the post—are you watchin' where we're goin'?"

He made the throw and pulled in the rope to tighten the noose. Alex stood there, his hand still entwined with hers and, for a moment, she wished they could stand like that forever. Then she took her hand away and faced him. For a second he rested his chin on the top of her head, then straightened again and went to get the noose off the post while coiling in the rope. She looked up at him in the fading light and saw nothing but kindness in his face, simplicity and gentleness that was most inviting. A smile spread across her face as he handed her the coiled rope and sauntered away, turning once to look back at her before he opened the gate. Emptiness filled her like a poisoned vapor seeking every corner of her being, and she stood with the rope in her hand listening to the ring of his spurs as his footsteps retreated.

****

With this uneasy and unspoken truce, mending was still slow work. After a few days of polite "Hellos" and "How's it goin's" Tom mentioned to Alex that Jesse had been sent up to Boyd line camp with Garrett to nighthawk for a while.

Nighthawking meant his days were free, if he could stay awake long enough to enjoy them. When Jesse heard Buffalo Bill's Wild West Show was over in Greeley, he thought of sending word to Alex to see if she and Cal would want to meet up, but Cal sent word back that Alex had already been asked to join the Yosts.

The men strolled around town before the show, mixing with the performers, talking to friends. They met an old acquaintance, a former puncher who went by the name of Stone Rodney who had once worked at the ranch; he was now in the show. Talking with him about life on the road, the man's eyes seemed to go beyond them. Cal and Jesse turned at the same moment to see where he was looking.

"Heck." Stone's eyes widened. "If that ain't the prettiest durned li'l gal."

Jesse didn't need to be told he meant Alex. She stood in the crowded street with Sue Ann, laughing at J.J. who had managed to get himself covered in some sticky candy.

"I think the same thing happened to me at the circus once." Alex met Jesse's glance. "Well, well, well, if it isn't the nighthawk himself," she said,

110

coming over.

"I sent word to invite you but Cal told me you'd be comin' in with the Yosts." His eyes sought hers. He was lost in her suddenly, ached for her. He could see the hazel flecks in the green of her eyes, and had that same feeling he'd had at the station the day he collected her—that his heart was quickening and part of him was lost.

Alex was filled with the sudden desire to kiss him there and then; she laughed. "I'm sorry." She giggled and covered her mouth with her hand as if he could somehow tell what she was thinking. "I might sit on your lap anyway," she flirted. "Just like 'of yore.'"

Cal stood there, his arms across his chest, slowly working the chicle in his mouth as his eyes darted from Jesse to Alex and back. To Alex he appeared to be waiting for something to happen.

Then Stone broke in with, "Ain't ya gonna introduce me, Jess?"

"Oh, sure. Lady Alexandra Calthorpe. Stone Rodney. Stone used to work at the Double F."

"Really?" Alex's smile was brief and disinterested. She faced Jesse as Tom and Annie came over to collect her. A bright idea hit her and she turned back to Stone. "I don't suppose I could sketch you, could I? I'll be coming into town while the show is on to do some pastels and drawings in the hope of getting something suitable for a painting."

"Lady Alex is a famous artist," Jesse put in. There was a big smile on his face as he said it but Alex's quizzical expression wiped it off. "Well, she's gonna be a famous artist. Soon."

Stone looked from one to the other. "Sure. How's about a trade? You be in my show and I'll be in yours."

Alex laughed. "What's your act?"

"You don't wanna be in his act, Ladilex," Cal said.

Jesse put an arm around her gently, almost possessively. "He's the trick whip cracker," he said.

Alex couldn't watch that part of the show. The idea someone could stand still with a cigarette in their mouth and let someone else whip it out was beyond her. She flinched at the very idea. Jesse took her out, stepping over the Yosts and others to get out of the tent into the fresh air.

"You didn't have to leave," she said at last.

"Not as good fun as the circus, was it? Pretend gunfights and all. Maybe them city folk like to see that, but I reckon we got enough of them out here."

"I haven't seen a gunfight!"

"No? Well, here's hopin' you never do—see a real one, that is." They walked on in silence. "I hear you been paintin' over at Miss Bea's? That musta been real int'restin'."

"Oh, very." Alex tried not to laugh but couldn't help herself.

"What?" Jesse stopped and looked at her. She was more woman now; somehow the child was slowly disappearing and there was an adult there instead. "She bin tellin' you tales?"

"Definitely not," she affirmed. "I asked, I begged her." She made a drama of her speech. "But she said she couldn't tell me a thing or it might ruin her business. Dreadful! Think of all the knowledge I could have gained, think of all the men I could be blackmailing—"

"Think of all the lies you might be telling...instead, of course, of the ones you're tellin' now." Jesse laughed.

He lifted his hat for a moment and ran his hand through his hair. Alex suddenly yanked the long bits at the back of his neck she had always liked to play with. "Why do you do that?" he asked. "You always

112

liked to do that, even when you were little." He shook his head pondering it for a moment.

Alex giggled. "I don't know really. I just... I don't know." They stood there for a moment on the boardwalk with the softening light of the late afternoon about them, each with their own memories, their own thoughts of the years that connected them.

"I have to get back," he said at last.

****

The Wild West Show sketches went very well over the next few days. Alex thought about bringing a rig into town to collect her things from Miss Bea's. Riding in the last day of the show, she spotted one of the Faringdon wagons outside the Benders' shop.

"Now, if you're still wondering 'bout them boots, Lady Alex," Mrs. Bender started as she entered the shop, "I'm afraid I'm still waitin' on news. All the bootmakers I've contacted are real backed up on orders at the moment."

"That's positively ridiculous," Alex shot back. "How long can this possibly take? Anyway," she continued, "I just came in looking for whoever was driving our wagon out front. Have they been in?"

"Oh, yes, it was Jesse Makepeace. He started to give me an order but then the sheriff came in saying something 'bout getting a posse to go out after the Darcy Brothers up near Boyd Lake, and Jess shot out of here like a bat outta hell. Went over to the liv'ry for a mount, I think. Said something 'bout Garrett Landry being up there on his own."

"Has he gone with the posse?"

"Oh, no I don't think so. Sheriff's still gathering men."

The door jangled as Alex left. She got to Ranger, checked she had cartridges for the Purdy, and that the rifle was loaded, and then loaded a sixth bullet into her Colt.

Chapter Twelve

Jesse feared the Darcy brothers would have smoked Garrett out of the cabin by the time he got to Boyd. They had twenty-odd horses up there, not to mention however many cattle the Darcys could rustle. Garrett had years more experience than he with handling rustlers, but Garrett was getting on a bit and his reactions now were often slow.

Then it went through Jesse's mind that if anything happened to him, he'd never see Alex again. They had eased back into something like their old relationship before the quarrel at the corral, but he had never told her what he felt, never been able to put his feelings into words, and never learned whether she returned those feelings for him. If he came out of this alive, he swore to put things to rights.

There wasn't any smoke so he figured Garrett must be outside somewhere. Tying the horse, Jesse listened for a moment, then slipped down through the trees closer to the corral. Birdsong had stopped and it was too silent. It even seemed the water had almost stopped lapping at the lake-shore. Suddenly gunfire rang out. He ducked, rolling about five feet to end up near the last little copse before the cleared area in front of the cabin.

"Well, what have we here?" said a voice behind him.

Jesse whirled around and looked up into Garrett's face. "I guess I made it in time."

"One is over yonder." Garrett pointed to the side of the cabin he had now abandoned. "But I've lost sight of t'other. He's prob'ly circling round to come up behind. I think we ought to try to get to the wagon there." He gestured to the cart several feet up toward the camp. "Be better cover."

"I'll go first," offered Jesse, and Garrett nodded.

Jesse pushed his hat down on his head and ran, gun drawn, to the wagon, then scrambled underneath. A shot rang out; Garrett's gun fired in reply. Jesse looked back to Garrett and signaled for him to come on, he was covering him.

Garrett lumbered as fast as he could toward the wagon, his leg giving way at the last moment and causing him to trip. Another shot sounded and he rolled toward Jesse who yanked him under the wagon bed.

"You hit?" Jesse looked his friend over.

"Hit? Hell no. I got me the arthritis, ya dang fool," grunted Garrett, looking about. "Dang pain'll kill me 'fore any damn Darcy will."

****

Alex heard the shots in the distance, saw startled, frightened horses milling in the corral, but as she approached, the guns went silent and she couldn't figure where Jesse and Garrett might be. She led Ranger into the trees a good distance from the cabin, tied him up and got her rifle out of its scabbard. Then she darted through the woods down toward the camp.

The guns fired again and she stopped in her tracks, uncertain what to do. After a few moments she realized some shots were coming from only a few yards down and off to the right, so she continued on her way. It was, indeed, Jesse and Garrett, hunkered down under the ranch wagon.

She threw a stone but it was absolutely no use. No one heard. She wished she could whistle but that was pointless as well. She ran up to the next tree and squatted against a large rock there, taking off her hat and gloves and casting them aside so she could best use the rifle, if necessary. Still hiding behind the rock, she pulled the Colt from its holster.

Behind her, there was a click. "Well, who have we here?"

Alex spun around and fired the Colt into the man's stomach. Blood arched out as he fell backward, his shot going into the branches as birds screeched away from falling leaves. Stunned, she turned back to see Jesse running but then another man came from the left. Alex lifted her rifle to fire and took him down also.

"Oh my God, oh my God," she kept repeating as she crumpled and slid down the bloodied rock. She was trembling and shivering and shaking; tears streamed down her face, both firearms thrown aside. Then Jesse's arms were around her, holding her tight. She couldn't stop sobbing, keening in his embrace.

"Are you all right, are you all right?" he kept asking. There was no answer, just the tremulous small body he held against him, and the gasping and shuddering that would not stop.

"She hurt?" Garrett came up and squatted next to Jesse.

"I don't know." Jesse sat back to try and examine Alex but she sobbed and rocked more. "Alex," he said gently, turning her face to him. "It's all right, it's gonna be all right. Are you hurt?"

At last he got a shake of the head in reply so he took her back into his arms and sat with her, leaning against the blood-colored rock.

"Jeez." Garrett looked down at the dead man. "She sure got a clean shot off both times. Good thing too. I think I was jus' 'bout outta cartridges."

Jesse just held Alex, whose wailing had at last subsided into whimpers. He rocked gently with her as he might cradle a small child.

The posse rode in at a gallop, pulling up short when they saw Garrett waving them down.

"'Fraid you missed all the action, Sheriff," Garrett said as the other man dismounted. He met Amos Dunn to talk quietly with him out of Alex's hearing. "This here Lady Alex done took 'em both down. Saved our lives, she did," he added with his own sense of wonder.

The sheriff walked over to see the one dead Darcy brother and Jesse and Alex huddled together nearby. Jesse nodded to him briefly as the sheriff shook his head and sighed. "Damnest thing I ever heard. Been huntin' them two boys for months now, and you tell me one small female—hell, where's the other?" Garrett pointed to where the other man lay. "Well, if I hadn'ta seen it, I wouldn'ta believed it."

The sheriff looked again at Jesse with Alex still in his arms. "Gonna need a statement sometime, Jess, jus' to square up the books." Jesse gave a small shake of his head in acknowledgement, but said nothing. "Well, I'll be. Damnest thing I ever saw. All right then, boys, let's clean this up and take these two carcasses back into town." He lit a cheroot as a few of the men got down and started to haul away the bodies to throw over horses.

"You can take that horse, Sheriff." Jesse gave a nod back to the trees. "Return him to Foote and Stoddard's Liv'ry for me, if you all don't mind. I'll settle with Virgil tomorrow."

By the time the men had tied the bodies onto the spare horse and gone, Alex was somewhat calmer but still nestled into Jesse's neck. Garrett crouched next to the pair and lightly rubbed Alex's arm to soothe her a bit. "You done a good thing, gal. I know it ain't feelin' too good at the moment but ya done a good thing," he said.

"I killed two men," she whispered. "It's horrible. Women are supposed to give birth, not cause death."

Tears tracked down the lead dust on her cheeks.

"Yeah, well, sometimes life has just got these fine lines init," Garrett said. "Sometimes you just have to make a durned decision lickety split, one side or t' other, and hope it's the right one, and mebbe you don't like havin' to make that decision but there it is—it's made—and ya jus' have to live with it. See, in your case, I'd say you done made the right decision 'cause here I am, and there Jesse is, and them two outlaws is dead."

Alex sat up for a moment, blinking back more tears. She made a small attempt at what tried to be a smile, then lay back against Jesse again.

"That horse of your'n gonna let me lead him down here?" Garrett asked. He got what looked like a nod and wandered off to where Ranger was tied.

The two men found Alex's hat and put it back on her head, though she pushed it off so it hung by its stampede strap. Jesse emptied the cartridge from under the hammer of the Colt and pushed the gun into her holster, then jammed the Purdy back into its scabbard on the horse. Garrett handed him his hat.

"You be all right here tonight, Garrett?" Jesse swung up into Ranger's saddle and extended his hand to help Alex up behind.

"I reckon. If I were a'feared of haunts, I might think otherwise. You all stay down at headquarters and I'll take care up here tonight." He waved them off.

****

They rode at a slow lope, Alex leaning into Jesse, her hands gentle about his waist. She felt again the solid strength of his body, and nestled her cheek against his back for a moment thinking of the things Miss Bea had told her, and wanting Jesse, wanting to know what his skin would feel like against hers, what his touch would feel like, or his kiss. The June evening was slow to come. The last hour of sunlight flickered through trees and then spread out on the horizon, a blood-red ribbon on the open range. A grouse sprang out of some sage and Alex started. Jesse patted her hand and then held it tight. She wished he wasn't wearing a glove.

After a time he said, "Alex, sometimes good people just have to do bad things. I've learned that now, and so should you."

"I know," she sniffed. Jesse's chest moved as he took in a deep breath and let it out.

"You know," he said, "when I wake up in the mornin' and I know I'm gonna see you, it sorta puts a whole diff'rent shine on the day. You know what I'm sayin' here?" She gave no reply, only a gentle movement of her cheek against his back. "I think...I think it's just a real honor to know you, Alex." And he held up her hand and kissed it.

****

Over the next few days Alex stayed inside, finishing some paintings in the studio she had made herself in an upstairs room. Oliver had been furious when he heard the story of Boyd camp, how she had followed Jesse knowing there was trouble ahead, but he eventually calmed down enough to note she was a "damned good shot" and the county was well rid of those cattle thieves.

Annie visited to see if there was anything she could do but only time would heal what Alex felt about having killed two men. The older woman tried her best, as did Tom, to assure the girl she had done the right thing but Alex only listened politely.

Jesse was back up at Boyd and Alex didn't want to see the punchers just yet, but then one day a surrey pulled up outside. At an upstairs window, Alex smiled to herself as out stepped Miss Bea, dressed outrageously in violet head-to-toe with purple feathers just about any place a feather could be stuck. Oliver was out, and a scandalized Wilson, the butler, started to refuse the madam entrance but was summarily pushed aside.

"Lady A., you get your ass down here this moment," Bea shouted up the stairs. "Or I'm coming up afta you." Alex appeared at the top of the steps. "Hell, gal, this place is worse'n any sportin' house I ever run. Who in tarnation designed this lot?" Alex laughed and cried all at once and gave her friend a big hug.

Wilson served lemonade out on the back terrace, setting it down as if his fingers might get burnt but both ladies ignored him. Bea sat back in her chair, her eyes narrowed at Alex. "You're missin' all the town news, sweetheart. When ya comin' in?"

Alex shuffled a bit. "Oh, I'm not sure. In a bit perhaps."

"You've left your things in my office. Ain't a whole lotta space in there, Lady A. I need ya to collect that junk."

Alex flinched. "I suppose everyone is talking about me. I don't know I can face all that just yet, Bea."

"Well. There sure are some jokes about the Lady-killer but you know you're stronger than that. Look-a-here, sweetheart. You all are gonna haveta come into town sometime, so you might as well come and get your things, make a quick trip of it, do me a favor will ya? You're gonna have to face people sometime. Just you act nat'ral like as if nothin' has changed and that's the way it'll be."

Alex hitched up the wagon the next day and went to get her paintings and oils. She found the alley door at Miss Bea's locked and so went around to the front, pushing the saloon doors open. There was total silence as she crossed the room. Barney nodded at her as he continued to dry a glass and then, one by one, men got up from their seats, removing their hats and some clapping their hands. Alex stopped at the foot of the stairs, looked back at them and said in her best Colorado voice, "I thought you only removed your hats when a funeral went by. I ain't dead yet."

****

Seeing the Faringdon outfit was going to be more difficult. She remembered the tentative way they had treated her after her fall when word had got out about her scars. Alex thought this would be far worse. It was J.J. and Sue Ann's joint birthday party at the end of the month that had many of them gathered together at the Homestead. Alex had told Annie she was learning from Mrs. Rackham, Oliver's cook, to frost cakes and would come over and frost one of Rackham's cakes at the party so it wouldn't get ruined on the way.

Most of the men were out the back when she arrived but Tom, Annie and Jesse came out to greet her, and Alex settled into the kitchen area to finish the cake. Tom and Jesse viewed the proceedings lost in their own separate thoughts.

"I'm wonderin' where we'll all be for their next birthdays." Tom took a deep breath. Suddenly he appeared older, more lined, worn.

"That bad?"

"Well...Calthorpe's talkin' 'bout holding the beeves over winter. Says the prices might pick up next spring."

"What do you think?"

"I think it's a dang bad idea. Prices go down as well as up. We could have a bad winter. Hot summer's meant grass is scorched in places. I'd take the money and run. Plus, of course, he's wantin' to cut back all the time. If we're short handed we jus' won't manage. Too many damn cows on that range anyways."

They stood for a while watching Alex try to find

things in the kitchen. Annie handed her various items and she measured them as best she could then stirred them in a big bowl.

"Does Alex know?" Jesse asked at last.

"Alex? I don't know it has anythin' to do with Alex, Jess. What can she do? She's makin' her own life with the paintin' and all and, anyway, Calthorpe wouldn't listen to me—you all think he's goin' to listen to her?"

"You taught her the business, Tom. She loves this ranch as much as anyone. She surely wouldn't want to see it go bust."

"Well, maybe not. But I don't reckon she has much influence on that man. It's the shareholders'll worry him most."

"Well, that includes you 'n me."

Tom looked at Jesse. "Yeah, but mostly that's Alex's father." They stood for a while as the action in the kitchen continued. "You don't see Calthorpe getting rid of none of his household servants. Punchers he can do without. Dang footmen or whatever you call 'em, that's another thing." A moment passed as they watched the two women laughing. "You gonna marry that gal, Jess? Don't you think it's about time?"

Jesse swallowed hard, glanced at his mentor, then back at Alex. "I'm ten year older than her, Tom. And aside from some savings from the shares and all, I hardly got enough to get a house and start a fam'ly."

"Well, money isn't ever'thing. And as for age, heck, I'm eight year older than Annie."

"You are?"

"I need a strong arm, Jesse Makepeace," Alex called across the room. "Someone who has muscle from throwing a lariat all day long."

Jesse wore a little half-smile as he sauntered over. "So what's your problem, lady?"

122

"My problem? My problem is mixing this because it has to get thick to frost the cake and I'm not strong enough to keep stirring it. That's my problem."

"I don't remember ever hearin' you say you couldn't do somethin'," he mused. "That's a first."

"Well, if you want me to risk dislocating my shoulder again—"

"No."

Alex put a finger in the bowl to taste the mix.

"Hey, watch it." Annie smacked her hand. "That's for the cake."

"No, it isn't." Alex went to offer some to Jesse but he pulled away and she caught him on his cheek.

"Alex!"

"Oh, here. It's like Indian war paint. Stop complaining." She searched for her hankie.

"You'll ruin that now," he told her but she took the lace hankie and started to wipe his face.

Jesse's hand came up to take the handkerchief himself but stopped, holding her gently about the wrist with her fingers just brushing his cheek.

The kitchen noises seemed to stop and Alex looked at Jesse as if she were seeing him for the first time. She was somehow aware Tom and Annie were both staring at them, yet she couldn't get herself to move.

Later, she would wonder if that was the moment she first realized how much she loved him.

Chapter Thirteen

To Alex's surprise, the men acted completely normal around her that afternoon, as if it had been decided that was the best way to handle the situation. Of course, no mention was ever made of that day at Boyd, and Garrett did seem particularly kind and friendly. The usual joshing went on unabated with Garrison and Cal getting their favorite digs in every chance they could.

"Well, heavens to Betsy, Lady Lex, I hardly recognized ya in a dress," Garrison said. "You're not goin' all feminine-like on us now, are you?"

"It's a party, Garrison. I wear dresses to parties. Usually."

"Heck," said Cal, "it couldn'ta been you, Ladilex, in that kitchen over yonder, in a dress. That would jus' have to be some other gal impersonatin' y'all."

"Impossible. I don't think anyone anywhere could impersonate our Lady Alex." Tom came out and started to throw steaks on the fire. "Chicken for y'all," he said to Alex, "knowing as living here on a ranch and all—"

"All right, Tom." Annie stopped him. "Alex go throw a coat on, it's a bit chilly out for your thin frame."

Alex marched back into the house then came out with one of Tom's light jackets.

"Got a tear in your pocket, Tom." Alex pulled out the pocket lining to show him. "Your woman's falling down on the job."

"Alex, any time you want to start mendin' for us, you just let Annie know," he replied turning a steak.

Garrison introduced her to his lady friend, Millie. Sara Beth was there, sitting primly by Cal's side, but not looking like she was particularly enjoying it.

The two children came running out with the presents Alex had brought them—puppets she had made from papier maché, with gloves for their hands which she had had Rose sew.

"Let me see that now." Tom pulled his son over. "You make this?" he asked Alex.

She nodded. "Had some spare newspaper, you might say." She pointedly looked in Sara Beth's direction.

"You sew it and all?" Tom asked.

"Well. I didn't actually do the sewing, no." She felt Jesse's hand on her shoulder as it slowly moved to around her waist. She wished she could turn and kiss him there and then, her body ached so much for him, but she just huddled further into the large jacket. "I fashioned and painted the heads and Rose sewed the bottoms. See, here you are Tom." She pointed out the one with which Sue Ann was currently playing. "Is it a good likeness?"

"I tell you it's a wonder what this woman can and can't do." Jesse looked at her lovingly. "One day we all are gonna have to just figure it out."

****

In the late afternoon heat of the following Saturday, Oliver and Alex stood at the corrals with Tom and Jesse, watching the boards go down, the torches and lanterns go up and the tables come out. The July Fourth party was that evening, and Oliver gave directions he needn't have bothered about, while Alex shrugged at Jesse as much as to say Oliver was wasting his time as everyone knew what to do. Tom was just silent.

Suddenly he said to Alex, "You know he's planning a big party for your birthday?"

"What?" Her eyes narrowed at Oliver who'd gone to direct work on the bandstand. "Is it supposed to be a surprise?"

"No, I don't think so. Said he was gonna discuss it with you. Alex? Alex!" Tom stood helpless as Alex marched to Oliver and started an almighty row. Everything came to a halt.

"I do not want a party!"

"Why ever not?" Oliver asked in true surprise. "It's your eighteenth birthday. That's a very big occasion here."

"Well, not in England!"

"We're not in England, we're in Colorado."

"I don't care if we're in bloody Timbuktu. I'm not having a party!"

"And may I ask why?" Oliver was keeping unusually calm about this and it infuriated Alex.

"Because such a party as you have in mind—"

"How do you know what kind of party I have in mind?"

"I know you, Uncle Oliver. I know it will be some sort of money-wasting extravaganza with all your bloody awful friends from the Cheyenne Club, or what remains of it, and I'll be miserable all night. It's my birthday and I am not having a bloody party. Parties like that are nothing more than asking people to buy one gifts one certainly doesn't want and which the givers can barely afford but are forced to try to outdo their friends and neighbors by giving. The whole thing is in bad taste, exceedingly bad taste I might add, when half the ranches are going bust—"

"You had a coming out party."

"Against. My. Will. And that was something totally different anyway. Frederic could well afford it." She stopped to see Jesse and Cal standing there amused, and widened her eyes, beseeching them for support.

126

"We've always had a birthday party for you, Lady Lex." Jesse raised his eyebrows a bit and she understood the signal he couldn't speak his mind in front of Oliver.

"No you haven't. Oliver gave dreadful dinner parties, which I abhorred, and Annie gave me a couple of delightful luncheons, but I'm not bloody twelve years old anymore. Anyway," she continued, turning back to Oliver, "I don't suppose you were counting the punchers in, were you? I mean, heaven forbid I have anyone at my birthday party I actually like!" She stomped off toward the house.

"You're swearing an awful lot these days, young lady, and I don't like it one bit," Oliver called after her.

Alex didn't turn back.

By evening, she was calmer. Tom came over while Alex was putting out some dishes.

"You settle the matter?" he asked.

"We reached a compromise—two parties in one. His grand guests over at the house for a dinner-dance, which I attend until 9 p.m., then I can come over here for the better part for the rest of the evening. Oh, dear, I do wish I hadn't agreed but he kept going on so. He said we all needed our spirits raised."

"That's so." Annie joined them and Tom put his arm around his wife. "Maybe he's right. Maybe we could all use a darned good party before fall round-up—"

"If there is one," Alex finished.

Cal wandered over, said "Evenin'" and nodded to them all.

"Cal, you sort of look like you got out of the barber's chair a moment too soon."

"Oh, Alex," admonished Annie. "You sure do call things as you see 'em!" She laughed and took Tom away to dance.

"Ah, heck, Ladilex, what am I gonna do when you're an old married woman an' stop bein' a smart-mouthed li'l gal?"

"Why would I stop, Cal?"

"Y'all'll have about a dozen chil'ren followin' you and you'll haveta give 'em a good example."

"Anyway, I'm not getting married, remember? So, no marriage, no children, smart mouth forever."

"Well, Jess may have a might to say 'bout that." Alex shrugged at him, before her eyes slid over to where Jesse was talking with Sara Beth. She raised an eyebrow. "She's my guest, Ladilex," he assured her.

"Don't go out with Sara Beth, Cal. You're far too good for her."

"Yeah, well…"

Alex gave him a squeeze and wandered off toward the stables. Music was playing and quadrilles formed for the dance. She noted that Garrison and Millie danced together for a while and she wondered what makes a man or woman fall in love with one person over the other. Why did she melt every time Jesse was near, but not with Cal? Jesse led Sue Ann out to join Tom and Annie, and she recalled how he had danced with her when she was that age, and how much more simple life had been then.

The stable was quiet, the horses calm. Alex moved down to Ranger's stall and fed him a carrot from a basket. She propped herself against the stall door and stroked his blaze, running her finger gently along its outline. The door opened and Jesse came in.

"I thought you were dancing with Sue Ann," she said as he came up to her.

"J.J. felt left out, took over my place. Anyway, what're you doin' in here? Everyone's lookin' for you, wantin' a dance."

"I was waiting to see if you'd kiss me." The words just seemed to tumble out. Alex tilted her face almost boldly toward him.

He hesitated, surprised. "I can't kiss you, Alex."

She looked away for a moment, but was drawn back to that familiar face. Jesse was so gentle, yet so strong. She knew now she had always loved him—for as long as she could remember, she had loved him.

"If I kiss you," he went on, "I won't be able to stop."

"We could have an experiment," she said softly, "to see if you could stop."

"Is there a prize involved?"

She thought for a moment. "No. Just the kiss. I guess that's the prize. Anyway, it's an experiment, not a competition."

He looked at her. "You jus' want your way. As usual."

"I won't deny that."

"No, don't. If I was to tell you the moon was shinin' tonight, you'd move heaven and earth to prove the sun were out, if that's what you believed. That's the way you are, ain't it?"

"Maybe. I don't know. You know me best, it seems."

"Yeah." He extended his hand to her. "Gonna dance then?"

"Mebbe," she said putting on her Colorado accent. "Mebbe I will, mebbe I won't." She took his hand and jumped down from her perch.

He laughed. "Yeah. That's what I thought. At least with dancin', there's no argument as to when the music stops."

Jesse led her back to the party. Alex saw Oliver look at the two of them across the corral dance floor; no doubt he was wondering exactly how involved Alex had managed to get herself with the young puncher. He nodded to Alex, waved good-bye and left. She considered for a moment what Oliver would make of her and Jesse, decided she didn't care a damn, and followed Jess to join the circles for the next dance.

They had just missed a two-step and now everyone gathered for a square dance to music that was no longer strange to Alex's ears. The men and women wove in and out of each other, formed couples, went round, formed quadrilles, and the whole thing started again. Every time Jesse took Alex's hands, he found he wanted to stop, just stop right there, and hold her. He wondered if the experiment was not so much if he could stop kissing her if he started, but whether he could resist kissing her at all. He knew he couldn't, not that evening, not with her looking like the first wild flowers of spring, something fresh and alive yet exotic and untamed.

When the music stopped they were not together and he politely nodded to the woman opposite him and turned to find Alex. A waltz was next and they moved toward each other as if someone had thrown a loop about the two of them and were pulling it tighter and tighter. He held out his hands but when she placed hers in them, he didn't hold them for the dance but stood there caressing them, their fingers moving in and out of each other's as if the hands had a life of their own. At the same time, his eyes lost in hers, Jesse had no sense of where they were, where they stood. Alex kicked off her shoes as she had done when she was young and stood on Jesse's toes when he slid his arms back around her and held her to him for a moment. She tilted her face up to his, brushing his lips lightly with hers before he sought her mouth. Then, for a moment, the magic was broken by a small voice to his side.

"Mama?" Sue Ann gave her mother a jab as Annie filled a plate for her. "Are they kissing or eating each other?"

From the corner of his eye, Jesse saw Annie look up. She gently turned her daughter's face back to the table of food and smiled. "Oh, they're just in love, sweetheart," she said.

Alex sensed Jesse guiding her back into the shadows, out toward the darkness at the edge of the dance floor. For a moment they stopped as the kiss got deeper. Yet Alex was suddenly aware of the people, friends and otherwise, around her.

"That's positively disgusting." Sara Beth turned to Millie, nodding in the couple's direction.

"Oh, Sara Beth, I wish I had me that kind of disgusting—and so do you!"

And then Alex heard the familiar voice as Cal stood with Garrison and just laughed.

"I guess that smart mouth of hers is learning its lesson at last," he said.

Chapter Fourteen

Jesse knew with Alex there would be no half measures, that once she accepted she was in love with him, she would want it all, the whole experience of love, the whole of Jesse in the same way she went at everything, a summer cyclone sweeping everything up into its vortex. But he also worried that, while what she felt was real at the moment, that cyclone could blow itself out. Without nurturing her love for him, without keeping that fire stoked, he would lose her. For Jesse, it was a conundrum. He needed his own independence, he needed to take charge, but he also badly needed Alex.

Independence was the key word. While Jesse was aware that Alex's feelings for him were intense, almost consuming, they would conflict sharply with her desire for freedom. From the moment she had pulled the trigger at camp Boyd, their lives had become permanently entwined yet she had no idea how to accept Jesse into her life while maintaining her independence.

When Jesse told Alex one morning in mid-July he was going into Greeley for a haircut, Alex did not ask to go, nor did she question it. It was only later it struck Alex as odd he had taken the rig rather than one of his mounts, but before she had time to dwell on this too long, Jesse returned, his hair still shaggy and long, but with someone in the seat beside him.

"David!" screamed Alex seeing him there. Her brother hardly had time to step out of the buggy before Alex jumped into his arms and practically toppled the young man over. "Oh, David, David! I'm so happy to see you." She cried and laughed all at once, gave Jesse a big smile and even her Uncle Oliver a happy glance. "You kept this as a surprise, the lot of you. Oh, how mean," she added, although she didn't really think so.

"Well, let him come into the house for heaven's sake, Alexandra." Her uncle gave his nephew a hearty handshake. "We all have a lot of catching up to do."

Jesse sighed as he heaved another great case off the back of the rig and helped the footman get the bags inside. It wasn't that after the two-hour ride back from Greeley he disliked David, but he had already ascertained Alex's brother was far truer to his background than was Alex. In believing this, he couldn't help but wonder if David posed a threat to Alex's happiness in Colorado and, consequently, to their relationship.

As it happened, he needn't have worried. Alex remained in her western pants outfit and David made constant good-natured jokes about his "hobo sister." Cal told Jesse it was like watching puppies playing together, and Tom added that it was a lesson in how the "leisured classes behave." David kept to his English attire for all occasions, riding in jodhpurs and hacking jacket, or otherwise wearing a white linen suit, which always managed, by some miracle, to stay clean. He had been visiting friends in Newport and Virginia prior to coming to Colorado, and so he came equipped with lawn tennis rackets and polo mallets. As Jesse and the punchers rode in from herd one evening, they stopped to watch curiously as the siblings hit the tennis ball back and forth across the lawn at the rear of the house.

"Lady Lex is sure better'n him," Garrett noted loyally.

"Yeah, she's real good with watchin' that ball,

that's fer sure," added Cal.

"Funny sort of fella," said one of the others. "Looks like a real dandy, talks sort of uppity like, but seems nice enough."

They all turned to Jesse.

"Well, don't look at me. I ain't got the answers."

"Yeah, but you brought him in from Greeley, Jess. You didn't sit in silence for them two hours?" prodded Terry.

"Well." Jesse thought a moment. "He sort of made polite conversation like. Said it was real nice to be back, good to see me again, that sort of thing."

"For two hours?" they pushed.

Jesse leaned forward and adjusted his seat, the reins loose in his hand. "Just what is it you all are askin' me now?"

"You know what the heck we're askin', Jesse," taunted Reb. "We're askin' if you were askin'!"

Cal laughed. He stuck a bit of chicle in his mouth and exchanged a look with Jesse. "Ladilex is more likely to tell us—if she knows—than Jesse is. You're wastin' your time here, Reb, if you all think Jess is gonna sit here and recount a conversation with Lord David."

But the chance hadn't presented itself as yet. It wasn't something Jesse felt he could discuss with Lord David directly after he had stepped off the train. And it wasn't until the day before His Lordship was leaving that Jesse finally found him alone at the corral having a quiet smoke.

For a moment, the puncher stood there in the path leading from the bunkhouse watching the man who might possibly be his future brother-in-law. His stomach churned. David wasn't as tall as he, and at twenty-four was three years the younger, but he bore himself like the nobleman he was. He was handsome in a very clean cut and manicured sort of way, with wavy dark hair neatly parted on the side, and pale blue eyes. The two men couldn't be more different, one obviously aristocratic in a clean white linen suit, the other dusty from work, a tear in his shirt, chaps caked with mud, his hair unkempt and long.

Jesse approached the young man.

"Ah, Makepeace." Lord David turned with a smile. "I wondered when we might have a good chance to chat. I was hoping it wouldn't be in the carriage ride back to the station. Sort of leaves things a bit on the late side, don't you think?"

"Sir?" Jesse was somewhat taken aback at this turn.

"Alex. We should speak about Alex. Shouldn't we?"

"I don't quite follow, sir."

"Oh, come now. I'm not my uncle Oliver here. Nor my father, thank goodness. Let's not beat about the bush, shall we?"

Jesse heaved a sigh and moved up next to Lord David, resting his arms on the corral railing. He took off his hat and gave his hair a shake with his hand before looking out into the twilight and breathing the soft night air. David reached into his suit pocket and offered him a ready-made.

"French, I'm afraid," stated David. "I can't really abide those American things."

Jesse smiled and shook his head, watching as David pushed the cigarette back into a pack and tucked it into his inside pocket once again.

"My intentions are honorable, if that's what ya wanna know," started Jesse, "but I ain't much with words."

"And yet Alex tells me you read every chance you get and could have gone on to the university here had you wanted." He waited for a reply. "Look, old boy." He turned to face Jesse squarely. "I know you're a good sort, I know you love my sister and I know she loves you. Despite appearances, I don't care a fig about the class differences, the background, nor the fact that—dare I say it?—you can hardly afford to keep her in the style to which she *should* be accustomed. Fact is, she had a damned miserable childhood until she came here, my father hated her from the day she was born, she was married briefly to the worst blighter imaginable, and you make her happy. Or so she tells me. And while she still likes her Worth dresses and Parisian finery when she dresses up, it *ain't* too often she wants to do that these days, now is it? She's far happier here in the middle of nowhere—though Lord only knows why."

He stopped to look Jesse up and down. "Maybe it's you. Maybe it's Colorado. It can be the bloody cows, for all I care, but I'm satisfied she's happier now than she's ever been. And I can always buy her the odd Worth dress, for goodness sake." He turned back to watch a young colt in the distance with its mother. "I wonder if Oliver's ever thought of horse-breeding to increase his funds?" He took a long drag on his cigarette. "Thing is, old boy, I can't give permission for you to wed my sister, and that's the problem. You have my blessing, of course, and I'll do what I can to try to persuade Father but I can tell you he most likely won't budge. You see, Alex is a card he holds…and he wants to play that card to his best advantage. And I'm afraid—"

"Some two-bit cow puncher in Colorado is not it." Jesse took a deep breath and adjusted his hat.

"Just so, old boy, just so." David dropped his cigarette to stamp it out with his heel, then carefully picked up the stub again and placed it in a small silver box he had in his pocket. "I'll do what I can, Jesse Makepeace," he said with somewhat less bravado. "I'll do what I can. But I also think you'll have to have a word with dear old Uncle Oliver."

****

"So?" asked Alex.

"So. So nothing. You know I can't do anything, and I told Makepeace that. Even if you cleaned him up, got him to stop saying ain't and stuck a few pounds in his pocket, Father would still never approve. And you know he wouldn't approve for the simple reason you love him. Our father, our dear old father, will do anything and everything to make you miserable."

Alex sat on the edge of David's bed. He had dismissed his valet and was checking his tie in the mirror before they went down for dinner.

"Do you know what I really think, darling?" David let out a long breath of exasperation as Alex picked at a nail. "I think you should go and get yourself accouchement—that's what I think. Father will disinherit you and you'll have your Jesse all tied up with a neat ribbon. How do you like that idea?"

Alex's eyes scanned David to see if he was joking or not.

"Of course, there's Oliver to consider," David went on. "He may throw you out, throw Makepeace out as well—"

"Jesse'll get another job. Annie Yost told me some ranches up in Wyoming and Montana have written to Tom asking him to recommend a reliable foreman. He told her he's asked Jess but Jesse didn't want to move."

"Well then."

Alex paced the room. "In any case, I know something about Oliver."

"That he's your father?"

"He doesn't admit to that, David. He says—"

"I don't give a damn what he says, Alex. I know what I saw. I was nearly seven, not a babe in arms—I know what I saw." David leaned back against his dresser and sighed. "Well, what difference does it make now, I suppose." He straightened up again. "So what is it? This information you have against Oliver."

Alex hesitated, then said, "He's fixing the books."

"He's what?"

"As far as I can see. I looked at the books one evening while he was away, the ones he keeps downstairs. I saw them out on his desk one day when I was chatting with him—well, chatting is rather polite, we were arguing actually, but never mind. I just thought, well, I wonder...so I went back and found them when he was out. I'm not good at maths, as you know—"

"So you're not even sure?"

"No. But I'm fairly sure what I saw meant Oliver had withdrawn funds from the Frederic Faringdon Cattle Company, which he has never really paid back."

"Why didn't you tell me this sooner? I could have tried to go look."

"What difference does it make?" Alex stopped suddenly, her frustration evident. "The biggest loser is Papa. So why should I care? But if I did get into a family way, and if Oliver tried to throw me out so he wouldn't lose his position, I can hold that over his head."

"Well then. Why don't you just force him into letting you marry Makepeace? He's your guardian here, he can do that."

"I thought about that. I can't—Papa would fire him and he would have to leave if he did that, you know that's true." She paced a bit more. "I can't...I can't ruin him outright like that. If I was carrying Jesse's child it would be different and, in any case, we could leave if we really had to. But to just ruin Oliver outright like that—I can't bring myself to do it. He hasn't hurt me, not the way Papa has. I just can't do it."

Alex loved her brother, loved his company, but also found she missed her time with the punchers, missed her visits with Annie and Tom, and certainly missed the lack of formality and the freedoms she had come to enjoy. What with dressing in the evenings and the extra social occasions David's visit had engendered, his stay, more than anything, marked the differences in her life between England and Colorado. So when the time went by, she was almost relieved when David finally went home to England.

Her paintings were now once again centered on activities around the ranch: the Yost children cuddling, the punchers in a card game down by the corral, Joe cleaning some tack, and Jesse leaning back against the office wall. She also did one of Oliver standing with his horse out on the range, but this was hung above the drawing room fireplace and not for sale or display in New York. By August, she was ready for Jonathon Strugis' visit and Oliver welcomed the news of a New York visitor rather more happily than he had her notice she intended to marry Jesse Makepeace. She had decided to test his resolve.

"Has he asked you?" he inquired when she told him.

"Not yet, but he will. We're in love," she said simply.

"And what, exactly, do you think your father is going to say?"

"I don't give a damn what my father says. It's none of his business now."

"I'm afraid it is, Alex. You cannot marry without your father's permission—until you are twenty-one."

"But I can marry with the permission of my guardian in Colorado, and that's you."

"I cannot do that. I'm sorry, I just can't." She

stood staring at him, anger rising in the set of her mouth. "I would lose everything, Alex, you know that. Your father would dismiss me if I let you marry Jesse Makepeace. I can't do it. I'm forty-seven years old. I can't start again. Where would I go? What would I do? This ranch is my life."

"That's ridiculous and you know it. You could…" Her voice trailed off. He was right—in her heart, she knew he was right. Oliver could never start again; he hadn't the guts for it. He'd built his little empire here and, such as it was, it was this or nothing. She let the matter drop. "Well, we'll wait until I'm twenty-one, if that's necessary. But I can tell you now, Uncle Oliver, if you try to send me home, I'll run away. I won't go back."

He stared at her and said nothing. Alex knew full well that if her father demanded it, Oliver wouldn't hesitate to comply. She tossed her head and walked out. It was a gesture Oliver had once told her reminded him of her mother. He seemed to be more or less resigned now to his inability to comprehend her nature or to build any kind of close relationship with her. Certainly she could not possibly resemble her mother in character.

For a moment she stood quietly outside the study door and pondered whether her mother ever really would have followed Oliver to America. Would she have left her wealth and her position behind for this rugged, wild land? What kind of woman had her mother been? Did Alex resemble her at all in character?

She heard the creak of Oliver's desk chair as he collapsed into it. A shuffling sound followed and, as quiet settled, she wondered exactly what he was reading.

****

Jesse stood on the platform holding hands with Alex as the train pulled into Greeley. It was a

Saturday afternoon and he had taken the day off to drive Alex in to meet Sturgis, knowing how nervous she was about the possible criticism of her work. Her nails were bitten down and smiles faded easily from her face. For a moment he felt threatened by this other part of her life, a part with which he had nothing to do, a part he couldn't even begin to understand or try to understand.

The train chugged slowly past him before coming to a halt. A porter sprang off and put the steps down, and a man in a three-piece tweed suit carrying an umbrella stepped off. Jesse laughed.

"Ssh!" whispered Alex, "It's not funny," but she was smothering her own giggles. "Jonathon! So good to see you." She extended her hand, then introduced Jesse as her *very best friend* and slipped her arm through his possessively, until he moved to take Sturgis' bag.

"Y'all have a good trip?" Jesse asked politely.

"I beg your pardon?"

"I said—"

"He asked if you had a good trip, Jonathon," Alex interpreted. She looked askance at Jesse and raised her eyebrows, biting her lip against another burst of nervous laughter.

Conversation on the way to the ranch centered mostly on Jonathon's journey out. He had never been beyond Chicago, so this was a first, a revelation, he said.

"Well, I've never been east of Nebraska," said Jesse. "And then there's Lady Alex who's been the whole world over, I reckon."

"So I can tell you Colorado is best and not to bother with any place else, really." She pulled his hair a bit from her place in the back seat.

Oliver went all out, naturally, to entertain this visitor from the east. He had planned a dinner party, which Jesse declined to attend, using the excuse of nighthawking again. Alex knew full well Jesse would have felt out of place and underdressed in his Sunday best with everyone else in formal attire. She didn't argue. She'd rather have been out with him.

Sturgis appeared greatly impressed with the house and grounds and ranch in general. He'd expected, he said, something rather more rustic and certainly not the servants and food he was offered. But most of all, he was here to see Alex's paintings as well as the world in which she now lived. She took him up to her studio the very next morning.

He was silent as he walked around. It made her nervous and she bit her nails as he first lifted one painting and held it out to view, then stood back from another one leaning against the wall, pulled the cloth from yet another on her easel, held another to the light. At long last, he stood and looked at her.

"Genius," he said quietly. Alex watched the dust motes dancing down a triangle of light to where he stood. "Sheer genius."

"Do you think they'll sell?" she asked uncertainly.

"Sell? Sell?" He looked at her as if she hadn't heard him, or was mad. "Darling girl, they'll be killing each other to own one of these."

****

The summer rolled on, the heat bearing down on them relieved only by the afternoon storms that seemed fewer this year than most. The earth was parched and flowers wilted early, the gardens around the house looking as if they had been hit by a plague. The cattle still had plenty of grass but if the rain didn't increase soon it might be a tough autumn.

Alex and Jesse tried to find time alone but it was difficult; either he was working or she was painting and couldn't just stop. The time they did have together grew increasingly intense and Alex knew Jesse would soon propose; she dreaded it. Telling him there would have to be a three-year wait was not going to be easy.

But Jesse already knew. Uncomfortable with not being able to ask her father for her hand, he finally got up his courage to go see Oliver. He stood uneasily in front of Calthorpe, who stayed seated behind his desk, never offering a seat to Jesse and obviously knowing full well the reason for the requested interview. Jesse would not be deterred.

"I cannot give you permission," Oliver said. "It's not mine to give."

"But you are her guardian here. Doesn't that—"

"No!" Oliver cut him off. "Even if I could, I'm not convinced this union would be in Alexandra's best interests."

Jesse stared at him for a moment, trying to keep his temper from boiling over. "You talk about it as if it were some business arrangement. You don't hold her happiness foremost then?" He kept his voice under control.

"Of course I do!" Oliver slammed the desk. "Of course I want her happiness." He got up and sat on the edge of the desk, looking at his hands for a moment, then back up at Jesse. "I want her happiness. Only, I'm not sure this union...what she feels...or what she thinks she feels for you is long term. I cannot believe someone born to the wealth and comforts she has thus far enjoyed can really see herself in a lifetime of second best. Third-rate if the truth be told."

Jesse looked at his boss and let the insult pass. "Mr. Calthorpe, sir, do you think you really know, really understand, your niece? I mean..." He let his voice trail away. Jesse felt Oliver's eyes burn through him, as if his boss were seeing him for the first time. "I don't mean to be disrespectful, sir, but maybe you should think of that little girl who first came out here when the ranch was nothin' but a hardscrabble set of buildin's. Think about the girl who wore pants and rode and helped at times with the horses and cattle, about the girl struggling to make her own way and—might I say it?—to be free of her father."

Oliver froze. A look crossed his face that Jesse remembered later as the look of a condemned man, a man consumed by guilt.

Oliver moved back behind his desk and lowered himself wearily into the chair. "Well, you have savings I take it?"

"Some. Maybe not a whole lot but enough to homestead I reckon."

Oliver shook his head. "I don't know what my blessing is worth, Makepeace. I cannot give permission. I would only lose my position as manager if I flagrantly let you go ahead and marry Alex. But for what it's worth, I won't stop you from courting her. It'll be a pretty damned long engagement though."

Jesse just smiled. "I'm learning to be tolerant," he said.

Chapter Fifteen

On August 27th while preparations were underway for Alex's birthday party, Jesse found her in the shaded walkway between the gardens and the front of the house.

"Well, fancy meeting you here, Mr. Makepeace. Was there someone you were looking for?"

"Yeah," he said. "All my life. And I finally found her."

Alex laughed a bit, then pulled him to her and kissed him. "So now what are you going to do—now you've found me?"

"Marry you, of course."

There was a long silence as each searched the other's eyes for some comment or statement or response. Alex still had her hands on Jesse's neck but she slowly let go and stood back.

"I hope you're a patient man," she said at last, but knowing he wasn't.

"I think I can be patient with you," he replied misunderstanding.

"No. I mean, I can't marry you until I'm twenty-one, Jesse. I—"

"I know. I know all about that, Alex. I spoke to Mr. Calthorpe, to get his permission, as I should."

"I should have realized—"

"Yes. He explained ever'thin' to me. I understand. It's three years."

"You'll be thirty-one."

"I know. Are you telling me you're not worth waiting for?"

"No, I..." She stopped. Her face was wet and

Jesse wiped it with his bandana.

"Well, I thought I was gonna make you happy."

"You do make me happy. You make me very happy, Jesse Makepeace."

"Well, you don't look so. Say, are you still gonna be Lady Alex?"

"Yes. I shall be Lady Alexandra Makepeace—with a few other names in-between."

"I ain't worried 'bout t'other names, Alex," he said gently. "Just those two." He bent to kiss her lightly. "I haven't a ring."

"Don't need a ring. I think you've got your lariat around me but good."

"Well, anyway, I did get you this a while back. Thought you might like it now." He unwrapped something from one of his bandanas and handed it to her. It was the silver cuff set with turquoise worn by the old Indian who used to sit outside the Benders' shop.

"Oh, my gosh! How did you get this?"

"Well, bought it of course. It was like you said, if he sold it he could eat, and he saw the sense in that."

"You've kept it all this time?"

"I had it to give you for your thirteenth birthday but you were gone by then."

"Oh, Jesse!" She threw her arms around him. "It's beautiful! It's wonderful! I shall never take it off. Really. I promise. Never."

****

Rose was just finishing Alex's hair when there was a knock on the door and Oliver came in. He looked the girl over as she sat there at the dressing table. Rose twisted her hair at the back and set the pins in.

"No pearls in it tonight?" he asked.

"No. No time I'm afraid," Alex answered. "Anyway, the gown has pearls." She stood to show him the shimmering gown, a pale pink evening dress with seed pearls embroidered throughout in designs of flowers right down the bodice to the hem. Rose gave her a final primp, and Oliver sighed.

"No doubt who'll be the belle of the Ball tonight. Is that gown by Worth?" he asked.

"Yes! Extravagant but it was a present from David. David always buys me Worth. He says I'm Monsieur Worth's muse and there ought to be a discount but I don't think there is!" She turned once more for him to admire.

Oliver motioned for Rose to leave them, and he waited for the door to close. "I know you said no presents..." He tentatively held out a leather box. "Don't consider this a present, then. I bought this for your mother...when I went back. Of course, she was gone by then and I didn't know, hadn't received the news on my travels. I'm not really sure why I kept this all these years. I suppose I thought for a while I would marry someone else and might give it to them. Then I realized I would never find anyone as lovely as your mother, Alex—until now, of course. She would be glad to know you had them. Really."

Alex took the box and slowly opened it, her eyes wide as she let out a breath in delight. It was a parure of a delicate diamond tiara, with a matching necklace and earrings. "It's magnificent," she sighed. "But Uncle Oliver, I can't..."

"Of course you can. I think you'll have to take off that bracelet, however."

Alex looked up at him. "I can't. Jesse gave it to me. I said I would never take it off and I won't, not for this, not for anything." She closed the lid and started to hand him the box, but he gently pushed it back to her.

"Let me help you get it on," he said.

****

When Oliver brought Alex down the steps from the French doors and onto the back terrace, there

147

was a united gasp. She stood there for a moment, laughing lightly before turning to search for Jesse, who said he would come over for a bit with the Yosts. She spotted him across the terrace at the far side but before she could even get off the steps people were coming over, engaging her in conversation, wishing her well, giving her birthday salutations. By the time she had reached the Yosts, Jesse had gone.

"He said he'd come for you at nine on the dot," Tom assured her.

"How will he know when it's nine?" Alex queried. "He hasn't got a watch!"

"Well, he'll know. Don't you worry."

"Can I have that dress when you've outgrown it?" Sue Ann asked.

"Oh, Sue Ann really. First of all," Annie told her, "Lady Alex won't be growing anymore and, secondly, just where do you think you'll be wearing something like that?"

"To my eighteenth birthday party!"

"I tell you what," Alex said, "you can most definitely have it when I've finished with it. When you're older. All right?"

She went to politely mix with the rest of her guests and moved from table to table to chat as they dined, but always she was waiting for nine o'clock and the chance to slip away. After dinner, the Yosts excused themselves when the dancing started at 8:30, and Alex told Wilson to let her know when it was nine. At his nod, she slipped into the covered walkway to the front.

Jesse met her halfway. "I thought you were a Lady, not a Princess," he said.

She laughed. "And I thought you were a cowpuncher, not a knight in shining armor!"

"I think it's you who's shining, lady. You got yourself some hardware there. You better be packin' your six-shooter if you're totin' that stuff about."

"It was to be my mother's, apparently." She looked at him, then showed him she was still wearing his bracelet.

"Come here, you." He pulled her to him. "I don't think I wished you happy birthday yet."

His kiss was devouring, overwhelming. With Jesse enveloping her, Alex felt like the world had disappeared. There was nothing more than their existence together. The more consuming his kiss became, the more she yearned for him. Finally she pulled away to catch her breath. "I can't wait three years, Jesse, I—"

"Hey, y'all," said Cal coming up behind them. "We're all waitin' for the birthday gal."

Alex took a deep breath, startled by the sudden intrusion, then collected her thoughts. "I'll be right there. I'm going to find champagne and glasses— none of that moonshine you all drink!"

"We drink good decent whiskey, gal," Cal told her. "None of that fancy lady's stuff."

"Ha! I'll be there in a few minutes," and off she went.

She found Jesse sitting on the grassy bank opposite the corral, the Yosts close by. Two ice-cold bottles of champagne and two glasses in her hand, she knelt down quietly behind him and touched the bottles to his bare neck.

"Darn!" He jumped and grabbed her hand behind him, pulling her forward and laughing. "What the heck?"

"Do you know how to open champagne?" She held out the bottles.

"Why, sure, we have it out there on the range every afternoon. Let me see that," he said taking a bottle.

Alex had to stop herself from giggling as Jesse tried to figure it out. She took the bottle back. The Yosts strolled over to join them.

"Just to prove to you I'm not totally useless, you first remove the foil then unwind this little bit here and remove the wire cage and cap. Has anyone got a bandana on them, or a hankie?" she asked. Jesse pulled a clean handkerchief from his pocket and handed it to her. "Then you ease out the cork, but hold one of the glasses up just in case." With the hanky around the cork she eased it out and quickly poured the first bit into one of the glasses, then into the other Jesse was holding in his other hand, and back and forth until they both were filled. "That's for Tom and Annie," she said. "We can share the bottle!"

"I'd never drank champagne before tonight," Annie admitted.

They all toasted Alex's health.

The other punchers gathered around, drinks in hand, wishing Alex well. Garrett pushed his way to the front along with Cal, boxes tucked under their arms. Alex didn't see Garrison come up behind her holding her hat.

"Lady Lex," Garrett started.

"I said no presents."

"Not to us, you didn't," Jesse corrected. "That was on them fancy invites. We didn't get those, did we boys?"

"Nope, sure didn't get no invite," Cal said. "Jus' sorta decided..."

"All right. All right, get on with it if you must." Alex slugged back some champagne, the bubbles going up her nose and making her eyes tear. Jesse gently took the bottle and put his free arm about her.

"So like I was sayin', Lady Lex," Garrett at last continued. "Aw, heck, boss." He handed the package to Tom. "You do it."

Tom took the two presents from Garrett and Cal. "Happy Eighteenth, sweetheart. From all of us." He handed Alex the two boxes.

One was small but long and thin, the other much larger but also long. She opened the small one first, tears already making trails down her cheek, which Jesse kept dabbing with the champagne hankie and laughing as he did so.

"You are about the cryingest dang woman," he announced as he wiped her cheek.

"Oh, shush. Oh, my gosh!" she exclaimed. Inside was the silver and feather hatband she had declined to pay for at Hope's Hats. She turned to Jesse and kissed him, full on the mouth.

"Hey, jus' a second lady." Garrison handed Alex her hat to put it on. "I think we all get one of those!"

Alex laughed. "Well, mwa!" she said kissing her hand and waving it at them. She pushed the band onto the hat, felt for her tiara and put the hat on over it, smiling up at them. Then she started to untie the bow on the other box. As she did so, she instinctively knew what was going to be inside. More tears fell.

Jesse dabbed some more. He looked up at the punchers. "Boys, we got more rain here than Colorado sees in a year!" They all laughed.

Alex poked him with her elbow, then pulled the ribbon off and lifted the top. There inside were her western boots, pointed heeled boots, in brown and white calf and snakeskin, made to order by a Dallas bootmaker. "Oh my Lord," she whispered. "You all are just the best friends any girl could ask for. Really. I mean it."

And the rain fell pretty steadily after that.

The party went on with dancing and food and entertainment. Alex took one of Cal's guitars and did an old duet with him of The Dyin' Cowgirl but declined an encore in favor of more dancing with Jesse. Toward midnight she realized she was going to have to go back to the house to say goodnight to her other guests and thank them for coming, but she was reluctant to let the evening end—and let Jesse go.

"Do me a favor," she said at last.

"For you, anything."

"Come with me up to Boyd to see the sunrise. You get to see sunrise all the time but I don't. I'd really like to do that."

"Alex, that's a two-hour ride."

"I know. So we'll have plenty of time to get there before sunrise. And, anyway, there'll be no one there now since they're all either down here or on herd. And the punchers will be clearing up here tomorrow morning."

"Don't you feel... Do you really want to go back there after the shootin's and all?"

"I can't tarnish the place because of what happened. It's so lovely. And you'll be there. It's not as if I were going on my own. Sunrise over the lake?"

He agreed. Alex went off to say goodnight to her guests and take off her jewels. She let Oliver know where she was going but got no response except to say he hoped Jesse had his gun with him.

Jesse changed his clothes and saddled up the two horses. He was surprised when Alex came back with only a duster over her gown, and her new boots on.

"I thought you were going to change," he said.

She shrugged. "Nope. Too much of a hurry!"

"You'll ruin your—" but she was up on Ranger, her dress hiked up, some bare stockinged leg showing above the boots as she rode off.

"You do know sunrise isn't until nearly 6.30?" But Alex was gone. Jesse took off after her, watching as her hair fell loose and the tendrils blew in the wind like fingers beckoning him. After a while she pulled up to listen. A coyote barked in the distance and somewhere an owl hooted. The sound of the train whistle was carried in the wind.

"I don't think I've ever been out here on the range this late at night. It's wonderful."

Jesse could only just make out her eyes glistening as she turned to him, but he leaned across and pulled her over, finding her mouth. "You're wonderful."

The camp consisted of a log cabin with a stone fireplace and a few bits of haphazard furniture for the men—a table and rough stools, two cots with bedrolls left. Cooking was done outside or in the fireplace, and an outhouse was nothing more than an enclosed pit.

"What now?" asked Jesse as they rode up.

Alex took a deep breath, dismounted and tied up Ranger while Jesse came and saw to the horses. She wandered about, pulling the duster around her in the cool night air. At last she went into the cabin. "Have you a match?" she asked sticking her head back out.

He came in after her and lit the lantern but it was low on oil and didn't give off much light. She took the duster off and stood there, silently facing him, then went over and took off his hat, placed it on the table, and turned back to him.

"Alex..." he started, knowing.

She didn't say a word, but just stood there.

"It's not...it wouldn't be right," he said softly. "You know, you know there ain't nothing more in this whole wide world I want at this minute but—"

She sat on a stool and pulled off first one boot, then the other and kicked them aside, then she stood and put her leg on the stool to roll down her stockings one by one. He marveled at her wantonness, her lack of propriety. "Alex, stop," he said gently putting his hand on hers. "Stop. You know..." But he was lost. She took his face in her hands and pulled him to her, kissing him so any resistance he had had was now shattered. His heart beat faster at the sweetness of her mouth, the softness of her tongue, the lack of air as they sought each other. His hands moved over her feeling the outline of her body, knowing its curves, its gentleness, its yielding. "Are you sure?" he asked at last.

"I want you so much, Jesse, I want you so much, I'm not going to wait three years. And if…if anything happens, so what? We'll get married, that'll be it."

"Yes, but Alex, you can't—I mean it'd be a 'shotgun' wedding, it's not how—"

"Ssh," she whispered. She put her finger to his mouth and then turned for him to unhook her gown. He ran his hands gently down her exposed back, feeling each scar, then kissed her neck.

"You have nothing on under…"

"It's how the gown is made. Monsieur Worth builds the undergarments into the gown." Her voice was at barely a whisper, a tremor showing her nerves. She turned and still held the gown up to her, then, looking at Jesse, let it drop to the floor.

His hand went to caress her breasts, gently touched their delicacy, their curve. He felt her nipples harden at expectation of what was to come. "You know how beautiful you are?" he said, quiet as the night surrounding them. "Do you?"

She got up on tiptoes and sought the warmth and wetness of his mouth while her hands found the buttons of his shirt. In the soft glow of the lamplight, their shadows became one even as they did so on their makeshift bed.

Alex awoke sometime in the early morning to find Jesse's face so close to hers she could see the specks in his eyes, and feel his breath on her face. She remembered then the awkwardness of his undressing, the surprise she had felt that his naked body looked so much like the marble statues she had seen. For a moment she had been mesmerized by him, silently watching him, entranced—she thought he was magnificent. There was the revelation his hands were so gentle as he caressed her body, as his fingers ran over her skin, slipped between her thighs to arouse her, and his manhood was so hard and yet softly skinned as she ran her own hand over it. He had entwined his fingers in her hair as he carefully pulled it loose and held her head as his kiss started soft and warm, going deeper as she yielded to him. She remembered, too, the comfort of the weight of his body, the feel of his skin next to hers, and the momentary shock of his entering her—and later the slight regret when he withdrew. But for now she was happy. She wanted Jesse and she felt a kind of belonging she had never known.

Alex pushed some hair from his forehead and kissed him.

"Do you know how beautiful you are?" she said.

"That's my line, woman. Men aren't beautiful."

"You are. Inside and out." She pushed him over and wound her legs through his, propping herself up to look at him. "I should do another painting of you. A nude!"

"Ha! No you don't. I wouldn't be able to show my face in the state of Colorado—in three states—if you did that!" He reached up to take her head in his hands and pull her in for a kiss.

"Don't leave me." Her voice was suddenly serious. "Promise you won't leave me?"

"Now where do you think I'm runnin' off to?" He wondered then if she felt any guilt, was sorry for what they had done, but her eyes said otherwise. It was he who felt the guilt, he who would never let her go now.

"I want to wake up every morning seeing you there beside me. I want— Have we got any paper and pencil here?" she asked abruptly. She slid off Jesse to the floor taking the duster they had thrown on top with her.

"Alex!" Jesse jumped off the cot to pull his pants on but Alex was already out the door getting something from her saddlebags. He stood in the doorway watching her. "Your feet are bare. You'll get bit, ya dang fool woman."

She pushed him back inside and sat on the tabletop by the lantern while he perched on a stool watching her. Her hand moved so quickly in the dim light it was a marvel to him. "How come I can't do that?" he asked. "I shoot pretty well."

"I don't know. Here try." She handed him the pad and pencil as she pulled on her boots to go back outside for a moment. When she came back in, he pushed the pad over to her to show her his drawing.

It was of two stick figures, one apparently in chaps and a Stetson, the other in what seemed to be her tiara but with western boots, bending toward each other and obviously kissing. Above their heads was an array of floating hearts and Xs. Below, he had written, Jesse and Alex Get Married 1889.

Alex looked at it and couldn't stop giggling for a time. "Well, let's hope maybe it'll be sooner than 1889." She looked at it again then leaned over to kiss him. "I tell you what, Jesse Makepeace—you hang on to this for me, and anytime you think I'm being miserable and *ornery*, you hand this to me and make me laugh."

Chapter Sixteen

September blew in with a chill that was ominous. The punchers had more trouble than they had ever had in previous years with wolves coming down from the hills. The birds, too, seemed to be leaving early on their journeys south. Terry took down a mountain lion, and a herd of wild horses was spotted coming south from Wyoming. The ranch had a round-up, but only to cut out other outfits' cattle who were sending them to the rail. Calthorpe had decided to keep his steers on until spring, take his chances that prices might go up.

Alex kept busy finishing her paintings and getting them crated for New York. Her exhibition opened Thursday, October 14th, although she had decided to go to New York in time to get there for the Monday before. She would oversee hanging the paintings in the gallery, stay for the opening as Jonathon wanted, and then come back. She planned on leaving Friday the 8th and being back around the 18th or 19th, taking Rose with her.

There were no further chances to be alone with Jesse. About mid-September she told him she was not pregnant so he shouldn't worry, but the disappointment was obvious in her voice.

"Alex, it's for the best," he consoled her, but she just shook her head.

She went in to see Miss Bea for commiseration, knowing it was not something she could easily discuss with Annie.

"Hell, child, any time you an' Jess want a bed for a couple of hours, you let me know. I can clear on outta here and get downstairs. Just say the word." Yet the organization to do this was not something Alex could contemplate at the moment. Her mind was now on her work and making money.

****

New York was strange after life in the country, crowded and busy and distracting—and frightening. Jonathon sent a hansom cab to the hotel for Alex and Rose every morning, and put them back into one every evening. Alex wondered how she had ever managed after Madame Helene had died, but then recalled she had been quickly whisked away by the horrible consular officer. She ate with Rose in the hotel suite in the evening, declining both Jonathon's various invitations to meet people as well as proposed reunions with family friends.

"This is business," Jonathon finally told her on the Wednesday afternoon. "You may get commissions, people want to meet you," he added with some exasperation.

"Then they can meet me at the opening tomorrow. I agreed to that, and I shall go, but that is it."

"You've already marked three paintings as Not for Sale. The one of the cowboy sunning himself has already had several offers from my special clients, and the children too. In addition to which, I've had to remove the painting of the nude madam for fear it would be considered scandalous for a young woman to have painted. You never showed me that in Colorado."

"It was hanging in the saloon in town, Jonathon. I..." She thought of her promise to make Bea famous but let the matter drop. Bea would never know anyway, and Alex felt she could not endanger her career.

"Lady Alex, please, please be reasonable," he begged.

"I'm always reasonable, Jonathon. Always."

****

She arrived for the private viewing party almost an hour late. Chaperoned by Rose who soon stood aside, Alex made a grand entrance, smiling good-naturedly at her audience. Everyone was captivated, everyone wanted to meet her, talk to her, know her—own her, she thought. Although some of them were either friends of her father's or David's, she found it wearing and couldn't wait to get home.

But it was the money. Commissions were requested. While virtually all the paintings sold the first night, it was the commissions where the big money was to be made. New Yorkers, it seemed, wanted nothing more than their own portraits hanging above their imported marble fireplaces, and for it to be done by the daughter of an English Duke was quite a bonus. To Jonathon's disgust, Alex declined them all—until Mr. and Mrs. Bell approached her to do a giant mural on the wall of their new home in Newport.

Alex proved a shrewd businesswoman; the money proffered for this fresco was five thousand dollars. Alex rejected it outright, saying it would take her three weeks and she wanted to get back to Colorado. They doubled the offer. Alex laid down her terms—there would be no socializing, no parties, no introductions to visitors, only work. She and Rose would have use of their private railway car there and back and, in addition, into New York for the unveiling of the statue of "Liberty Enlightening the World" on October 28th. The deal was made.

She sent two wires. To Oliver Calthorpe: *Staying three extra weeks STOP Visiting friends in Newport STOP Alex.* To Jesse Makepeace: *Persuaded to take important commission STOP Three extra weeks STOP Huge amount money STOP Start building dream house STOP I love you STOP Alex.*

Jesse didn't compare telegrams with Oliver Calthorpe but he heard about Alex's alternative version from Tom. He envisioned Calthorpe as thinking "At least she has the sense to mix with the right people. Maybe this will put that puncher out of her head."

Jesse read his and his heart sank but when he showed it to Tom, the older man said, "So where you gonna build that house of yours, Jess?"

"I can't live on her money, Tom. That's not right."

Tom sighed. "I think, Jess, if you want the girl you're gonna have to take the whole package. I knew the first day I met Alex, when she was eight years old, she was never going to be easy, she was going to try Annie and me constantly, but she'd always be worth it. She's a dang perfectionist. Not for others, not for her surroundings, but for her—herself. And she doesn't want to be dependent on you any more than you want to be dependent on her. Marriage is a partnership, anyway, give and take, half and half all the way. I know you got your pride. We all do. But Alex has got hers too and I tell you one thing—she's not goin' to change. Since that dang marriage her father forced her into, and since Madame's death, she's like some wild thing. Calthorpe don't pay her no mind, and she certainly doesn't listen to Annie or me much."

Jesse grimaced thinking Tom didn't know quite how wild Alex actually was.

"So where you gonna build that house?"

On November 11th Jesse got to the station a few minutes after the Express had left. He spotted the luggage but no Rose or Alex, so he loaded the bags into the wagon and waited, wondering where they had gone.

"Jesse?" said a voice behind him. It was Barney from Miss Bea's. "Miss Bea said she had to see you real quick—said it was urgent and to take the back stairs."

But Jesse knew it wasn't Bea. He ran up the stairs and knocked on the office door. "Come on in, cowboy," simpered a phony drawl.

He opened the door to see a trail of Alex's clothes leading to the bed where she was comfortably ensconced. "Now what would you have done if it weren't me, is what I want to know, Alexandra Calthorpe."

Alex laughed. "Been very embarrassed, I guess."

"Where the hell is Rose?"

"So many questions."

He sat on the edge of the bed, charmed by her shamelessness, her lack of a girl's prim modesty as she reached to unbutton his shirt.

"Rose is conveniently visiting relatives in Chicago. She'll be back next week," she said at last.

He bent to pull off his boots and remove his pants, then slipped under the covers, pulling her over to him. "Oh Gawd, I missed you!"

Their lovemaking was self-perpetuating—the more they made love, the more they wanted each other, couldn't get enough of each other, couldn't stop. His body heat enflamed her, while the generosity of his lovemaking captured her heart and made her more giving. Alex had a white-hot heat that only Jesse could satisfy; his power over her was manifest. Only Jesse could make her body sing. Time and again his hard sex found the soft damp center of her core, their two bodies moving together to fulfill each other.

Two and a half hours later there was a knock on the door. "You still in there, sweetheart," came Bea's voice through the door.

"Which one of us are you calling sweetheart?" Alex called back, lying sated in Jesse's arms.

"Time's up, Lady A., less'n you all wanna be

sharin' that bed with others. You got twenty minutes to clear out or it'll be a foursome," to which she added in a lower voice, "Don't suppose it'd be the first time here, neither."

Alex laughed and said, "Yes, Ma'am!" She looked at Jesse. "I missed you so much. I couldn't believe how much I missed you."

He kissed her breasts then gently ran his hand around the curve of them.

"Not much there, I'm afraid."

"No, but what there is, is prime quality." Alex laughed again and Jesse held her face just looking at it. "You know how much I love you?"

"About half as much as I love you, I think."

"Now what makes you say a thing like that?"

"Because I learned one thing while I was away, one very important thing."

"Which was?"

"Being independent doesn't necessarily mean not wanting someone with you always. All the time in New York, working, meeting people, dealing with Jonathon and his clients and their, oh, I don't know... I did it all, but all the time it was like there was a part of me missing, a huge part. I don't think I can live without you, quite honestly."

She sat up to get dressed, wondering if she had told him the truth, knowing now that a career as an artist wasn't only doing enough paintings for two exhibitions a year—it involved being away from home, taking those commissions which would make her name. Where did having a family fit in with all that? She looked across at Jesse again. Jesse with his intense blue eyes and his shaggy fair hair, Jesse slipping his shirt on over the taut muscles of his lean body. And she wanted him again, wanted all of Jesse, 100% of Jesse, even though she could never give him 100% of herself. "No, I can't live without you. Does that make you feel lassoed," she asked quietly, "or hog-tied or corralled? Or just plain trapped?"

"No." He reached across and kissed her again. "It makes me feel loved."

Two days later all hell broke loose.

Chapter Seventeen

On November 13th it started to snow and continued almost solidly for nearly thirty days. The reduced number of punchers had trouble getting feed out to the increased number of winter cattle, and after what had been a very dry summer, the grass under the snow cover was virtually gone. Cattle perished, the fat on the steers disappearing almost by the day. Then, around the end of the first week of December there was milder weather and a thaw began of the deep lying snow. Rose managed to get back from Chicago at last, and Christmas festivities were planned in the belief the crisis was over.

But on Christmas Eve it snowed again. Oliver and Alex were left alone while the men were sent out to trail feed the cattle that followed each other and huddled to stay warm. As the days went by, thawed slush turned to solid ice as temperatures dropped to minus 30. Horses plunged after the cattle in the deep snow, their legs cut and blood freezing on their coat as the wounds opened. Cattle feed was buried and the herd started drifting with the wind, walking and lowing, bawling, with empty stomachs and nothing more to eat than underbrush, bark from the few trees, lower branches and twigs, if they could find them. Hair wore off their legs to the hocks and soon it was hide peeling off from frostbite. Tails froze like icicles and snapped off. In many cases, their hooves froze and dropped off and they limped on with hoofless stumps while others became encased in the solidifying crystals and unable to go further. Those endless plains Alex had so admired now proved deadly with their lack of woodland as the snow eddied and swirled into the great emptiness.

In January, there was a three day blizzard, and on the 14th, the temperatures plummeted to forty-seven below. Alex was frantic for Jesse, whom she hadn't seen since before Christmas Eve, and also worried for the Yosts in their much smaller home. Firewood and coals were running out, as was food, and she tried to keep herself busy with endless sketching rather than watch Oliver pacing the floor and shouting every time he was asked a question.

In late January, a Chinook melted the top layer of the crusted snow. Yet the winter was not over, and it turned cold again. On the third of February, another two-day blizzard started. The feed sleighs were practically useless now.

The men had been moved into the house to camp when they weren't out, as the bunkhouse proved too cold for human habitation. Ropes ran from the stables to the house and outbuildings because the wind was so fierce at times it could blow a man off his feet, and the billowing snow was blinding. Food had to be rationed and snow melted for water consumption. In the evenings the men became almost sentimental for the old days, the trail rides, the hardships of a land that was filling with a civilization they did not want. They told Alex stories of this past and, although she had heard many before, she still loved to hear them—the Indian raids, the rustlers who hit the herd coming up, the river crossings and wild nights in cow towns (although these were toned down somewhat for her female ears). Alex almost knew the stories as well as the men remembered them, and would say to one of them, "tell me again about the time you did so-and-so" or "let's hear about the..." and they would laugh and sit a moment and repeat the tale again.

She busied herself during the day looking after

one of the men who had gone snow blind and a couple of others who had frostbite. And there was sketching, always the sketching. She talked with Jesse briefly but only long enough to know he was still all right, unhurt, and still had something of a sense of humor. "Ain't you knittin' for us all?" he asked.

The cattle looked like ghosts of themselves, Jesse said. Tom told her the men were nothing less than heroes, riding all day without a hot meal, in blinding snowstorms, their horses slowly plowing through the blizzard to try to get whatever feed they could find to the cattle. They mostly had to ride sideways into the wind, often unable to breathe in the inhuman temperatures, sometimes having to cup their hands over their noses and mouths to keep the wind and snow out in order to get the frozen air into their lungs.

Jesse came back in with Tom and Cal one evening in late February, and all humor was now gone. Alex was with her uncle when Tom told Oliver he believed they had lost between 60 to 75 per cent of the herd, the cattle had lumped together in places against the weather, heads lowered and crusted with snow, and starved or froze to death. Out on the rivers and lakes, they had drowned in numbers down air holes. Ravines and draws were filled with dead cattle, nothing but horns or noses sticking up through the deadly snow.

Alex fled the room to Oliver's study. She couldn't cope with all this loss, all this misery, and what she saw as probably the end of the ranch. She grabbed a pencil from a cup on his desk and looked wildly for paper to sketch on, opening drawers in his desk, pulling things out, shuffling through, trying to find any blank page on which she could work.

But instead of blank paper she found something unexpected, something she never imagined he would have—letters. A pile of them tied up with string, aging now, yellowing somewhat, but nevertheless there.

And she knew what they were.

****

In March, as Alex made her way to the stables to see Ranger, she heard what sounded like the gates of hell opening, steel screeching against steel. Joe came in to the stables. "It's the ice. Breakin' up on the rivers. It's a thaw."

The snow at last melted exposing a barren wasteland of earth and dead grass, a range that looked as if it had never been anything more than dirt. Jesse told her you could almost walk from the Cache to the Thompson never stepping off the carcasses of dead cattle, and the ones that were living were emaciated, hollow and listless, searching aimlessly for food. He said the sight and the stench were unbearable and he hoped he would never live to see anything so miserable again.

Alex listened, hollow-eyed and gaunt, lethargic almost, unable to take it all in. Jesse believed she was worried about the ranch, about being sent home, about the two of them being separated, but he, too, was numb and unable to give her much comfort.

She rode out to see Annie but their meeting was strained. Annie and the children were fine but Alex couldn't show any feeling. She felt languid, lacking any life, empty—and try as she might to talk to Annie about what was wrong, she couldn't tell her dear friend about her discovery.

Things were slowly getting back to a semblance of normalcy. One evening, after all the men had moved back to their quarters, Tom came in to the main house with Jesse. Wilson opened the door but kept the two men in the hallway while he attempted to let Oliver know they were there. Alex and Oliver's raised voices came from the study.

"You BASTARD," Alex shouted, "you bloody bastard. You denied your own daughter, time and time again. You denied me, you bastard. How could you, you, you...how could you?"

"Alex, please, believe me, I wanted nothing more than to tell you..."

"How many times did I ask you? How many, FATHER? How many times did I come in here and ask you straight out, and still you denied it. And not only that, you denied me the right to hear my mother's voice, to read her letters. Do you know what it is like to grow up without a mother? Do you know what it is like for a young girl not to have that woman who unquestioningly wants her in her life, to have someone to talk with, to love her, to hold her, to cuddle her, to kiss her goodnight? Do you know what it is like to grow up with a father—a supposed father—who hates you, hates your very being, hates the very sight of you, who wants nothing to do with you? And now I know why! I wasn't even his. I was yours. What agreement, what deal had you reached, FATHER, that you couldn't let me know, couldn't recognize me as your daughter? Did he offer you money, you son of a bitch? You bloody bastard. Greed. That's all it is, bloody greed. It's run your life from start to finish—or at least I hope you bloody well finish it off because, believe me, I have a good mind to finish it off for you, you bastard. Really I do!"

"Alex please," Oliver pleaded, "listen to me!"

"Listen to you? Listen to your excuses for not telling me the truth? My goodness, but we are— what? Tell me, I want to hear these excuses, these reasons you never told me you are my father. Please. Go on!"

Jesse paced in the hallway. What they were overhearing was upsetting him to the point that his flesh crawled. His anger spread like a disease until he clenched his fists and stood facing the study door. He inhaled deeply, ready to intervene.

"I think we ought to go," Tom said.

Alex stormed out of the study, stopped, surprised to find them there, started to say something but didn't, and ran up the stairs.

She laid in her room for days, barely touching her food, the letters, which she read and re-read and read again, lay scattered about her bed. She couldn't understand how her mother could love this coward, this feeble, self-centered, covetous man. Then she realized she didn't know her mother, not from the letters, certainly, which just went on asking Oliver to come back, then apologizing to him for her own weakness in marrying Frederic, and finally telling him their last reunion had resulted in her being "with child." What a quaint expression, Alex thought, how refined and decorous for someone who had broken her marriage vows. No, she would never know her mother, never understand a woman who had loved one man yet wedded another just for the security and position he offered, someone who had ostensibly accepted without question all the rules and regulations society laid down yet managed a clandestine affair outside of her marriage. To Alex it was incomprehensible for someone to be so hypocritical, so duplicitous as this.

****

Jesse came in one evening, was permitted to go upstairs to see her and found Alex lying there, fully dressed, a plate of food uneaten on the floor, her red-rimmed eyes staring at the ceiling. He sat on the edge of the bed and took her hand.

She looked at him blindly. "What's happening with the ranch?" she asked after a time.

Jesse was reluctant to tell her. "Well, it's pretty bad. Tom says it'd be nothing short of a miracle if we can keep going."

Alex sat up a bit. "I don't even know who I am anymore. Do you know that? Who am I, Jesse? Where do I belong? If the ranch goes under—"

"If the ranch goes under we'll get that dream house of ours and start our own."

"Living in sin for the next three years?"

"Well, it's almost two now," he said with a small smile. He caressed her hand for a bit. "I know who you are, Alex. And so do Tom and Annie and Cal, and the rest of the punchers. You're that durned wonderful gal who paints and rides and cracks jokes with the best of us, who makes us all think every day is worth living jus' because you're here. Don't you go takin' that away from us when we need you the most, don't you do that."

Oliver came in to see her the following afternoon. He quietly took a chair opposite her, nodding for Rose to leave them alone. Lying on her bed, Alex continued to stare up at the ceiling.

"Listen to me." He spoke very calmly and steadily. "It's important you listen. I've been into town to see Higgins, the lawyer. Frederic will soon put me out for mismanaging the ranch, but I've settled my shares in the Faringdon on you, signed them over some time ago so they can't be sold by my creditors when they come calling, as no doubt they will. It won't be enough to out-vote your father— Frederic. He still has the controlling percentage. But perhaps you can reason with him, put some pressure on him to let the ranch continue."

"Is it worth continuing?"

"That's up to you. You do what you want now."

"What will you do, where will you go?"

"Oh, back to England, I suppose. I've received a letter from David. It's taken a while to get here of course but it says Frederic's health is failing. He may be more, well—"

"Well disposed toward me? Toward you? Please!"

Oliver got up then sat back down heavily. "I never meant to hurt you, Alexandra. Believe me, I wanted to tell you everything. Your mother meant the world to me. When I heard she had married Frederic, I was devastated. She said, as you no doubt read, she believed I wasn't returning, that I would never make anything of myself—"

"So you spent your whole life trying to prove her wrong, is that it? It wasn't greed, just wanting to be as good as Frederic? Really, Oliver—did you think you could compete with a duke whose money and holdings are beyond encroachment? The ranch's losses will be nothing to Frederic, but he will close the company to spite me. Or you." She kept her voice monotone, quiet. She no longer had the strength to fight.

"Well, when I eventually got back and saw your mother, some six years later, she believed she had made an awful mistake. We planned on running away together, coming back here to America and living as a couple. Of course, I realize now it would never have worked, she would never have left David, first of all. And with so many people in the vicinity with connections at home, well... But that was the plan. I came ahead to start the ranch—"

"Mostly with Frederic's money!"

"Yes. Well, be that as it may, that is what we were going to do. Frederic and I had already founded the company. The shares had been sold. The money was there. Then Elizabeth found she was carrying a child...you. By the time the letter found me and I headed back, it was too late. She was gone and you were there, a small helpless bundle."

"Please, spare me the dramatics."

"Surely you can see it was for the best. I couldn't have taken you with me, not a baby. Frederic knew, of course. He suspected you weren't his but we made a deal and I was conveniently sent back here as manager. For your mother's sake that her name not be sullied with this…this indiscretion—"

"More likely Frederic decided he didn't want to be known as a cuckold."

"Frederic said he would raise you as his own if I kept my mouth shut, but the deal was I could have you with me when you were old enough—"

"Hence the four years from eight to twelve."

"Exactly. He said you must come back to mix in society, be presented at court, make your debut and get married. That was it. I would have no other say in your upbringing except I would have you for four years."

"You knew then, when I came, how long I would be here."

"I knew, but I didn't know if he would be good to his word. With Frederic, as you well know, nothing is ever written in stone if he cares to change it. I got letters through the earlier years, written mostly by his steward, telling me how you were. You didn't find those, I'm not even sure where they are now. I knew, according to them, you were, shall I say, 'a handful'? I knew you were headstrong and ungovernable, that you had gone through a line of governesses, driven David's tutors to distraction. Maybe what you call my 'greed,' my self-centeredness, has come out in you in this manner?"

Alex took a deep breath. "What now?"

"Well." Oliver rose to his feet. "Now, while I'm still manager, I'm just going to take a ride and see the devastation, see if I can do anything at last."

For a time Alex continued to lie there. She picked up a letter and started to read, then put it down and thought maybe it was time to bathe, to change her clothes and start again. She pulled the bell rope to call Rose, but as soon as Rose came in the door, she knew. Like a bolt, it struck her, Alex absolutely knew. She pulled on her boots, pushed past a startled Rose and started down the stairs. Breathless, she ran out the door, down the path to the stables, running faster, running...running.

"Don't!" she screamed. "Oliver, don't!"

And then she heard the shot.

Chapter Eighteen

Tom had asked Alex to move into the Homestead with his family for a while, at least until after the funeral, but Alex declined. From somewhere, somehow, she found some inner strength to deal with everything, knowing Jesse and Tom and Annie and everyone else at the ranch were there to help her. Jesse worried she was wasting away, not eating, and hardly sleeping. But he worried, too, that she would leave and not come back.

She gave instructions for nearby ground under trees overlooking the Thompson to be consecrated so Oliver could be buried there. She said if the shareholders decided to pull out and sell the ranch, the new buyer would have to take Oliver with it. So on a windy, cold afternoon in late March, Rose helped her into a black dress, coiled her hair back, and pinned a hat and veil upon her head. Jesse and Tom and Annie all called for her in their Sunday best, Annie insisting Alex put a coat on. As they got to the vestibule, Alex stopped and picked up a small reticule, then Jesse opened the door.

Outside were twenty-five or so men of the Faringdon. The plumes on the horses in front of the hearse wavered in the blustery weather but there was silence except for the suspiration of the wind and a door slamming somewhere in the outbuildings. Jesse led her down the path, holding her tight, his arm about her shoulders. They stopped at the carriage and he made to help her in but she shook her head.

"I'll walk behind the hearse," she said quietly. And so, they walked in silence to the grave site, the wind at times lifting Alex's veil as if it wanted to dry her tears.

Outsiders, friends and townspeople, other ranchers were all there. The minister from the English Church talked about how Oliver had been a man of vision, a leader who had put his mark on an untamed country and made it his own. Flanked by Tom and Jesse, Alex hardly moved throughout the service, hardly heard what was said, just stared ahead and listened to the wind. Tom whispered to Alex that he would help her lift the first shovel of earth for the grave, but she just shook her head and said, "You do it." When Jesse went to take the shovel next, she moved forward to the edge of the grave and stood there for a moment, then opened the bag she had and took handful after handful of torn papers from it and let them fall into the grave or fly out on the wind, as they might.

Many of the mourners, including the punchers, came back to the house for refreshments and Alex moved among them, accepting condolences, playing the hostess, trying to act normal. She had removed her hat and veil and Jesse could see how worn and tired she looked, how red her eyes were, how thin and pale she had become. He was standing with Cal when she finally made her way over to him.

"Higgins says he wants to see us when they all start leaving. I think he wants to read the will."

"Well, do you want me there?" he asked.

"He mentioned you himself, and Annie and Tom and the servants." She looped her arm through his and smiled at Cal. "No punchers, I'm afraid."

"Well, we'll just count ourselves lucky to have jobs at this point, Ladilex."

Alex nodded and wandered off again.

They assembled in the study, Alex leaning in to

175

Jesse as if she would fall asleep.

"You may want to set yourself down, Lady Alex. It's been a long day," the lawyer said kindly. Alex shrugged and sat in the chair in front of the desk with Jesse standing behind her. Higgins made himself comfortable at the desk and cleared his throat. "I have to tell you before I begin, this will is dated only ten days ago. That may serve to answer some questions you have arising from the bequests in this will. I must also tell you that, as far as I can now ascertain, the bequests are virtually...well, they are worthless. Oliver Calthorpe died owing more money than can be raised from his goods and chattels. Only the Homestead was actually in his sole name as per his filing with the government. This house, of course, belongs to the Frederic Faringdon Cattle Company and was therefore not his, although the furnishings and décor were his responsibility. It would appear he borrowed large amounts of money from the ranch accounts to that end, which he never re-paid. The shareholders will naturally want to claim back these funds from his estate and will no doubt employ a lawyer to do so, most probably putting a lien on the Homestead."

Higgins started by reading the small bequests to "my loyal staff who have served me faithfully over these many years." This included, of course, Rackham, Wilson, Rose and several others. To Tom Yost, "the most honest man I have ever met and who I, without reservation, trust to serve *in loco parentis* for my daughter, Alexandra, until she comes of age, I leave, free and uninhindered, that property known as the Homestead."

Tom and Annie both gasped. "Good Lord," Tom started.

"I'm afraid, Mr. Yost, it is as I said at the beginning. Oliver Calthorpe died owing more than he had—"

"What does that mean?" interjected Alex. "Surely you can't sell the house out from under them?" Oliver would have known. Of course he would have known. It was his last flamboyant gesture, sending messages of affection and respect without any substance behind them.

"I'm afraid that may be—"

"No! No, never," said Alex, getting up.

"Alex...if it's law." Tom's voice had a note of resignation in it.

"No, no." Alex moved to the door. "I'll see you in your office tomorrow, Mr. Higgins." She made to leave.

"Lady Alexandra? I'm not finished. There's more." He waited for Alex to turn and re-seat herself. Her mind was already working, forming plans, figuring what might be done to keep the ranch going.

"To Jesse Makepeace," Higgins continued, "who has sworn to look after Alexandra and care for her always, I leave the sum of One Thousand Dollars." Now it was Jesse's turn to gasp. "As I said." Higgins looked up briefly. "These bequests are worthless."

"Finally, to my beloved daughter, Alexandra, I leave the bulk of my estate and that letter written to her which here attaches as codicil to this will. Signed this day etc. etc. etc." Higgins put the paper down, looked over at Alexandra and handed her an envelope. She stared blankly at it, then folded it and held it between her hands. "As you know, Lady Alexandra, Oliver's shares in this ranch were signed over to you some time before his death. Those cannot now be touched by his creditors, and you will find he set up a separate account for you in which the dividends have accumulated. Everything else here that belonged to him I'm afraid may have to be sold, although I hasten to say the full amount owed is not yet known." The group watched as Higgins picked up his briefcase and stuffed the papers back into it.

Tom said, "How long have we got? At the Homestead, I mean. I have a family."

"Oh, it will be months yet. Probate has to be filed, amounts worked out. A year maybe, if you're lucky."

"If Tom is now...what was it you said?" asked Jesse.

"*In loco parentis*?"

"Yes, that. Does that mean he can now give permission for me and Alex to marry?"

"I'm afraid not. It means he is only a local guardian. Her father would be able to sue him if such a marriage took place against Faringdon's will. In actual fact, it was not Calthorpe's place to appoint Mr. Yost. And I don't think you would want a man as wealthy and powerful as the Duke of Faringdon suing your friend." He started toward the door.

"But Faringdon isn't Alex's father," Jesse persisted.

"I'm afraid, in the eyes of the law, he still is."

"Tomorrow in your office, Mr. Higgins please," Alex called after him.

Four days later a telegram arrived from David telling Alex their father was critically ill and begging her to return forthwith. She knew she would have to go back, if only to be there for David, and so instructed Rose to pack certain items and get them both ready for the journey to England. She told only Tom.

Life at the ranch was returning to a routine although at times, when the wind direction dictated it, the stench from the dead cattle blew in. There was not a lot the punchers could do but leave the carcasses as carrion and get on with saving the living.

Tom, now manager, and Jesse, as foreman, worked out a plan of what might be sold to bring the ranch down to a manageable size, where fences could be put up, how much extra forage could be bought in, how many extra acres they could give over to growing winter feed and where storage could be built for all. Tom also envisioned diversifying the ranch and slowly changing over from Longhorns to Herefords. He wrote to the Duke's steward to outline his plans and awaited a reply.

Alex rode out to find Jesse on the Thursday afternoon, Ranger being about as unmanageable as he could be after staying inside virtually all through the storms. Jesse watched as she came in at a gallop toward him.

"He really wants to go, doesn't he?"

"I should have put the damn hackamore back on him or more steel in his mouth, damn horse."

Jesse shook his head at her, then leaned across to kiss her gently. "Awful lot of damns for one young gal."

Alex looked away to watch the other men for a moment; they were putting in fence posts. "The end of open range," she said softly. "I don't know if I can bear it." She looked back at him. "I'm leaving my bedroom door to the garden open. Will you use it?"

"I'm an early riser, lady. You gonna keep me awake all night?"

"If I can, if I can."

****

Their lovemaking was different, slower, gentler, as if they were each trying to memorize the other's body, draw maps of every muscle and sinew and joint. To Jesse, Alex's body was still like satin, smooth and flowing and curved, but he felt he was somehow not reaching her, her heart or mind were somewhere else, she was holding something back. As he entered the damp center of her awakening and she pulled her legs up to take him further into being, he sensed a part of her was not with him, she was withholding herself from him, keeping something back. Their bodies moved together to find release, but it was purely physical—without emotion. There was still tension in the air, like electricity after thunder. Jesse propped himself on his elbows and looked down at Alex, taking a tendril of her hair and wrapping it around his fingers for a moment. "You're leaving, aren't you?" he said at last.

"For a while. I have to. There was something in the letter from Oliver I have to tend to, and of course David has begged me to return to see Frederic before he dies—if he dies, or if he is still alive. Whichever."

"When?"

"I-I don't know. Soon."

"You don't know or you won't say?" He rolled over and looked at the bedroom, suddenly aware it was too neat and uncluttered. "When, Alex?" He turned back to her. "Tell me, dammit!"

"Soon." She kissed him, brushing his lips and then pulling his head down to hers. "Soon."

In the chill of morning, when the punchers had ridden out, Tom called for them with the buggy. Wilson, trying to be stalwart, and holding back tears, loaded the rig and stood aside. Alex held a box she had tied with a pink ribbon and handed it to Tom. "For Sue Ann," she said.

"Is that the dress?" Tom asked. Alex nodded. "But you'll be back to wear it for your twenty-first."

"I'll come back with other dresses, new dresses, and we'll have a huge party again." She smiled and her eyes scanned Tom as if she were trying to memorize his face. "And you'll give this to Jesse," she said handing him an envelope.

"I will. Of course I will. But he'll be mad as all get-out. So will Annie and the rest of them."

"I can't say good-bye. Anyway, it isn't good-bye. I'll be back."

"I know that. I want to do that *in loco parentis*

business. Can I get you to eat beef once and for all?"

Alex laughed a bit. "Well, mebbe."

Tom helped the two women into the buggy and the three rode in silence to the station through the morning light. Mist had settled on the river and the wet grass sparkled like a green carpet with jewels thrown across it. Alex looked up to see a hawk gliding on an air current and looking for prey. She thought perhaps one day she would start painting animals and birds rather than people, landscapes before they disappeared forever.

On the platform she turned to Tom and said, "I'll be in New York a few days, of course, to settle matters there. Don't forget what I said."

"Alex, I—well, Annie and I, we can't thank you enough..."

"Don't say anything more, Tom. I don't want to hear anymore. I don't know what I would have done all these years without the two of you."

"Yes, but this is different."

"Oh, no, oh no, it's not." She gave him a quick kiss on the cheek, then followed Rose onto the train.

****

3 April 1887

My darling Jesse,

Please forgive me. Goodbyes are just too torturous, and the thought of not seeing you for so many months is far more than I can bear. It is not so much I need to see Frederic before he passes, but I need to know my story, if there is anything more to know. Oliver said there are possessions of my mother's at Bayfordbury and he believes Frederic prevented me from getting an inheritance, which was rightfully mine. David, of course, was only seven at the time of her death so would probably not know much, but he may help unravel the mystery at least.

Jesse, I can't tell you what this is doing to me, to be separated from you like this, but at least I know when I get back we shall never be separated again—I promise. Please write as often as you can, as shall I. If you find someone else, if you decide you don't love me, just write to say so. I wouldn't be able to bear not knowing, not hearing from you. These last months until the winter were the happiest of my life. You have given me so much. I only hope I can someday give back something in return.

I will wear the bracelet always. I will love you forever. I am,

Your Alex

Part Two: 1889

Nineteen

Sky.
Space.
From the train window Alex could see the bare breadth of earth and air that always affected a sense of wonder in her. That so much land could be so vacant was a fascination, that it could be so unending, that the sky could wrap itself around the earth like the curtain in a theatre giving the expectation of action absorbed Alex completely, yet within sight nothing but the grass and the clouds moved. Like dancers caught in a ritual, the grass swayed in the constant wind and the clouds scudded, sailing on above more prairies, more land, more open space. And the colors—so different from the deep greens and rich blue of England. Here the colors were so neutral as if the Maker Himself feared to offend by drawing from a palette too vibrant. Here were tones that pulled the earth into a pale chiaroscuro against the mottled blue sky. The Plains seemed endless, as if no habitation would ever appear on this blank canvas.

Yet she knew it would. She knew what lay ahead. Craning her neck to see further, she couldn't tell whether those were mountains or clouds in the distance, couldn't tell where the next town lay, but she knew they would appear. She would be home soon. And while life wasn't going to be easy—nothing worth having ever was.

****

Alex saw him as the train pulled in. Standing with his thumbs in his belt, his hat tilted back, he watched as the cars ran past him. He looked the same to her in that fleeting glimpse, older maybe, very slightly thinner maybe, but the same. She gathered her things, took the porter's proffered hand to step down off the train and turned to face Jesse Makepeace at the far end of the platform.

It was obvious from his stunned expression he hadn't expected her, that in fact she was the last person he had expected to see step off the train on that breezy May morning. As she walked toward him, his expression changed slightly and he moved his arms as if he might embrace her. Then, without thinking almost, her hand rose and she used her full strength to slap him across the face.

Both of Jesse's hands went to his cheek in stunned disbelief. His face reddened as anger rose. "What in the hell...what was that for?" He stared at her as if he still couldn't comprehend it was Alex.

"That was for deserting me," she said hoarsely, barely above a whisper, "that was for stopping writing, for leaving me when I needed you most. That was for not having the guts to tell me you didn't love me anymore." She breathed heavily for a few seconds. "Now take me home." She walked past him and turned back to look at him, challenging.

He stood there for a moment uncertainly. "I don't know what you're talking about. You're the one who stopped writing. I wrote three dang letters you never answered, three of them, Alex, the last one only a couple of months ago. I got two letters from you asking me to write but I was writing all the time." He stopped and looked at her to try to ascertain if she was taking this in. "Where's the new owner?" he asked suddenly remembering why he had come.

"I'm the new owner," she replied. "Now take me

home."

Jesse stood with his hands on his hips, his eyes narrowed in disbelief. "You're the new owner," he echoed. "You're the new owner? You bought up the major shares an' all? Tom sure as hell was keepin' that one a secret!" His anger rose as he tried to make sense of it all.

"Tom sent you?"

"Who the hell you think sent me? I sure as heck didn't just come here on my own. You didn't let *me* know you were comin'!"

"No, I don't suppose...." She stopped and went to get her bags and bring the conversation to an end.

"Oh, for goodness sake, Alex—or should I call you Lady Alex now, seein' as how—"

"You can call me whatever you goddamn please, I really don't care. Just take me back to the ranch, or send someone else, whichever you're more comfortable with."

"You gonna sit here for four hours while I sort that?"

"If I must!"

"Get in." He held out his hand.

Alex pulled herself up into the buggy on her own and sat staring straight ahead while Jesse picked up the rest of her bags and got in beside her.

"You're the new owner, huh?" She nodded. "Well, I quit!"

****

They rode in silence for the two hours, the only movement from Alex being when she removed her hat and shoes, and then pulled the shoes back on as they approached the house. They were both greatly relieved to see Tom there waiting, although from Jesse's reaction Tom wouldn't have known it.

Jesse got down and grabbed some bags to storm into the house with Wilson trailing behind with more. He didn't say a word to Tom, who embraced

Alex and held her at arm's length to look at her.

"Well, ain't you a sight?" Tom gave her a gentle squeeze before letting go.

"What's left of me." Alex looped her arm through Tom's and they walked a bit down the path to the front. Alex stopped to greet Rackham and Rose, who had returned to the ranch some months earlier.

Wilson came back out with Jesse, who walked by and went off to take the rig away. "It's so good to see you, M'Lady," Wilson said. "So very good."

Alex smiled, then turned back to Tom. "I understand you haven't told anyone."

"No, thought it would be our little surprise."

"Right." Alex mused on this for a moment. "I'll come down while they're all in for dinner then. And I'll see Annie tomorrow."

****

Jesse banged open the door to the ranch office and marched right in. He planted himself in front of Tom's desk as the other looked up, but there was a moment before he spoke.

"That was some dang trick you pulled on me, Tom. You mighta told me it was Alex. Leastways I'da been prepared."

Tom pushed some papers aside. "I thought the two of you would see each other and just sort of—"

"Sorta fall into each other's arms? Just sorta pick up right where we left off, as if no time at all had passed, as if she hadn'ta stopped writin'—is that what you were thinkin'? You know what that woman did to me, Tom? She laid off and hit me, right across the face. Woman hates my guts. Says I didn't write her for the last year."

"Oh, now, Jesse, she didn't mean anything by it. You know Alex—act first, think later."

"Yeah, well I'm thinkin' now and what I'm thinkin' is, I'm givin' you notice. I quit. I can't stay on with her. It just ain't goin' to work."

"Hang on now, Jesse." The older man looked up. "You can't do that," he said.

"Well, you tell me why not. Just give me one damn good reason for me to stay. You know what it's gonna be like tryin' to work with her, to see her every day?"

"I guess it isn't going to be easy for either of you right now. But you can't just up and quit, Jess. She needs you, and she needs you now more 'an ever."

"Needs me? Needs me?" Jesse snorted. "That woman ain't never needed no one. That woman is more self-sufficient than any dang puncher I ever knowed, even if she can't boil water to save her soul."

Tom was ever one to find a way out of a sticky situation and negotiate a resolution quickly. Jesse paced the length of the office a few times waiting to see what Tom would come up with.

Tom said quietly, "You can't go, Jess. I need you as foreman. Alex isn't going to manage. I could give you a dozen good reasons to stay but—"

"Well, give me one then, just give me one reason I shouldn't walk off this ranch right here, right now, this minute."

"Because it's Alex as been keeping this ranch afloat, Jess. It's Alex who's been payin' our wages, puttin' food on our tables. And it was Alex who paid off Calthorpe's debts so the ranch wouldn't go bust. The shareholders could have been held accountable for his spending on the ranch, and if they refused to pay—which they surely would have—the operation would've been shut down. You know he took money from the ranch accounts, you know what Higgins said."

Jesse stared at him, feeling like a trapped animal. Alex had never told him this. The Yosts had never spoken of what Alex was doing.

"After the funeral, Alex went into town and

settled matters with both the bank and the attorney. Annie and I woulda been out on the road there without a home if it hadn'ta been for Alex. Calthorpe had so much debt, everything he owned was to be sold off—you know that. Alex took all that money from her paintings and transferred it to me to pay off Calthorpe's accounts and told Higgins to sell off whatever he could to clear the debts and keep the house. She also sold her jewelry—the diamonds Calthorpe gave her for her birthday—while in New York, and wired the money back. Then she went ahead and sold some property or other Calthorpe had in London she'd inherited and wired that money back. Every last dime she had, every cent she could lay her hands on, she put into this ranch. That's why you can't leave."

For a while the only sound was the squeak of the door in the wind. "Dang door," said Tom, "keep meaning to get some oil and fix that." He got up and slammed it shut. Jesse had still not spoken. "She's had a real bad time, Jess." He seated himself again behind the desk. "You can't just leave her now." He waited but still Jesse had not spoken. "Her brother signed over all the shares to her—said it was the inheritance she should of gotten from her mama. That's how come she's got them 'cause she sure as heck don't have the money to buy them." He let this sink in for a bit. "Anyway, truth be told, I don't even think she'd take your resignation. I tell you what, if you really feel this way, if you really want out, you go see Alex. If she takes your resignation, then fine, I'll accept it. Well, where in hell you gonna go anyway?"

"I've had offers," Jesse said at last. "You know that. Up in Wyoming and Montana."

"Is that what you want?"

"Change might do me good." Jesse looked out the window. His friends, men he had worked with for years, were riding in or saddling up, changing shifts. His heart wasn't in leaving, that was for sure.

Tom took a deep breath. "Well, you go see Alex. If she accepts your notice, fine, go if that's what you want. But I'm sitting here telling you this thing is gonna work itself out between the two of you. I don't know what happened, who wrote what or when or what the hell went on, but I can tell you sure as hell that woman needs you. She's just had a real bad time of it, Jesse. Let her settle."

"Oh, when the heck hasn't Alex had a real bad time? Bad times just follow her aroun'."

Tom rubbed his forehead. "Well, that may be true but I can't rightly say any of 'em has been her fault—not her birth, not her parents, not her marriage, and not anything that followed. Been a complete mystery to me how Faringdon could blame her for killin' her mama that way—beyond my understanding. And, as for Calthorpe, denying her…"

Jesse yanked the door open and slammed it as he left. In his heart he knew he could never leave Alex. The guilt he had always felt for laying with her was too much. He didn't regret it, not for one moment, but he couldn't put it behind him either. He had wanted her then, and he wanted her now. For just over two years, he had waited for her, waited for her letters, waited for news of her, waited for her return. He had felt the loss of her so keenly, felt the ache of her departure with such force, he had hardly known himself.

And now she was back.

****

Alex heard the hum of the men's voices in the chuck house as she came over, still dressed in her traveling clothes. There was Joe's smoky voice saying something about Ranger acting up and kicking his stall, and Reb's southern drawl telling

189

some story or other. Then there was Tom calling for them to hush up and behave because the new major shareholder was on the way, and it was then she swung open the door.

Tom stood at the front with Jesse, who leaned back against the wall in that way he had. Cal sat over on a windowsill, the light behind him, having been talking with some new men up at the front. The room went dead silent, then the old hands started hollering and clamoring, and banging the tin plates. Alex could hardly make her way to the front for hands reaching to shake hers, have a few words with her, but at last she stood beside Tom, who waved his hands to quiet them all.

Cal started to say something but one of the new men in the front said, "Heck, we gonna be bossed by a mere slip of a gal?" Before anyone else knew what was happening, there was screeching of chairs and benches and five other men surrounded the puncher.

Alex looked on steadily but it was Tom who said, "Settle down now, settle down."

Jesse still hadn't moved.

"I guess I still have some friends in Colorado," Alex said barely audibly, but staring the man down. "Of course if anyone isn't happy working for me, you can see Tom or Jesse, and take your wages and go." She waited.

"Ah heck, Ladilex," came a familiar voice. "I'll work twice as hard for you as I would for anyone else."

Alex smiled over at Cal. "I don't plan on any changes here. Tom is still manager and...Jesse is still foreman. So I'll hope to see you all much as usual." She nodded and started to go, the emotion suddenly becoming too much. Then she thought of something and smiled a bit. "Of course I do expect you to put cowbells on all the herd and wear pink ribbons on your hats," she jested as she closed the door.

Standing there a moment she heard Tom say, "Don't you even think about it, Cal Jenks. Don't you dare!"

Then there was laughter.

****

Standing in her study the next morning at the house, there was a knot in her stomach when she heard Wilson tell Jesse he would announce him—and Jesse's spurs ringing down the hallway as he shoved Wilson aside.

"It's all right, Wilson." She barely looked over as the door opened. "Mr. Makepeace can come in."

They faced each other across the room, Jesse noting how frail Alex looked, how her Levis and shirt hung on her, how gaunt her face had become. He hesitated for a moment but there was no point in delaying. Alex sat in the big chair that had been her father's, and leaned back, her hands clasped in front of her.

"I'm quittin', Alex. I can't work here." He waited for a response but Alex was biding her time, thinking things through. "I can't stay on and work and…and see you every day. I ain't made like that."

"But you can leave me in the lurch, leave Tom in the lurch, you're made like that, are you?"

"Tom'll manage. You'll manage. You always do."

She stared at him with tired eyes devoid of life, and he wondered if owning the ranch was what she really wanted.

"You're supposed to give a month's notice, Jess." She suddenly sat up. "It's in your contract." Realizing Jesse might leave permanently, might never return to the ranch, a vice gripped her heart. She had wondered time and again what their reunion would be like, considered over and over whether she wanted to see him. Now, faced with losing him once and for all, she was stunned.

191

He planted himself in front of her and shook his head. "What damn contract? I never signed no contract, and you know that. Any foreman on any ranch'll walk off at a moment's notice. What contract are you talking about?"

Alex thought quickly. "Well, if you didn't sign a contract you certainly should have. Maybe in the wake of...of everything Tom just never got around to it."

"Oh, don't give me that!"

"All right. A gentleman's agreement then," she hedged.

Jesse paced a bit. "I can't stay, Alex. I wrote you those damn letters. I wrote letter after letter and I didn't get replies to the last three. I have no idea what's been goin' on..."

"Will it help if I apologize for slapping you?" she asked quietly.

He stopped and looked down at her. "It's not the point. I can't wake up in the mornings and—"

Alex rushed on, "I need you here. I can't manage, and Tom can't manage the ranch without you. You've been foreman now for over two years. No one can replace you. You have to give a month's notice. If you're still not happy and want to go at the end of the month, I'll accept your resignation. Surely we can have a working relationship?" She tried to keep her tone quiet and reserved, business-like, her hands folded on the desk. But inside she felt like screaming. Her tension mounted.

"A working relationship?" Jesse spat. He shook his head, unbelieving. "My, but you are one hard woman," he said, staring down at her. "You got one month and then I'm outta here, lady, you hear? One month!"

He slammed the door as he left.

Chapter Twenty

"He practically kicked down the stall door yesterday," said Joe, stroking Ranger's muzzle. "He sure is glad to have y'all back, Lady Lex. As are we all."

"Thank you, Joe." She led Ranger out, then stopped. "I thought he was in Jesse's string now."

"He was. Jesse took real good care of 'im for you. But he left him here t'day. Said you'd want to ride him now you were back."

She rode out to see Annie who gave her a big hug and had a little weep and held her out, as Tom had, to look at her. There were no tears from Alex, though, just a little half smile as she put her arm around Annie and went with her inside.

"So, no major changes to the house this time, I see. How are the children?" Alex realized the tone of her voice must sound stilted but she couldn't help it. Her reunion with everyone was proving more emotionally draining than she had foreseen.

"They're fine. Growin'. Sue Ann's quite the young lady. She keeps saying she's going to wear that dress you left her."

"Oh. Yes." Alex just stood there in the kitchen as if she were a formal guest waiting to be asked to be seated. "And J.J.?"

"Still readin' books. Tom says he thinks he's going to be a lawyer the way he reads everything." Annie waited for some response but Alex didn't move. "You goin' to have some lunch with me?" she asked.

"I don't think so, Annie, I really have to get on

and see—"

"David said you need to—"

"I know what David said, Annie!" Alex snapped. There was a moment before she said, "Sorry. I didn't mean...I know you mean well. I'm just tired of people telling me what I have to do, what I can do."

Annie stood there patiently.

"I have to go," Alex said suddenly and she turned for the door.

"Just a moment, young lady." Annie's voice came back at her. "Don't you do that, don't you do that to me. This is me you're talking to here and I'm not having this. I'm not being shut out like I don't matter, like nothing matters. You sit yourself down and talk to me."

Alex stayed where she was, her back to Annie.

"I know all about what you done, both good and bad, I know all about you saving us, saving the ranch, and I know about the bad things too. Don't you go marching off like that and think you can just leave me with no words spoke. You sit down, Alexandra Calthorpe. This minute."

"I'm not a child anymore," came Alex's hoarse reply. "I'm not eight years old, and I can't be reprimanded or bribed with chocolate cake anymore, Annie."

"No one's bribing anyone here, nor reprimanding you neither. I'm asking you to talk to me. I thought we were friends."

"We are friends. We'll always be friends I hope."

"Well, you sure as heck aren't acting like it!" Annie stood there waiting.

Alex moved toward the door then stopped, looking out at the grassland, at some horses grazing off in the distance. She shook as tears forced their way out, a dam bursting. Annie laid a gentle hand on her shoulder.

"I have to go." said Alex, shrugging her off. She

grabbed the door handle.

Annie moved quickly and slammed it shut. "You talk to me, Alex."

Tears blossomed then trailed down Alex's face. "What do you want to talk about, Annie? You want to talk about what it feels like when the man you love, the person you love most in this whole world, just stops writing for no reason when you need him most? Or maybe you just want to talk about what it feels like to lose a child? To feel like you've lost everything you ever wanted all at once, to have the bottom fall out of your life?"

"You tell Jesse yet?"

"No, of course not. Tell Jesse? What does Jesse care? He stopped writing."

"No, he did not, Alex. He was in here saying he was getting letters from you begging him to write and he was writing all the time. I told you that!"

Alex moved to a chair and finally sat down. "I didn't get them. I don't know how three letters or however many could go missing. No one stole them. No one intercepted them. My father was dead— Frederic that is—he was dead by then and David certainly wouldn't have given orders for letters to be intercepted. Maybe Jesse dreamt he'd written."

"Jesse wasn't dreaming and Jesse wasn't lying, Alex. You know him as well as I do. If Jesse says he wrote those letters..."

Alex put her head in her hands. "What difference does it make now, Annie? What possible difference? It's over. You see me. You know what I went through, what I did. Jesse would never understand that, Jesse—"

"Jesse has a right to know, Alex. Leastways 'bout the child. Jesse loves you!"

"Loves me? He doesn't love me now. It's been more than two years. It's too late, it's too damn late for anything now except going on and making a life

195

that doesn't involve pain."

"You don't want a life that doesn't involve pain. Such a life doesn't exist. What you want is a life that doesn't involve love, Alex. You're afraid of being hurt, that's your problem. Well, if love doesn't hurt, I can tell you it'll be something else, it'll be not loving, not being with Jesse, seeing Jesse with someone else. You think on that for a while." She waited for a reply but got none. "And Jesse has a right to know," she repeated. "You're going to have to tell him sometime." She went over and held Alex's face against her chest, her arms around her, soothing her. "According to David's last letter, Tom's still *in loco parentis* until you're twenty-one. Goodness, loco sure is the proper word!"

****

For the better part of two years Alex had attempted to eradicate her feelings for Jesse any way she knew how. Even when his letters were arriving, the pain she felt at reading them was so intense she could not deal with it in any manner except to try to put him aside, even knowing, as she did then, she was carrying his child. She wrote back lovingly at first but, as time wore on, more sparingly and with less emotion. Then, when his letters had stopped, she felt she had pushed him out of her life, realized her mistake and wrote begging him to write again. Letters never came back.

She knew before returning to Colorado she would see him, he was still there, and Tom had claimed Jesse still loved her. But for Alex it was too late. The last year had taken its toll and now all she wanted was her independence and freedom from all emotional ties. And yet...when she saw Jesse she knew she hadn't eradicated those emotions as well as she had hoped.

The house was almost as empty as she was. There seemed no rhyme or reason to what had been sold and what was left. The study was complete. There on her desk was Oliver's set of engraved crystal and silver decanters. She sat staring into the faceted whiskey decanter, noting the way the light from the window filtered through the amber liquid and changed its color from pale yellows to golden browns. Fascinated, she turned the glassware around slowly, then sat back and stared at it a moment before returning to her work. Having agreed with Tom to have a meeting at the house with Jesse to bring her up to date on all the various ranch matters, Alex tried desperately to get her emotions back under control. Wading through a pile of work when Wilson showed them in, she felt incredibly tiny behind the stack of paper, her feet on the desk. She didn't look up, but continued to turn pages as they entered.

"Coffee for the gentlemen, please Wilson," she said as they sat down.

"You goin' to manage all right with the reduced staff?" Tom seated himself in front of the desk.

"Of course," she answered, looking across at him for a moment. "I'm not exactly having house parties here, Tom."

"No, but it's a big house."

"We'll manage." She turned another page as Wilson came in with a tray, set the coffee out for the men and put a glass of milk in front of her.

She stared at it for a moment, putting the papers aside, sitting up, and leaving. Her hand went slowly out for the glass, turned it around toward her as she brought it to her mouth for a quick gulp. "Ugh!" She gagged getting up, turned from them, reached for her hankie and spat it out. She yanked on the bell pull.

"Is this your idea, Tom?"

"David says—"

"I know what David says. I don't have to be told

anymore. I'd rather stuff myself with potatoes every day than drink that."

Wilson came back in.

"What the hell is that, Wilson?"

"Milk, M'lady. Mr.—"

"What kind of milk? Milk that's never seen a cow?"

"Eagle Brand, M'lady."

"Well, take it away. Or put some chocolate in it or something. And go find a milk cow for goodness sake. We've got enough of them out there."

"You going to milk it?" asked Tom.

Alex sank back in the chair. Jesse just sat there, his face blank, unreadable. "There must be someone on this damn ranch who knows how to milk a cow?"

"I'll find out, M'lady."

"You can take that as well." She pointed to the silver tray of decanters. "I don't think I'll be entertaining anyone from the Cheyenne Club any time soon. It's a wonder these weren't sold." Alex settled back in her chair. "What're rail prices like at the moment?" she asked, getting down to business.

They went through the papers: the much reduced size of the ranch now pulled down to the border with the Thompson, fences put up all around, the reduced head of cattle they were running, the increased head of horses, the lower number of men, the change to Herefords from their Longhorns, and the additional acreage given over for winter feed. The railway freight prices were down for the moment as so many ranches had gone bust, but beef prices were slightly up. They were just turning a profit again. Alex looked up from her papers.

"I haven't said thank you," she said quietly. "I owe you both so much, your management and your foresight, it's the only reason the ranch is still going."

Jesse had been monosyllabic throughout and

198

still just sat there, a hand across his mouth, looking at her. She was still wearing the Indian cuff he had bought her but she had moved it to her left wrist.

"It was a joint effort," Tom said, "The three of us. Without your money—"

"Never mind that." She went back to look at the papers. "Who's bought Boyd?" she asked suddenly.

Jesse changed position slightly and Tom looked at her for a moment. "Why? I don't rightly know. Why do you ask?"

"I want to buy it back. I like it over there. The light is good for painting. How can you not know who bought it, Tom?"

"Higgins handled the sale. You'd have to ask him." His voice had a nervous edge to it. "I don't mean to pry, Alex, but have you the money to buy it back?"

"No. But...I don't know. Maybe David would lend it to me." She straightened the papers into a neat pile. "Who bought Cattail?" She referred to one of the other camps.

"Well, Garrison bought it actually. You know, he and Millie got married last year."

"I think I did know that. You wrote." She almost said, "unlike some," but thought better of it. "Garrison still working for us?"

"He is. He's handling the horses and throwing his cattle herd of about four hundred head in with ours. It works for him. He's doing well."

Alex sat back and rocked in her chair for a moment. "Can you find out who bought Boyd?"

"Some businessman from Cheyenne, I'm thinking," Tom said. "Yeah, I reckon that was it. Wanted a hunting cabin."

Alex stared at him. Jesse looked up at the ceiling.

"I'll ask Higgins," she said.

****

"Confidential, Lady Alex," Higgins told her.

"How can it be confidential, Mr. Higgins? It was my property. I have a right to know who bought it. I want to buy it back."

"Buyer has a right to remain confidential. His lawyer acted on his behalf. Anyway, it wasn't your property at the time of sale."

"Who was his lawyer then?"

"Hmm. Well, I'll have to get the papers out and see. Don't rightly recall. Papers are in the vault. Come back, in a couple of weeks, why don't you. I'll try to find it for you by then."

She went to say hello to the Benders and then went on to the saloon. There was no one to stop her now from wearing her denims into town, no one to tell her where she could and could not go, and she didn't care what people thought. Tom took his guardianship seriously, but so far it only seemed to extend to her health and the need, according to her English doctor, to put on weight. She swung the saloon doors open and looked up at the painting above the bar.

"Still there." Barney smiled and extended his hand.

Alex shook it, then noticed a table of her men, Cal and Reb included, along with the new man who seemed to still be working for her. She slapped a couple of bills on the bar. "Bea upstairs?"

Barney nodded. "What's this for?"

"Give my men over there whatever they're drinking." She started up the steps.

"The only person who knocks like that," called the voice from the other side of the door, "is the merest wisp of a girl who—"

Alex swung the door open.

"Good Gawd!" Bea got up from her desk. "You're even smaller than you used to be. What they been feedin' ya over there?" She enveloped Alex in a bear hug. "Lemme look at ya." Alex stood there patiently and turned around as if showing off a dress. "Not much to look at, kid, not much to see. You're disappearin'."

"Well, some might think it was for the best."

"Now what in tarnation is that supposed to mean? You feelin' sorry for yerself? That ain't right. When'd you ever feel sorry for yerself?"

Alex stood there smiling at her friend. She went and hugged her again. "You're so damn wonderful," she said, holding her.

"Yeah, I know—whore with a heart of gold. Give me a break, sweetheart." They sat on the edge of the desk. "You got tits now, I see, thin as you are. Where in hell did you get..." She stopped, suddenly serious. "Oh, I see." She ran her hand gently down Alex's back. "Wanna tell me 'bout it?"

"Nothing to tell." Alex's mouth formed a hard line. "Baby died."

"You tell Jesse?"

"No. And don't you tell him either, Bea."

"Man's got a right to know, Lady A." She rubbed Alex's back a bit. "He ain't been in since he lay right there with you that time. Jesse's—"

"Oh, Jesse, Jesse, Jesse." Alex got up. "Everyone's worried about Jesse. Jesse can take care of himself. I'll take care of myself—"

"And you'll jus' go on regretting everythin' for the rest of your life, is that it?"

Alex looked at her sadly. "I have to go," she said.

"You have to go because you don't want to hear. Yer boys told me you and Jesse split. Let me tell you, that is one of the dumbest damn things—you gonna throw him out because of some letters?"

"It wasn't the letters, Bea. I needed him. I needed to know he was there for me, even if he was on the other side of the world, I needed to know he still cared."

"So you're blaming him for the U.S. postal service or Wells Fargo or maybe the defunct Pony Express, or whoever the hell lost them letters? Hell, lady, you are some dang fool."

Alex took a breath and smiled at her friend. "Good to see you, Bea."

The door closed behind her.

She stopped on the way home, looking back at the mountains, dark against the unending blue of the sky, snowcapped still and standing there as they had for the ages. An eagle was gliding overhead and she watched it as it hung in the air, flew in the current, then swooped down for its prey.

The wind got up again and it looked like rain in the distance and she thought how Jesse actually liked the rain "because it made the flowers grow" and provided for the earth.

Jesse. What now?

Were Annie and Bea right, or was it finished between the two of them? Or should she just go and tell him she'd been wrong? Or had she been wrong? Alex could not decipher her feelings anymore. The only thing she felt right now was hurt, and a burning desire to be left alone once and for all.

The sun came out for a moment but the clouds were scudding, which meant the weather would change soon enough. What sounded like a hammer reverberated through the air. She looked around and saw some of the men in the distance fixing the fences. An indefinable sadness swept over her. Their world had changed, their lives had changed so much since that storm. The trails were closed now, the open range finished, the ranches brought in to manage. It wasn't progress, it was simple adaptation in order to cope with the changing world. It angered Alex that so much beauty, so much freedom was now gone.

The hammer echoed again and she looked to see

Tom waving. She started Ranger toward him but the sound came again and she realized it wasn't the hammer this time but a shot. Looking around, she saw the eagle in free-fall toward the earth and started off at a gallop in the direction of the gun.

"Alex!" Tom chased after her. "Alex!"

She came into a broad expanse of pasture past some trees and pulled up, suddenly aware Tom and Jesse were both right behind her.

"Over there." Jesse pointed.

There were three horses, one with a sidesaddle, which puzzled Alex for a moment until she saw the riders. English. Someone's guests, no doubt. Two men smartly dressed in hunting tweeds and a woman in proper ladies' riding attire, veiled top hat and all. Alex rode up, the men behind her.

"Good afternoon," one of the Englishmen called pleasantly. "Looks a bit like rain."

"Did you take that eagle down?" Alex dismounted, her voice deceptively agreeable.

"No, my daughter here did. Jolly good shot, don't you think?"

Alex gave the woman a smile and held her hand out for the gun.

"It's a Purdy," the woman said in her cut crystal voice. "They're from England."

"Yes, I know." Alex kept her tone pleasant. She looked the shotgun over, checked it was no longer loaded, then took it by the barrel and swung it smartly into a tree, CRACK!

"Now, wait just a minute!" the man began but both Tom and Jesse had drawn their Colts.

Alex checked the next one wasn't loaded and swung that, too, smashing the barrel from the stock. She put her hand out for the gentleman's next but he held it tight, cradling it against his chest.

"Just what in the world do you think...?"

"The gun," said Alex quietly. "You're

trespassing. Hunting on private property. You're on my land and—"

"Those guns are worth over three hundred dollars apiece!" the older man asserted.

"I know," replied Alex calmly but threatening. "I own two myself."

"You're English!" the woman noted with surprise.

The younger man, the woman's husband, had been quiet all this time, just leaning back against a tree taking this all in. "You're the Calthorpe woman, aren't you?" he asked at last.

"That's right." Alex put her hand out for the older man's gun. She grabbed it from him before checking if it was loaded, then she bashed that, as well, into a tree.

"You're crazy!" the older man said. "I'll get the law out here!"

Tom and Jesse both smiled broadly. Tom said, "This is the law. She owns the property. You're trespassing. You're darned lucky she didn't blow your heads off."

Alex was now looking over the fourth gun as if she were considering keeping it. "On second thought," she said, taking a good swing into the tree. She threw the pieces down. "Where're your guns?" she asked the younger man.

"I don't hunt. It's my wife's sport," he said looking Alex up and down.

"Good! Then I'll just take the derringer you're hiding up your sleeve." She held her hand out for the small gun. There was a moment's hesitation in which Jesse's gun clicked behind her. The husband rolled back his cuff and removed the derringer, dropping it into Alex's hand. She gave it to Tom. "I'm not good at throwing."

She looked back at the three trespassers. "That was a golden eagle you took down. They generally have a wing span of about seven feet and can fly at great speeds. I'd rather see any one of you dead than that bird. Now get the hell out of here before my friend here accidentally but conveniently lets his gun go off."

She gathered Ranger's reins and pulled herself up, then sat there watching until the three rode off.

Jesse looked over at her. "You feel better for that?" he asked.

Chapter Twenty-One

Over the next few days the men would spot her in the distance. Alex rode the fences to see her property as it was now, started some drawings to get her hand back in, and tried to come to terms with how she felt about Jesse leaving. She was one week down.

Spring round-up was underway, and although it was a much reduced affair with far fewer Reps around, it was still round-up. There was late calving going on too, since late snowstorms had postponed some breeding, and the men were riding from rounding up to the cows still giving birth. Alex came up to a group of them down by the creek. Cal was there with the new man who'd complained about working for a woman.

"What's happening?" asked Alex getting off the horse.

"We think it might be breech," said Cal frowning. "Gonna lose one or t'other."

"We need small hands," said the new man.

Alex tied Ranger to a tree. "What's your name?"

"Coates."

"Coates, huh? You don't like working for women?" She squatted, not expecting an answer, pulled her gloves off and tossed them aside, then took off her silver cuff and threw that into the pile. Then she rolled up her sleeves. "You have a wash?" she asked. They handed her a bucket with the wash in it. She splashed it up her arms and on the cow, then reached into the cow, feeling around. "One leg is back. It isn't breech." The men stood by as she manipulated inside the cow, then brought the cupped hoof forward in her hand.

Jesse rode up. "What the heck is going on?" No one answered. They all looked at Alex. "You know what you're doing?"

She stared back at him. "Do you think I'd be sitting here like this if I was..." The cow lowed and the calf inside her moved. "Tom taught me, remember?" She turned back to the cow.

Jesse raised a questioning brow to Cal who just shrugged.

Suddenly Alex shouted, "Pull!"

Cal grabbed the calf as it came out covering Alex in all the mess of a birth.

She stood up and assessed herself while the men finished up and got the calf to its mother. "Can you take my belts off please?" She stood stiffly in front of Jesse, arms out to the sides. His eyes widened. "Your fingers won't burn, Jess. Just take the goddamn belts off, please, so I don't get my gun wet."

"You sure your pants won't fall down?" There was a smug look on his face as he gingerly opened the buckles at her waist.

"My hat, please. Off," was her reply.

When he had lifted her hat from her head, she stepped on her boot toes and pulled her feet out, then marched down to the creek and dove into the chilly water.

Jesse stood there, his hands on his hips, waiting. He waited some more but there was no sign of Alex coming up, and then, as he was about to run to the bank, she reappeared, turning her head side to side to shake water out of her hair. She pulled herself out by some branches and marched back. A shock of desire ran through him as he took in her wet clothes clinging to her body, her breasts outlined by her shirt. He knew that body, had loved that body, but knew there was something different, not just that she was so much thinner, but she had changed somehow.

Shivering, Alex quickly rolled down and buttoned her cuffs before stooping to pull on her boots, then pick up her hat and gun belt. Lastly she slipped the silver bracelet on her wrist.

"You don't like working for women, huh, Coates?" she asked the new man again.

"Yeah, well."

"Well, welcome to the Faringdon." She climbed up on Ranger and rode away.

****

It bothered Jesse overnight.

He had never wanted anything or anyone the way he wanted Alex. He knew her, he knew what motivated her, what ran her, the way she thought. He knew the way she looked and the way she moved and the way she pushed food around her plate. Alex was the family Jesse wanted, the best friend, sister, the mother who looked after him, and the lover he desired. Alex was the ranch and his world. Since she was eight years old they had had a bond, a bond he thought was stronger than blood ties, more than friendship, greater than love. Now something was changed, something was lost and he had to find the missing piece or it would be lost forever.

He went to see Annie, holding his anger inside him like a rotten fruit he couldn't digest. In truth, he told himself, he understood why Tom and Annie hadn't told him, if they knew. Surely they knew. Alex would've said—if he was right about what he thought had happened.

Annie was hanging wash outside as he rode up. "I was wondering how long it would take you." She pegged another shirt to the line, moved her basket along, then stood looking up at him. "You want coffee?"

Inside, he sat and put his hat on the table. "Why

didn't you tell me?"

Annie put the coffee down in front of him and sat opposite. "It wasn't for us to tell you, Jesse. You know that. Anyway, we thought she would write. We thought the letters would eventually get through, that she would tell you." He looked at her without expression. "I think you have to go and discuss this with Alex, Jesse. I'm not the one to be talking 'bout this."

He never replied nor touched his coffee but picked up his hat again and left.

****

Alex was in the house discussing with Kenny, the new ranch carpenter, how three of the old servant's rooms on the top floor could be turned into a better studio for her. She heard Jesse with Wilson in the front hall, and asked Kenny if he could call another time. Leading him downstairs, she stopped at the top of the final landing and watched him go out as Jesse stood there looking up at her. She walked down the stairs slowly then went into the study with Jesse following her and closed the door behind.

"I won't ask why you've come." She seated herself behind the desk. "It's obviously not ranch business, is it?"

"Why, Alex? Why didn't you tell me? I had a right to know. It's my child too."

"Yes, well." She played with some paper on the desk for a moment, folding it and unfolding it again. "How could I tell you, Jesse? In a letter? I couldn't do it. It was something that needed to be said in person. Then when I hadn't heard from you, I decided you didn't care and therefore...well, I didn't tell you."

"I had a right!" he repeated, slamming his fist into the wall.

She stared at him for a moment. "What was I supposed to write, Jess?" she asked quietly. "'Dear

209

Jesse, you might like to know I had a baby that died.' Or perhaps later, 'I realize you hate me since you haven't bothered writing so you'll be happy to know I lost our baby...'"

"Stop it!" He slammed the wall again. "How 'bout the letters that went, 'Only you make me happy. Nothing else matters.'"

"Yes, when you bothered to write!" She fumed at him for a moment, then calmed down. "I don't know what happened with your letters any more than you do. All I know is I-I lost two...fathers, I was alone six thousand miles away trying to sort out the ranch, trying to find out about my mother, trying to find out who I was, and having a baby at the same time, hiding away in that great house, knowing David was buying off people so there would be no scandal. And you weren't there, you weren't writing, and as far as I was concerned you had opted out of any rights you may or may not have had. Do you think—"

"Do you think for one moment I wouldn't have moved heaven and earth to go there, to be with you, if you had just said? Do you think I didn't want to be with you? You tell me, Alex, for one moment, just think on it, do you really believe I wouldn't have dropped every last thing here and gone to England had you but asked? Scrounged any dime to be with you?" He stood there, as if the wall were holding him up, his eyes burning at her. "Jeez," he said at last, "do you know what lovin' you is like?" He put his hand on the door.

"It was a boy." She spoke as if it were a secret still. "It was a boy. I went full term and then...I don't know, the doctor said he strangled." She put her head in her hands. "I named him Oliver Calthorpe Makepeace and he's buried in the family vault. David didn't stop me. There was no one to stop me." She started to sob.

Lightning flashed outside suddenly before heavy

rain hit the windows. A late afternoon summer thunderstorm was clearing the air, refreshing the plants, and giving energy to everything living. Jesse stood there looking at her, his own eyes pooling, unable to help her but listening to that thunder outside and the rain beating against the panes for a solid minute, then stopping almost as soon as it had begun.

Alex pulled her hankie out at last and wiped her face. "I'm sorry," she whispered.

"Because of letters, Alex," he barely uttered.

"Three."

****

Alex packed her things into the saddlebags next morning, left Tom a note as to where she was going and went to saddle up Ranger.

Cal came in to the stables. "Taking off?" He propped himself against the next stall.

"Day off?" she asked as she busied herself with the tack.

"Nice bracelet," he continued.

"Are we playing a game here, Cal? Guess the answer, or something? What is it exactly you want? Shouldn't you be out on round-up?"

"Jess sent me in for some things."

"Then get them," she practically ordered, throwing the saddle on Ranger's back.

"You and I used to be good friends."

"What is it you want?" She stood at last facing him. Yes, they had been good friends. Was she going to lose everyone now, everyone she had ever loved, cared about?

He reached for her left hand, but she pulled it back. "I had a sister once. Went to live over in Kansas, married a man while she was still down in Tennessee and they decided to move up to Kansas. Couldn't take it—life in the cow towns weren't for her..."

"I'm sorry to hear it. I didn't know." Alex started to cinch up Ranger's saddle.

"Had them same markings on her wrist after the first time she tried it." Alex stopped. "I want you to tell me there ain't gonna be no second time, Ladilex." He waited but there was no answer, no movement. "Dang foolish thing to do when so many people love ya. You, I've known since you were but eight year old. Jesse I've had as a brother since he were fourteen. I don't want to see neither of you hurt." He stared at her a long moment. "Jesse know?" She looked away and shook her head. "I want yer word here." He waited some more but there was no movement. "He's gonna find out at some stage. You know what that'll do to him? You better come up with some good explanation, you know." Alex took Ranger's reins and started to lead him out of the stable. "I mean this, Ladilex. You promise me here and now there ain't gonna be no second time. I may be nothin' more than a-a good for nothin', uneducated puncher, but I know what's what 'roun' here. You give me your promise, now."

Alex was at the door. She had Ranger behind her and turned back to face Cal. "You're such a good friend, Cal. Really you are, but…"

She never finished the sentence. It was all too much. She just left.

****

There was a new homestead up at Boyd, though the old camp was still there, its door hanging off, the room damp and smelling of animals. Alex decided to trespass in the new house. If someone found her on their property it wouldn't really matter if it were the house or the camp so long as she didn't steal anything.

The inside wasn't quite finished. There was a large brass bed, which surprised her. Why would something so fancy be in a hunting cabin? The table and chairs were of a polished wood, while the kitchen had an indoor pump. She had expected something far more basic, rustic; this looked like a home. It reminded her of the Homestead except it was single story with the bed in an alcove opposite the kitchen, and only a small fireplace catty-cornered onto the main room. She dumped her things, looked about and set up her easel outside. The dilapidated camp was interesting now, worth a painting certainly, with so many memories attached.

Those memories played through her head as she worked through the day. She would find her eyes wet and herself just staring at the camp, then she would suddenly come back to life and resume the painting. Sunset took her by surprise with its failing light and she realized she was being bitten by the mosquitoes off the lake, and a chill had set in with the cool evening air. She reluctantly packed her things to go inside for an early night, eat her bread and cheese and get into her bedroll.

A clatter woke her. The gun was on the floor by the bed but, half asleep, Alex lay there listening: the spurs, the movement that was unhurried but competent and knowledgeable, not unfriendly nor menacing. She opened one eye, squinting into the insistent mid-morning light.

"What are you doing here?" she asked Jesse.

"I knew you wouldn't eat 'less someone cooked for you." He lit the fire. "You do know you're trespassing, don't you? Could be shot."

"I'll deal with that when it happens."

She pulled herself up and he could see she was wearing her chemise and knickers but nothing more. He stood in the kitchen and started to gut a trout. Alex stomped into her boots and went out the door.

When she came back in, Jesse was watching the fish and potatoes fry. She sat on the edge of the table. "You eating?" she asked.

"No, I had breakfast about two hour ago. I'm making sure you eat and then I'll leave."

"I didn't know babysitting was part of the foreman's duties." He got a tin plate and pushed the food onto it.

Jesse sat at a right angle to her, noticing she had put on her silver cuff. He started to make some remark about dressing with a bracelet before she put on her pants but thought better of it. He knew she was completely oblivious to the fact she was half-dressed, that she was not attempting to flaunt herself. Alex would never stop being a child, he thought, she would always be part child, part-woman. She had been the same at eight.

"You might compliment the cook," he said at last.

"Yep. It's good." She smiled, putting another forkful in her mouth. "So when did you learn to cook?"

He didn't answer but just sat staring at her, desiring her so much he wondered if he could get out without kissing her.

"I can't eat any more potatoes. You'll have to finish for me." She pushed the plate toward him.

Their eyes locked, each waiting for the other to speak. At last Alex sat back and said, "I have to tell you something."

Jesse got up and put the plate in the sink. He stood looking out the window for a moment, listening to geese and ducks out on the lake. He thought she was going to say she'd had an affair, coming over on the boat unchaperoned as she had been—that would be it, though he didn't know how he could bear it.

"I tried to kill myself."

It came so starkly he thought he hadn't heard right for a moment. He walked slowly back to the table, gripping the edge with both hands as his eyes bored into her. She removed the cuff and showed him her wrist, then she pulled her legs up and rested her chin on her knees. Jesse remained speechless, and the silence was like an icy wind making the two of them shiver.

"They put me on laudanum," she continued at last. "I didn't know what I was doing. I was beside myself after the baby. They thought it would help." She ran a hand though her hair. "Then I started to drink. I just...drank and drank. Anything in sight, everything I could get my hands on. Rose couldn't cope with it, that's why she returned here before me. David hired someone else and that drove me further away. I-I was out of control. They hid everything. I ended up in London in some opium den or other, and David had to come and find me and take me home. That was it. That was the low, the bottom. This nurse, Margaret her name was, she found me the next morning just in time.'

"I just didn't know what I was doing, I-I don't remember very much but I don't remember wanting to die, I just didn't want to feel anything, I wanted...to be numb, I guess." She stopped for a moment. "I suppose I wasn't going to tell you but then, Cal had figured it out. It's not very well hidden, you would have seen sooner or later."

"That's why you're telling me?" Anger etched the question like the scrape of a knife. Alex didn't answer. Jesse started to throw some things from the kitchen back into the sack he'd come with. "I can't do this, Alex. I'm leavin'."

"Oh!" She was somewhat puzzled by the response.

"No, I mean I'm leavin' for good. I can't watch you destroy yourself like this. You want a perfect world and it's not a perfect world. Nothing's ever gonna be good enough for you. You can't accept nothing's ever gonna be ideal and you're gonna destroy yourself trying to make it so. You just don't understand that not everything turns out the way you want it to, not everything in life is perfect."

"No, I don't understand!" she retorted. "I don't understand why people have to kill golden eagles for sport. I don't understand why a snowstorm has to come and kill half a herd. I don't understand why lightning strikes an innocent man just sitting out there on his horse and kills him. I don't understand why three letters go missing, or when someone says they'll never leave you, they up and go. And I sure as hell don't understand why a baby, born of the love of two people, has to die before it's even drawn a single breath. Do you understand that, Jesse? Because if you do, please tell me, please give me the explanation, I would certainly like to know that answer!"

"It's life, Alex. And I can't go on watching you all the time, wondering if you're gonna do that again."

"I'm not going to do that again. I told you, I was drunk and on laudanum. David took me to Italy and I recovered, if you like. I haven't had alcohol at all since Italy." She curled into a ball looking small, and vulnerable.

Jesse leaned against the door for a moment. "You remember that time when you were eight and had just arrived, and you shot out your arms and I picked you up?"

She looked at him, her brow creased. "I remember. Madame Helene was so astonished. I had seen some child at the station in New York do that and I thought it was a good idea." There was a weak smile for the sentiment.

"That was so out of character," he replied quietly. "You never seemed to need anyone after that. You want to do everything yourself and you want everything to be perfect. That's you, that's who you are, Alex."

She ran a hand across her face. "You're

confusing my desire to be independent with not needing anyone. I needed you. I thought you needed me. And I need you now." Her admission surprised herself and she looked away.

"For the ranch!" he shouted. "The thing with you, Alex, is you don't want to need anyone, you may need me, but you don't want to admit it, you can't deal with it—"

"I just did! I just said—"

"Yeah, but you don't believe it, do you? You think—"

"Don't tell me what I think, Jesse. That all happened because I needed you and you weren't there." She slammed her hand on the table. "No, I don't want to need you, I don't want to need anyone. You're right. I want a perfect world in which I can deal with everything on my own. That's my perfect world. Does it exist?" she asked, getting up at last and going to find her clothes. She heard the doorknob turn. "My father killed my mother, you know." There was utter silence for a second before she continued, "Well, he was responsible for her death, if he didn't actually murder her." She pulled a shirt on as he closed the door again and turned back to her. "All those years..." She sat on the bed and pulled on her denims. "They told me she'd died in childbirth. All my life he blamed me. But she had been ill and Frederic was afraid of her losing the baby, which he no doubt hoped was another son— 'one must have an heir and a spare,' as the saying goes—so he had the doctor bring about the birth, my birth. He didn't even care apparently whether the baby was his or Oliver's so long as it was a son. What a disappointment I must have been. A girl. And then he knew he had killed her, the infection from that killed her. Frederic never told me that part, did he? All that time he was blaming me and he had done that. And for spite, I should think.

Because she loved Oliver more and he knew it." She stood and started buckling on her gun belt. "He couldn't live with that. It's amazing he didn't kill me but maybe that was what he was trying to do all my life by making me miserable." She bent to search for her socks, grabbed one from under the bed and stood up to face Jesse. "I don't know why I tried to kill myself. It was a stupid thing to do. But I do know I'm not my mother. I'm not trapped—I'm free."

"H-how did you find out all that?"

"Oliver's letter told me to go back to discover more about myself. But it all came out after Frederic's death because there were papers regarding her will. She had made a will prior to her death, just days before, just like Oliver did, leaving me and David equal parts in an inheritance. She must've known what might happen, since he was forcing her to do this. And she had written her baby—me—a letter. It wasn't much—just an apology basically, for not being there to take care of me." Alex stood there staring across at Jesse. "Yes, well. I come from a complicated family so you're really best rid of me."

He looked at her, still speechless, still trying to deal with the complexity of her life.

"This is yours, Jess, isn't it, this house? You bought Boyd, didn't you?"

"You told me once to build my dream house. I had money saved. I was getting a higher salary. Higgins worked out a payment plan." He was still numb—the words were just tumbling out.

"Well. I won't trespass any more. Sorry."

She bent to pick up her bedroll as she heard the door close.

Chapter Twenty-Two

Jesse went to see Tom the next day to tell him he had decided to leave early, but Tom just shook his head.

"You said once you wanted to provide for her. Well, dang it, provide for her. None of this makes sense, Jess. You're leaving because she really needs you now?" He waited for an answer but Jesse just stared blankly at the wall.

Tom got up, his aggravation keen and sitting heavily on him. He looked out the window. Alex was in the distance, coming up from the main house. "You know," he said swiveling back to Jesse, "we've all let that girl down. You, me, Annie. Alex's like one of them fine thoroughbreds you read about, sensitive and...sort of nervy-like, but they give you so much back in return. Trouble is, they have to trust you, and that there's where we've failed." He glanced at Jesse briefly. "First I let dang Calthorpe send her back when she was little and I should of stood up to him."

"You couldn't have done anything, Tom. No one could. You know that."

"And then Annie and I let her spend all her money—all that money she worked so hard to save, and she went and spent it on us, on buying the Homestead." He leaned back against the windowsill for a moment, shaking his head as if it puzzled him he could have done such a thing. "I've been a fool. A dang selfish fool."

Jesse stayed quiet as the older man walked back to his desk and sat down as if he'd returned from a long journey. "She's kept the ranch goin', you said. She hasn't done it just for you and Annie."

Tom looked up. "Maybe so, but maybe it's my fault she doesn't believe you sent them letters. Why should she believe any of us, Jesse. Why?" He busied himself with papers on his desk, as Jesse pulled the door open to find Alex standing there.

There was a moment's hesitation as they stood facing each other.

"I just received a letter from David," she said at last, "with this in it." She pulled out a crumpled envelope addressed to her. Jesse took it, turning it over in his hand, then gave it back. "It arrived after I left," she said. "So that's one."

Tom watched the scene from his desk and shook his head.

"You haven't read it," Jesse mumbled. He hesitated, as if he wanted to say something more, than stopped. He noticed a small tremor. The letter fluttered in Alex's hand like a moth finding the light. Alex looked down at the sealed letter. "No. I suppose I'm a coward. Does it matter now?" She searched his face for an answer.

"Looks like we've got a caller." Tom nodded toward the window. Jesse and Alex moved to see Nigel Henderson getting off his horse.

Alex strode out, the two men behind her.

Henderson was a stocky figure with a large square head, which sat on his body as if it had been dropped there. He had a neat little moustache, too small for his face, and round deep-set eyes, invariably squinting. Alex hadn't liked him when she first met him when she was eight. Her feelings for the man had not changed through all the social occasions Oliver had made her attend.

"Ah, Mr. Henderson, what can I do for you?" Alex stood with her thumbs in her belt, her face masked with a smile.

"Yost. Makepeace." He nodded to the men. "Lady Alex, I heard you ran into a few of my guests the other day?"

"Oh, were they yours? That's too bad. Me, I've stopped having guests here at the ranch. Don't really like people on my land."

"So I hear. Is that why your treatment of my friends wasn't so special?"

"It wasn't meant to be special. We have fences now. They were trespassing."

"By accident."

"Accident? There's an old English proverb, Mr. Henderson, 'good fences make good neighbors.' You should know that."

"Yes, well, it was your choice to put up those fences, Lady Alex. I can understand the drift fences, but the others? Out of respect for Oliver—"

"Ah, my uncle sometime father. I'm never really sure."

"You certainly are one tough lady now."

"Yes. I've learned my lessons well."

"You haven't had it easy, I'll give you that."

"If you've come here to commiserate, you're a bit late, Mr. Henderson. I never felt sorry for myself and I sure as hell don't intend to start now. In fact, things were really looking up until you came along."

Henderson was silent for a moment. Alex's hate for the man welled up inside her as she remembered the last dinner party with him, to which Oliver had brought her, against her will. The man had sat staring down her dress and then accused her of being arrogant and judgmental. And he had always stunk of whiskey.

"If you've come for an apology I'm afraid that's not forthcoming either," she continued. "In fact, I'm thinking of sending over a bill for that golden eagle. I hear hunt outfitters make quite a bit of money from these easterners and Europeans."

"Why, you…"

Jesse shifted behind her.

"I really think you ought to go now, Henderson. My foreman here, he gets a bit itchy sometimes, if you know what I mean. Has something of a short temper, I'm afraid."

"Yost, can't you talk some sense into her?"

Tom guffawed. "She's got a sight more sense than the most of us, Mr. Henderson."

"These men practically brought me up," Alex went on. "Everything I know about this land I owe to them."

Henderson shook his head. "I know you don't have two dimes to rub together now, Lady Alex, but an apology for ruining those guns might've been nice."

"Well," replied Alex, considering this, "I guess I'm as stingy with my apologies now as I am with my cash."

The three of them stood there for a moment as Henderson rode off. Tom gave Alex's shoulder a squeeze and went back to his office.

Alex faced Jesse. "I thought you were going."

"It's the children's birthday party next Saturday. I'll go after."

Alex stood there for a moment, thinking. She heard the horses coming in, Garrison and Coates running a small herd into one of the corrals. Jesse went to the corral fence to watch, but Alex stood as if glued to the spot. She began to tear open the letter but changed her mind and stuffed it back into her pocket. She wasn't going to start crying out here in front of Jesse, as no doubt she would. She started back to the house when Coates came up to her and stopped her.

Jesse watched the two of them from the corner of his eye. He saw Alex shrug and nod as if she were sorry about something, then head toward the house.

Coates came over and put a foot up on a rail, pushed his hat forward a bit scratching the back of his neck, and then leaned against the fence next to Jesse.

"She is one dang woman, that one," he said at last.

Jesse looked at him. "What d'ya mean, Coates?"

"Well." The other man turned to him. "I got up my courage, like, and thought I'd ask her to the church social next Sa'day. Thought all she could do was say no or fire me for oversteppin' the line."

"So she accepted and now you're stuck?" offered Jess.

"No. Wish she had." His forehead creased. "Heck, wouldn'ta asked her if I hadn'ta meant business. No, she turns to me and says she's been in love with the same man since she were eight year old, ain't about to stop loving him now and since the sonovabitch don't love her—"

"Did she say sonovabitch?"

Coates' brow creased again. "No, why? She said 'the gentleman concerned.'"

"Just curious," said Jesse moving off with a smile.

Chapter Twenty-Three

Alex was late. No one had offered to drive her so she knew the men were coming in off herd to the party. A chilling rain fell and she'd pulled the hood over the buggy, but had still got wet and entered looking somewhat bedraggled. They were all inside and Tom was just showing Millie the painting of the two children that hung above the fireplace.

"Well, there's our artist now." He greeted Alex.

She shook herself a bit and stood there uncertainly, a waif at the door. The others all stared at her.

"There's our boss, ya mean, Tom." Cal was obviously trying not to laugh. "Bit of a sorry sight, Ladilex."

"I don't care what I look like, Cal, I'm more concerned I've just ruined the gifts for the children."

"Oh, what are they?" Sue Ann rushed over from her spot next to Jesse on a sofa.

"Sue Ann! Give Alex a minute and don't be so rude!" Annie came with a towel for Alex to dry herself off, and led her toward the kitchen. Alex stopped and took something out of a folder she carried. She opened a handmade book, glanced at it to see if it was dry and intact, then handed it to Sue Ann.

"Happy Birthday, darling." She bent to kiss the girl. "There's another for J.J. I hope they're all right." J.J. came and got his present, pecked Alex quickly on the cheek and went back to a corner. "Growing up," she said to Annie with a smile.

The presents were each a series of little water

colors of the ranch: the men at work, the children on horseback, Annie in the kitchen.

Sue Ann showed hers to Cal.

"Did you see these old photographs, Ladilex? The ones that were taken back in the seventies by that Huffman fella? You should come and look."

They were spread out on the table in front of Jesse. He looked up at her as she approached and handed her one. In it, she was sitting on Jesse's lap on a bench in front of the chuck houses, his arms about her and his chin resting on the top of her head, huge matching grins on their faces, with Cal looking on and laughing. She studied it for a time as Jesse watched her, knowing they felt the same things there, in that moment, the same connection, knowing they had never stopped loving one another.

She laid it back down on the table as her eyes started to well when a voice behind her said, "I think photography will soon make painting extinct." It was Sara Beth.

"I guess I'll just be a dinosaur," countered Alex.

As the rain let up they all drifted outside and Tom started the cookout. Annie and Alex hung back in the kitchen, not talking about anything in particular, avoiding any discussion of Jesse. Millie joined them for a while.

"I meant to say congratulations on your marriage," said Alex, "though I think congratulations is not the proper word for the bride."

"Thank you." Millie smiled graciously. "Your turn next!" She patted Alex on the shoulder. "I saw the retreat Jesse built y'all up at Boyd. It's lovely there, isn't it?"

Alex didn't say anything. She supposed people would know soon enough. Annie glanced at her. "It'll work out." She spoke quietly so Millie couldn't hear. "He's not going anywhere."

They brought some salad bowls outside along

with plates and cutlery. "Lordy, Ladilex is doing her female stuff again," quipped Cal. "Will wonders never cease?"

"You know some ranchers would fire you, Cal, for a remark like that," she retorted.

"Yeah," said Garrett, "but we ain't workin' for some ranchers."

Alex crossed her arms. She watched J.J. flipping through the pages of the book she had given him. The wind blew her hair and for a moment she shivered.

"Go get a jacket, Alex," advised Annie, "it's a cool day."

She wandered back inside and found Garrison and Millie kissing, shook a finger at them and got Tom's jacket off a peg. "So the honeymoon's not over, I see," she said to Garrison.

"No, ma'am, and no intention of it ever being over!"

Millie raised an eyebrow at her as they went back out. Alex stood for a second in the empty house, shrugged the jacket further onto her shoulders and pulled it tight, then thrust her hands into the pockets as she stepped outside. Her finger jagged in a hole.

"Tom," she said with a smile, "you have that same tear in your pocket you had three years ago!"

"Tell the wife!"

Alex felt something in the hole and pulled it out. She looked at it, thought she was seeing things or it was some sort of joke, turned it over in her hands and kept staring down at it. She walked off toward the swing at the far end of the yard and sat down.

"You ain't very friendly," Cal called after her.

There was no reply. Alex ripped open the letter and read, turning the pages over slowly as she swayed on the swing.

"Oh, whatever is she doing? Jesse, go get her to

come and eat," said Annie, with not a little contrivance.

Jesse rose from the table and looked over at Alex, puzzling at what she was reading. He sauntered down to the swing. "Want a push?" he asked.

"This is from you to me," she said looking up. "It was in Tom's pocket. What was it doing in Tom's pocket?" They stared at each other for a moment. "Jess?"

"I-I have no…" He stopped. "No. I gave him a letter to mail for me once, when he was going into town. Do you think he forgot?"

"He certainly wouldn't have not posted it on purpose." She looked back at the letter. "Well, that's two now out of three. Huh." She folded it up and shoved it back in its envelope. "Don't say anything to him. He'd be devastated if he knew, if he thought— you know—that he had been the cause, been instrumental…"

"Yeah. I know." He watched her swing for a moment. "Come on." He extended his hand to her. "Everyone's waitin'."

****

Alex couldn't figure Jesse anymore, what his intentions were, whether he was staying or going. Between the ranch and her painting and his duties as foreman, there was just no time to talk to him alone. But he was still there, still at the ranch, and that was enough for now.

From her eyrie in the former servants' quarters, she heard shouting and tried to see what was going on from the window. Rushing down the steps and outside, she just made out Cal and then saw a wagon with someone laid out in it. A group of the punchers was gathered about the wagon in which Garrett lay, one leg draped over the side, the other flat but in a shape no leg should be.

227

"Oh my goodness, what's the matter, how badly is he hurt?" Alex went to Cal.

"Broke leg. Dang bronco throwed him, then stomped on him for good measure."

"Garrett?" Alex walked over to the wagon. "How are you doing? Mind if I take a look?"

"I'm in real pain, Lady Lex. And I can't afford to be outta work."

"Who said anything about losing pay? Man gets hurt on the job working here we look after him. You know that." She pulled herself up on the wagon. "Cal, go up to the house, please, and ask Wilson for a couple of bottles of whiskey. And tell Rose we need linen sheets cut into wide strips for binding. Coates?"

"Ma'am?"

"Go find Kenny and ask him to mix up some thin plaster if we have any. And tell him we need a stretcher out here and we're going to need some sort of hook in the ceiling above the sick bay bed. Is there a sick bay?"

Someone said, "Not anymore. Sick bay apparently became the foreman's room. Sign's still on the door."

Alex looked to see who had said this. It was a young puncher with a chubby cherub face, and a shock of white-blond hair falling from beneath his hat. Alex almost laughed. She felt as if she might be looking at Jesse when he was that age. "When did you arrive?" she asked.

"Arrive? You mean, sign on, Ma'am?"

"Yes."

"'Bout a week ago."

"How the hell old are you?" She was tempted to say, "son," but stopped herself.

"Sixteen."

"Crikey, Garrett." Alex turned back to the patient. "I must be getting old." She heard a laugh like croaking come from the older man. "Have you a knife? We've got to cut his pants."

It was then she noticed Tom, Jesse and Annie had arrived with a stranger, and were standing off at a distance watching. She didn't wave or acknowledge them, but saw Cal come out of the house, stop to talk with them a moment, and come on carrying the whiskey.

"Rose is on her way with the linens," he said coming up. "How we doin'?"

"Cut him out of his pants." Alex stood up again on the wagon and walked down its length. "We have to get his boots off, too."

"Jeez," Garrett moaned.

"Yes, it won't be easy. I'm not going to lie to you—it'll hurt like hell. Get him drunk," she advised Cal.

"Can I join him?"

"You do and you'll be riding for other wages."

She looked again at the visitor with the Yosts and Jesse. He was an older man, with a neatly trimmed moustache, and well dressed, yet dressed for riding. She thought he looked weathered but handsome, fatherly in a way, yet also stern and business-like. She wondered why Annie was with them and figured it must be some relative.

Cal had a knife and was slitting Garrett's pants leg while Garrett guzzled the whiskey, half propping himself up to swallow. Coates came out with Kenny and a stretcher.

"Crikey," Alex said again, looking over the exposed break. "It's swelling up. We need ice. You, kid, what's your name?"

"Beesley."

"Beastly..."

"Alex!" Cal admonished.

"Go up to the house, see if Rose has the linens ready and get as much ice as you can carry. Cal, you're going to have to get this bone back into place."

"Why me? Why do I get the doctoring jobs here?"

"Because you're strong and I can't do it. You can do it quickly so it won't hurt him so much. Though I have to tell you again, Garrett, it's going to hurt something awful."

Cal looked at the break. He raised a questioning brow at Alex who had positioned herself opposite.

"Wait for the ice to numb it, I guess," she said.

"How come you know so much, Ladilex?"

"I don't know. David broke an arm once. I guess I just took it all in."

Tom came over. "You got everything under control?"

"I think so." Alex got to her feet for a moment. "Who's your guest?"

"Old friend. You'll meet him tomorrow, if you have time."

"Ah, here's Beastly." She placed the chunks of ice around Garrett's leg and they waited a few minutes before Cal quickly pulled off Garrett's boot, then smartly pushed the bone back into alignment. Garrett let out a roar of pain but slugged back more whiskey. Alex shuddered in sympathy, then got down from the wagon to let the men ease the patient onto the improvised stretcher.

"Jess said they should put Garrett in his room—that he'd move back to the bunkhouse for a spell," said Cal.

Alex followed them into Jesse's quarters and watched as they maneuvered Garrett onto the bed. "Better take his pants completely off. I have to plaster up the leg. It's better than splinting it, and he'll be able to hop around in a few days. Plus it'll heal better."

"You gonna see me undressed?" Garrett slurred.

"I have a brother if it's any consolation."

"You see him in the altogether?"

"No. Look, just keep drinking and forget about it. I'm only going to see your naked leg, Garrett. Anyway, as I recall, you saw me in my chemise so we're equal."

She faced the wall while they stripped off Garrett's pants. That's when she noticed the photographs. Jesse had tacked some of the old photos of the two of them to the wall. He had to have done it after Saturday since the ones she had seen then were now here. It stunned her for a moment.

"Now what, doctor?" Cal asked.

Alex turned back and noticed Rose and Kenny waiting outside. "Now we plaster him up!" She took the bucket of soft plaster, and the bundle of linens from Rose. "Roll your sleeves up, Cal, we're going to have fun. The rest of you can get back to work please! Beastly included!"

"Alex! Y'all are gonna make that kid real unhappy. He's already having a hard time with the punchers."

"Yes, and I bet you're the worst of the lot!"

She thought then of what it must have been like for Jesse at fourteen, a young boy forced to leave his family, a boy with a chip on his shoulder ordered to eat dust out at drag and all the time trying to be a man, trying to be one of "the boys." Cal stared at her, waiting, looking as if he might be reading her mind.

She brought herself back to the present and looked again at Garrett. "I think we have to shave his leg you know."

"What?" Garrett croaked.

"Maybe not. Maybe we put the linen on first, then the plaster on other linens and just bind. All right, let's go."

A few minutes later there was uncontrolled laughter between the three of them. Garrett was so drunk he could no longer speak at all, and Alex and Cal were covered in plaster mix, mostly thrown on each other.

Jesse walked in. He looked from Alex to Cal, then at Garrett. Alex tried unsuccessfully not to giggle. A thick strand of hair hung down with a lump of plaster in it, like a bauble on a cap. Jesse looked her up and down.

"What's up?" he asked mildly. "Place smells like a durned distillery."

Oh here it comes, Alex thought, he's going to ask me if I've been drinking. She said somewhat belligerently, "I thought you were leaving."

Their eyes locked for a moment. "Well, I figured you had kept your promise about never takin' off the bracelet, so I better keep my promise to you."

"About staying a month?"

"No, Alex, the promise about never leaving you."

****

There was a positive bounce in her step as Alex came toward the group the next morning, a stack of papers in her hand. She stopped every so often to look something over, then walked on again. Glancing up at the Yosts, she quickly took in Jesse and the visitor, then went back to the papers, before the corral caught her eye.

"Garrison, cut those two paints and the two Appaloosas out for me and I'll run them up to Wind River."

"Oh, now, Lady Lex, you don't want to be doing that," he moaned. "I had my eye on that Appaloosa."

"Cowpuncher on an Appaloosa just looks darned silly, Garr. Cut them out!"

"Lady Lex—"

"Two paints, two 'Loosas, Garrison!" she said good-naturedly.

"But..."

"But nothing. Look at that grulla. That's a puncher's horse for sure. What are the 'Loosas doing here anyway? They're pretty far from home. I may send them back to the Nez Perce where they belong."

"I only see one Appaloosa," Garrison lied.

Alex went over and spoke to Garrison so the others couldn't hear. She tried hard not to laugh and to be stern with her old hand but it wasn't working. "I want those four horses, Garrison," she said turning the pages and coming over.

"Alex," Tom started.

"We're going to have an American company!" She smiled looking up at him. "Oh, hello Annie," she said as if she'd just seen her friend.

"Alex," Tom started again, "this here's Norris Beckett come up from Texas. He's—"

"Goodness!" Alex took a step back. "Isn't that... Aren't you the... Weren't you the boss of the trail outfit that started this ranch?"

Tom laughed and Jesse rubbed the back of his neck, trying to keep a straight face.

Beckett smiled and put out his hand. "That's right. Only we brought up Longhorns. I see you're moving over to Herefords."

Alex shook his hand, noting he pronounced it "Hurfords" as Jesse did, and almost laughed. "Well," she replied, "that was my manager here. But I think it was a good decision."

"Oh, I can see the sense in it. Fine looking beasts too."

"Alex, Norris is thinking about going in with an English outfit who want to back a ranch down in Texas. We all thought you might know some of the names involved?"

"Maybe we could talk over dinner tonight," Annie put in. "Mr. Beckett is staying with us. Why don't you come over?"

"Oh, Annie, you're always cooking. Rackham complains she does nothing but salads and chicken for me. You all come over to me—the four of you," she clarified, "and give Rackham a field day!"

****

It was strange to be dressing up in finery for a dinner party. Strange to be giving a dinner party, entertaining guests and using the social graces to which she had been bred. When Oliver was alive, Alex disliked intensely the rich foods the cook had prepared, and all the formality of his parties. But today, she and Rackham had settled on a meal of venison, of which they still had some hung, with a trout pâté to start. Then Rackham insisted on whipping up ice creams for dessert now that they had the milk cow. This would definitely put weight on the girl, the cook had remarked.

Jesse waited downstairs and watched Alex carefully descend, shimmering like the moon on water, yet looking as if she were trying to remember what she was supposed to do. He didn't have a chance to say how lovely she looked. The others arrived just then, and they all started chatting at once. It was pleasantries in the drawing room with sherry for Annie and bourbon for the men. Alex told Beckett how she had heard endless stories of the trail ride up from Texas when she was young, and Beckett had become something of a mythical figure to her, the way Jesse and Cal had told it.

"Well," said Beckett laughing a bit, "they were pretty young punchers, quite wild for a time there. But they were good boys. Fiery in Jesse's case, angry at being stuck out there at drag, and too much fooling around on Cal's part. But they were good."

They went into dinner where Alex had put Tom opposite her at the other head with Beckett to her right and Jesse to her left with Annie between her husband and Jess. She withstood the usual jokes about living on a ranch and not eating beef, which completely astounded Norris Beckett. He kept repeating he couldn't believe it, that they were having him on, until the venison was brought out, and that seemed to settle the matter. Alex briefly described her plan to buy out the remaining— British—shareholders and form an American company, if they were willing. "Though of course it'll cost a bit, and it's money I haven't got at the moment," she explained, "unless I sell some paintings."

"You do the one of Calthorpe above your fireplace?"

"Yes."

"Well, maybe you'd like to come on down to Texas and paint a few things for me."

"I'd love to but I think my traveling days are over, though I have to admit Texas is rather tempting."

"I haven't been back for, what, sixteen-odd years now." Jesse slipped his hand gently over Alex's. "Must've changed a bit."

Annie and Tom leaned back in their seats as if some nagging worry had been lifted from them both.

Norris Beckett sat a moment, then said finally, "Well, I been meaning to ask you, Lady Alex, if you knew any of these men who are forming this company. Not personally perhaps, but I understand your family may have connections with them."

"Yes. Who are they?" She sat back so Wilson could remove her plate.

"One is a Jamison Rowe."

"Oh, I met him once! Father—that is Frederic, had dealings with him in London. I-I'm not sure what to say. I mean, I can't vouch for the man's honesty but his business acumen should be all right if Frederic dealt with him. But if you want a character reference, that I can't do. I was too young and uninvolved to know him any better than as a brief houseguest. Good shot, though, I seem to remember," she added with a smile.

"Well, that's something." Beckett sat back in his

chair as the ice creams were set in front of each guest. He waited as Alex took up her spoon. "What about a Lord Hayford—John Hayford?"

Alex's spoon clattered to the plate, splattering ice cream on her dress. "How clumsy of me," she said quietly, taking her napkin to rub off the stains. She suddenly felt suffocated, as if the room had become airless. "Is he here? In this country, I mean," she finally said.

"Why, no. He's on his way over to see the location I believe."

Alex sat back and looked across at Tom. Jesse patted her hand again. "His character I can vouch for," she said at last. "It's despicable. As for his business sense, well...he's a gambler, a womanizer, a drunk and—oh yes, a wife beater. At least he was for the four days I was married to him."

Chapter Twenty-Four

July fourth fell on a Thursday but by Saturday, when the party was to be held, the heat was so intense the men claimed sweat was drying before it showed. Cattle had either pushed each other into the river or lain down on the grassland as if ready to sleep. Alex looked over the herd briefly but everything shimmered in the distance like a watercolor that had streaked. She wore her hat way down on her face and her hands in gloves to protect her skin from the ferocious sun, but later decided the best thing was to sit in a bath all day. Men working to put down the boards and tables for the evening's party had stripped off their shirts, the first time she could ever remember seeing them do that—although when she rode back in, Beesley hurriedly pulled his shirt back on.

"What'll it be like with torches lit?" she asked Tom who was helping out.

"Lord only knows. Hopefully it'll be a might cooler after dusk but maybe we'll use more lanterns and light fewer torches."

Alex liked the July fourth party. In fact, she decided, she loved it. She loved the regularity of the seasons as they came around, the special holiday dates, the ranch year, the knowledge of what lay ahead relieved by what one couldn't foresee. It gave her a sense of belonging and community, of continuity, of place and time. It gave her a sense of permanence.

Sunset spread itself on the horizon like a fire through the trees. As she walked across from the main house she guessed that everyone was there, including Garrett hobbling around on a crutch with his one-legged pants and his cast. "Better late than never," he observed as she stopped to chat with him. "I thought you wore dresses to parties."

"Couldn't pull myself out of the bath, as it happens, and then the thought of all those petticoats... Which reminds me, don't get that plaster wet. It'll disintegrate and we'll have to do it all again."

Coates came over to ask her to dance and she went off, observing Jesse and Cal across the floor with Sara Beth and the Yosts. They waved as she went out on the floor and took her place in a line. Jesse took Annie out while Tom took his daughter, but the heat soon got to Alex and she excused herself at the end of the dance.

She helped Garrett to a plate of food and stayed by him to give him company. Various punchers came over to talk with them and would then wander off but Alex just liked watching. Jesse, she saw, kept busy with Sue Ann and then Millie and Sara Beth, gentleman that he was.

"I hope you're gonna eat," said Annie, suddenly behind her. "Look at these ribs. You'll like those."

"Did you make them?" Alex asked.

"I may have," Annie replied coyly, coaxing her friend. "Look, they're pork, and the sauce, Tom says, is my best."

Alex gingerly lifted one from the platter and bit into it. The sauce dripped down her chin and she laughed, bending slightly over the table so it wouldn't go on her shirt. There was a quick tap on her shoulder and she straightened up but knew from Annie's expression it was Jesse. She turned to face him, rib in hand.

He shook his head disparaging of her, took the rib from her hand and put it on a plate, then shook out a handkerchief and wiped her chin. "Want to dance?" he asked.

She looked at him a moment, taking in the burn he had got on his nose, the shaggy hair that was bleaching from the sun now, and the freckles that were darkening. Her heart lurched. "I thought you'd never ask," she replied.

He put an arm around her and pulled her to him, but just stood there for a moment as if they might melt into each other. She thought he might kiss her but instead he said, "Want to get married?"

Her sun-up smile spread across her face and she gazed at him for a long moment. "I thought you'd never ask."

Jesse's hold got tighter but before Alex knew what was happening, he lifted her and put her over his shoulder. Alex laughed. "Jesse, put me down," she giggled. "Put me down!" He moved off toward the shadows with her, into the dark, and she couldn't stop laughing. The whole party was laughing for the most part, watching Jesse walk off with Alex thrown over his shoulder.

"Jesse Makepeace!" She giggled trying to be stern, hammering on his back. "You put me down this minute! This instant! Jesse! Jesse! I'll be sick," she threatened, "I'll be sick all down your back!"

But he kept on going. He had her now and he wasn't about to let go. Not until he got her back to the house.

****

Everyone at the Faringdon knew, of course. They knew about the empty space in the bunk house, knew about the garden doors left open for more than a summer breeze, knew about the arrangements being made for an August wedding. A discreet silence encircled the couple. What happened at the ranch was no one else's business as the men had always maintained. And if Tom and Annie knew, they also knew August was just around the corner.

The 27th fell on a Tuesday but it was Alex's twenty-first birthday and Jesse insisted that was the day. The wedding would be held late afternoon and people could take time off work as if it were a Saturday. David had been wired although it was doubtful he could now arrive in time. Tom would give Alex away and Cal would be best man. Arrangements went ahead.

Alex threw herself into it—invitations only to people they both liked (Miss Bea but not the Hendersons), hothouse flowers, champagne, food, extra staff, a request for the dress wired to Monsieur Worth in Paris, along with measurements of Sue Ann and Annie for bridesmaids. It would be similar to Alex's eighteenth birthday party with the ceremony in the garden and the reception over at the corrals done up for a sit-down dinner. They just hoped they could pay for it all.

They went to see the minister to get permission to hold the wedding at the house.

"Ah, Lady Alexandra, just the person I wanted to see," he said as they entered his study.

Alex panicked for a moment and threw a quick glance at Jesse. She thought she was about to be scolded for her immoral behavior so she tucked her skirts about her and primly sat, as if a newfound decorum might put things to rights. "You wanted to see me?" she inquired at last.

"Yes, I have a huge favor to ask." The reverend sat forward in his seat a bit, clasped his hands on his desk and cleared his throat. "I wonder if there is any chance of you donating a painting for the church drive. You see, we're trying to raise funds for a new roof and we're having an auction in a couple of weeks. I thought perhaps a small painting of yours might be auctioned off. People are donating all sorts of things, mostly items they no longer want, but—"

"Really, Reverend, say no more." Alex breathed with relief. "I'd be delighted. I have a view of Loveland, which I just finished and I think will do."

"That would be perfect. Thank you!" He sat back. "But I take it you came to see me about something?" His face lit with a slight smile.

"Yes," said Jesse. "You may have heard that Lady Alex and I are gettin' married." He waited for the minister's acknowledgement. "We're hopin', of course, that you'll perform the ceremony but, thing is, we'd like it over at the house, in fact out in the garden if the weather holds."

"I don't see why not," the minister said amiably, "as long as it is held in a Christian manner and everyone behaves."

Alex looked at Jesse and he knew what she was thinking: Miss Bea. Neither of them said a word. By the time the minister would be aware of their guest, it would be too late. "In any event," as Alex said to Jesse later, "what could be more Christian than to have a fallen woman as a guest?"

"Well, the dang bride's a fallen woman, if you ask me. Half the state knows what's been going on," Jesse replied, though he said it smiling.

Alex liked having Jesse in her bed. Even in the searing nights of the July heat wave, she liked the comfort of his body next to hers, his arms wrapped around her, his breath on her neck, their legs entwined. She inhaled the scents he brought with him, of leather and grass and sweat and smoke. She loved his weight on top of her and the rhythm of their two bodies moving. She didn't mind the sweat that trickled between her breasts or dripped sometimes from his face to hers, nor the whole messiness of lovemaking. She loved listening to his breathing, to his sighs, to the quiet little gasps of pleasure, and loved that he knew her, too, knew her body intimately, what she was comfortable with, what pleasured her. And most of all she loved being able to lose herself with him, to let everything go and to forget whatever demons held her past because now there was a future—a beautiful, endless, happy future.

And yet...

And yet at the back of her mind was a sense of losing something, a part of herself, her freedom, the liberties she had been granted in leaving England. Weighing up those losses against having Jesse forever she knew she would choose, always choose Jesse. And yet...and yet...

****

The church auction, held in the town hall at Loveland, garnered a big attendance. All the men who were off from the Double F, including Cal and Garrison along with Millie, came in to see if there were any bargains to be had or small items they might purchase for a sweetheart. Ranchers, including the Hendersons, and townspeople like the Benders were all there too. The Yost's couldn't make it because J.J. had come down with a fever and Annie wouldn't leave him, so Alex and Jesse took the buggy in on their own to see how her painting sold.

The number of people gathered in the early August heat made the room so oppressive that Alex thought it best to stand at the side near the open doors rather than be seated. Jesse, in his Sunday suit, was also uncomfortable, and although Alex told him to take off his jacket, he said if she could stay in that fancy French dress of hers, he could stay in his suit.

The minister had got in an auctioneer from Denver for the occasion and it turned into quite a show. There were saddles, both used and hardly used—"Should have got rid of the blasted side saddle," commented Alex—old gas lamps, fine china, odd pieces of silver. People had a good laugh at a doll with which someone had sadly parted, a set of lace antimacassars, and a pair of sheep shears, which got booed by the ranchers. Alex spotted Cal and Garrison standing together at the other side of the room near the back door, and she saw them stomp and catcall when the shears were offered.

"Anything you want, you let me know," said Jesse, rubbing her neck lightly.

"I don't want anything except you," she replied looking up at him with a smile. "Anything you want?"

"Oh, I might bid on that painting by that funny woman. What's her name again?"

Cal bid on some silver spurs but didn't get them, and Beesley timidly raised his hand once for an old Army Colt but gave up. Garrison bought Millie an embroidered reticule, which made him hero for a day, and Terry managed to get himself a silver slide for his bolo. Alex's painting had been touted as the highlight of the evening, which seemed somehow to go on forever. A few people had left, which made the room less cramped and stuffy in the heat, but the clanging of the back door with people coming and going gave Alex a headache by the time her painting came up for auction.

"And now," called out the auctioneer, "last but most certainly not least," he said in his resonant voice, "we have this beautiful painting, aptly titled Loveland, by Lady Alexandra Calthorpe."

"Good thing I sign my paintings Alex," she remarked to Jesse, "or I'd have to think about changing them all."

"No, you wouldn't." He pulled her to him and put his arms about her waist so she could rest her head back against him for a moment.

"I understand Lady Alexandra's paintings sell for a good deal of money in New York City," the auctioneer went on, "so I hope you've been saving up for this. Let's not be shy. I'll start the bidding at twenty-five dollars even."

"Fifty!" shouted Jesse shooting his hand up.

"Oh, for goodness sake, Jess, we haven't got that kind of money with the wedding and all. And I can paint you another one."

"Two hundred," came a voice from the back.

Alex stiffened. She turned slowly as Jesse shouted out, "Three!" but when Alex turned back to him, the color was drained from her face. She swayed slightly as he looked down at her and the other man shouted, "One thousand dollars!"

The audience gasped.

Jesse saw the well-dressed stranger at the back and understood. In that moment, such hatred welled up in him, he felt himself losing control. There was a rifle in the buggy but he wasn't wearing a sidearm and his hands went sweaty with the knowledge.

Alex just stood there staring at him, her face becoming more ghostly by the second. Jesse made a movement with his head, signaling Cal. While the auctioneer waved his hands to quiet the audience, Cal and Garrison moved to either side of the stranger and hustled him out the back door. Alex suddenly moved to the side door. Jesse followed.

As Jesse grabbed Alex's hand and the couple came around from the side of the hall, the stranger tried to struggle out of the grasp of the two punchers, forcing Cal to trip him. Lord John Hayford fell, and then looked up at the two men before spotting Alex.

"Ah, Alexandra my darling, my angel," the young lord scorned her from his place on the walkway.

"What are you doing here, John?" she almost spat.

"Come to see you, of course, my precious, my

dear wife."

Jesse flinched but Cal and Garrison still stood guard either side of the almost prone visitor.

"Why now, Johnny, why now? I'm not your wife, you know that. The marriage was lawfully annulled nearly three years ago. I have the papers." Jesse paced a few steps away from her, then turned back and watched. "You know that, Johnny, you're wasting your time here."

"But my sweetheart..." he continued.

Cal gave him a hard kick in the side. "Let's not get too friendly. I think your business here might be finished, mister."

"Oh, I think not." John Hayford rested back on his left hand, while making a grand gesture with his right. "You see, I'm really used to having what I want, paintings and artwork. Or women..."

But it was at Jesse he was pointing.

"No!" Alex rushed to push Jesse out of the derringer's line of fire.

The shot rang out.

Alex gasped and sank in Jesse's arms.

Jesse just held Alex, rocking her as he had when she was small.

Chapter Twenty-Five

"Metal stays," said the doctor, noticing how the corset built into Alex's dress was almost like a suit of armor. "Dang bullet just bounced right off them things, thank the Lord. Poor child, fainted dead away."

When Jesse had realized there was no blood anywhere on Alex, he carried her to Miss Bea's with the doctor at his heels. Smelling salts soon brought her around and Miss Bea offered her a shot of whiskey, which Alex declined.

"That bastard," Alex said when she had revived a bit. "He put a hole in my Worth gown, didn't he? I won't be getting many more of these."

Jesse laughed. Then he laughed a bit more and a little bit more. "You crazy woman," he said, holding her to him, "what am I gonna do 'bout you?"

"Marry her for chrissake, Jess," Miss Bea advised, "'fore the whole town comes out to tar and feather you both. Church auction, indeed. I tell ya, if ya hadn'ta gone to arrange your wedding that minister would be ex-communicatin' the two of yous. Or whatever it is they do in that stuck-up Church." Bea took a swig of her own liquor. "Jess ever leaves you, sweetheart, I tell ya, you come work for me."

****

"I don't know," moaned Alex. "You'd think with electricity and telephones now over in Utah and Kansas there would have been some way of contacting David. The whole bloody northeast of the country has got all those things. This is a modern world yet I still can't locate my brother. Nor

Monsieur Worth. What do I do if we don't get the bloody dresses in time?"

"Well, for a start," answered Jesse gently, "let's hope they're not bloody dresses. We don't want them ruined 'fore you've even had a chance to wear 'em."

"Funny, very funny."

Jesse kissed the top of her head. "You'll manage. You always do," he said as he went off to work. Yet he knew she was getting wound up over details, and if things didn't improve she would panic badly.

When Tom asked later that day how things were going, Jesse replied, "We should've eloped, truth be told, but we wanted ever'one to be with us, to celebrate. Sooner this is over, the better."

"Well, I got some good news anyway," said Tom, and he showed Jesse a telegram he was holding.

****

They had decided to have a rehearsal and dinner a few days before the wedding so Alex could thereafter relax and calm down a bit, and Jesse could be entertained to a last bachelor night by the men. With the dresses still not arrived, and no word from David, Alex was wound like a guitar string tuned too tight. But that wasn't the only thing bothering her. What was bothering her she could no longer put into words. She was too absorbed in the minutiae of planning the wedding to define what niggled her, fretted her constantly and drove her to tears for no reason at all. Jesse was aware of this, watched the growing signs, and kept his thoughts to himself without worrying. He tried to keep a steady influence on Alex and calm her down the best he could.

The night of the dinner, Alex came down in her gray silk evening dress, her auburn hair falling in tendrils from one side, flowers set in it, already looking like a bride. Everyone was gathered in the drawing room, the minister included, and the company of such good friends composed her.

"We're moving one of those small organs, for Miss Hegarty to play, into the area by the door there if that's all right," said Tom.

"I saw the Allen sisters in town," said Annie, "and they say the flowers will be perfect. They're coming out early on Tuesday to put everything in place."

"I don't really mind if I haven't got a Parisian dress," Sue Ann said encouragingly. "I'll get one another time!"

Alex had to laugh; she knew they were all trying to help and she knew things would be fine. Most of all, she knew it didn't really matter. She could get married in any old dress and her friends wouldn't care, just so long as they were all together.

Jesse took her hand and gazed at her a long moment that ended with a decisive sigh. He turned to the minister. "Rev'rend," he said. "You know them bits the bride says about love, cherish, honor and *obey*?"

"Of course. The vows."

"Yeah." Jess looked again at Alex. "I think we gotta leave out that obey bit if y'all don't mind. We don't wanna make a liar outta the bride on her wedding day."

There was knowing laughter before the minister asked, "Well, shall we start? I shall be waiting at the end of this walkway, is that correct?"

Jesse showed him how the curtains would be drawn open to the French doors from the house into the garden and the bridesmaids, followed by Alex and Tom, would come down the path between the seating for the guests. He and Cal would be off to the side at the front by the other little steps down to the covered walkway. "Shall we try this, then?"

Cal, Jesse and the minister got into position, Cal humming some tune no one recognized for the bridal march, and Annie followed Sue Ann at a slow walk down the path. Alex moved past the curtains to the head of the path and an arm slipped through hers— but it wasn't Tom's. She looked up and there was David, smiling mischievously. Everyone laughed.

Alex burst into tears.

"Hello, what's this then?" David asked, taking Alex into his arms. "I thought you'd be happy to see me."

"I thought you weren't coming," she sobbed into his shoulder. "I thought you couldn't make it, that the wire didn't reach you." She sniffed. "I hate surprises, David!" She stomped her foot. "You know that!" She took his proffered handkerchief, then turned to look down the aisle at Jesse. "You're horrible!" she said, trying not to smile. "And you, Tom Yost. It was plain mean to do this to me."

"Oh, now, Alex," Tom said soothingly, "the dresses are here, too, so everything's going to be just fine. No more surprises. I promise."

"Oh, the dresses are here!" Sue Ann said excitedly, "Can I see mine?"

Alex wouldn't have Jesse in her bed after that evening. She was too superstitious, she said, to tempt fate. In any event, Jesse threw himself into work the last few days trying to put things in order before they went on their wedding trip. They had thought about Texas after Norris Beckett's visit, but Jesse decided it was best left until the air had cleared a bit over John Hayford and his fellow British investors. They considered going to see San Francisco and the Pacific Ocean since neither of them had been far west and, certainly, Jesse had never been in a large city, but Alex said she'd rather go someplace that didn't require dressing up evenings and dealing with fancy hotels. So, in the end they happily decided on going up to the Boyd retreat for three nights and then continuing on to the new Yellowstone National Park to see the geysers and the country up into Montana.

The day of the wedding Alex was up at 5 a.m. pacing her room, trying to think things through, be sure everything was as it should be. She could hear the men going out on herd and the servants moving about downstairs, speaking in low voices thinking she was still asleep. She sat at her dressing table to look at herself, and noted the darkness under her eyes from lack of sleep and the light honey color her skin had taken on from the summer sun. She got up and opened the French doors to let the air in and heard the birds calling to each other like neighbors in a tenement as they started their day. The view down the garden was glorious. It was going to be perfect weather.

Alex strode the length of the room a few minutes, took a deep breath, then rang for Rose. Soon she heard her maid coming up the stairs, a teaspoon dancing on a saucer.

"You're early," Rose commented, setting the tray out on the dressing table. "Shall I run your bath now, M'lady?"

Alex stood there looking at her faithful, dear old Rose. She plunked down on the bed. "No. Yes. Oh, no, Rose. I don't think so. Later maybe."

"Maybe? Maybe? You do know, M'Lady, you're getting married today. I think perhaps there is no maybe about having a bath."

"No. Yes. Yes." Alex put her head in her hands.

"Oh, dear." Rose looked down at her. "I wouldn't think you'd be having wedding nerves, I'm sure." She stood there a moment. "You haven't a headache, have you?"

"No, no. I think I need to sleep some more. That's it. I have to go back to sleep." With that Alex crawled back under the sheet and waved Rose away.

"Oh, for goodness sake," Rose commented as she

went out.

But Alex couldn't sleep. She lay there, her eyes wide open, staring across at the wedding dress hanging on the front of her linen press, the lace mantilla she had chosen to wear instead of a veil thrown over the shoulder. Annie and Rose had worked the last several days on doing minor adjustments to both Alex's and Sue Ann's dresses—Alex's because she had gained a bit of weight since sending M. Worth the measurements, Sue Ann's because she had grown a tiny bit. The only one that had fit perfectly was Annie's, and she had been so delighted with it, it almost moved Alex to tears. "A Parisian dress," Annie had exclaimed putting it on, "me in a real Parisian dress at my age!"

"When I grow up," said Sue Ann, "I shall have dozens of Parisian dresses, just like Lady Alex, and wear them all the time."

And Alex had said the dresses didn't make her happy, they were just adornment. Only her friends made her happy—which was true.

They were such good people, all of them. Studious, quiet J.J. Ebullient Sue Ann, who was reaching for the stars—and why not? thought Alex. And her dear surrogate parents, Tom and Annie. They only wished her well, only ever wanted her happiness. As did the punchers—not a bad man in the lot, the dearest best friends a girl could want.

And Jesse. Her Jesse now. Her best friend, her lover, her soul-mate, her life. What was more important, making Jesse happy or her freedom, her independence? Were the two mutually exclusive? Did they need to be wed for Jesse to be happy? She knew she loved him more than she would ever love anyone, knew she couldn't live without him there in her life, knew she wanted his children, wanted to see him every single day, be with him, make love to him. Annie had once said freedom was having a choice, but was marrying Jesse the right choice? Could she have a career and still keep Jesse happy? An artist's career was not just about exhibitions in galleries—she knew this now. There were commissions, commissions that took you away from your home, from your family. Would all of that be fair to Jesse?

At one pm, Rose knocked on the door again to find Alex just sitting, staring at herself in the mirror, breakfast still untouched. "I'll run the bath now, M'lady. It's three hours to go and there's ever such a lot to do."

Alex listened to the rumble of the pump kicking in downstairs and the water filling her tub. She heard the voices of the Allen twins as they set out the flowers, made adjustments, discussed a few changes. The perfume drifted in on the breeze making her slightly somnolent as she sat with her head in her hands. When she heard the familiar screech of Rose shutting off the taps, she rose as if sleep-walking and went to bathe.

"M'lady?" Rose called through the door a while later. "Are you all right?" she asked somewhat nervously.

Alex took a deep breath. The water was rapidly cooling as she continued to just sit there. "Yes, Rose, I'm fine."

Rose helped Alex dry off and dress into her pantalets, stockings and a dressing gown while her hair was done. They had decided, against all fashion, to pull it as straight back as could be, letting the natural curls frame her face with ringlets at the back. Since Alex had come to believe curling irons ruined the hair and burnt it, Rose brushed it back, fixed it with combs and wound thick strands of it into numerous ribbons so it would dry into tendrils.

"You should eat something," Rose said as she fixed in the last ribbon. "You don't want your stomach grumbling as you say *I do*." Alex didn't reply so Rose put the brush down and left to get a tray. "The Yosts are here now," she said as she returned a bit later. "Wilson has shown them to the blue guest room to change for the wedding. I told them you weren't dressed."

"It's fine," said Alex. She picked a bit at the food set in front of her while Rose shook out the dress, checked it over, and got it ready to put on. She pulled Alex's new shoes from the wardrobe and laid them out. "I can't eat any more." Alex pushed the tray away.

"All right, I'll take it down. You sit a moment and then we'll dress."

Alex sat wearily listening to Rose's retreating footsteps. She knew she was being uncooperative, that Rose would be worrying and might approach Annie for help, yet she couldn't seem to shake the niggling qualms. Trying to show some inclination to be dressed and ready for the wedding, Alex started to remove the ribbons from her hair, which was still damp.

"I thought we were leaving that for last," Rose muttered as she entered.

Alex stopped, got up and put her hands up for the dress to be slid over her. She stayed silent as Rose hooked up first the inside corset, then the outside, nor did she speak as Rose stooped to push the shoes on her feet. She sat back down, without a word for the hair dressing to be finished when there was a knock on the door.

"Nearly time," called Annie through the door. "Do you need any help?"

Rose hesitated, saw Alex in the mirror shake her head, and called back, "No, Mrs. Yost, we're fine. We'll be down in a minute."

Alex knew Annie was still standing there a moment, then heard her proceed downstairs talking quietly to Sue Ann as she did so.

"That's it then," said Rose as she pulled the last ribbon from Alex's ringlets. She took down the matching mantilla and fixed it into Alex's hair to just cover the curls at the back, then gently put her hands on the girl's shoulders. "You look beautiful," she whispered. "Now all we need is a smile."

But there was none. Alex stood up and Rose lifted her train and followed her to the top of the stairs where she stood for a minute listening to the happy bantering going on in the drawing room— Tom telling his wife he still owed her a wedding trip and if she was going to look like that, it was probably time he paid up; David inviting them to visit him anytime they wanted and suggesting England might be a nice belated wedding trip; Sue Ann twirling around and singing to herself. It was Sue Ann who first saw Alex at the top of the steps and gasped. Everyone rushed to look and just stood there gaping up at Alex.

"Well, I'll be," whispered Tom.

David smiled. "Yes, she cleans up rather well, my sister. One is always surprised when one sees Alex out of that cowboy outfit she insists on wearing."

Alex started slowly down the stairs, the train flowing behind her like a silken river. She saw the expectant, happy faces, heard the low hum of guests settling into their seats and the hurried movements of last minute adjustments going on outside. Then she stopped. Two-thirds of the way down she looked at Tom and David, her face slowly creasing as if invisible hands had pressed it in. She burst into tears and sat clumsily on the step.

"I can't do this!" she cried, her hand to her mouth, "I can't marry Jesse. I can't!" She sat there sobbing uncontrollably, everyone looking at her.

Tom and David rushed to either side of her, Annie standing below. "Alex, sweetheart," she said soothingly, "it's just nerves. Why, all brides get them. You'll be fine. It will all be fine."

"Of course it will," Sue Ann said brightly, but Annie waved her away.

"No, you don't understand," moaned Alex. "It'll kill him. I'll just make him so unhappy. I can't do that. He'll end up hating me."

Tom looked briefly at David who mirrored his own perplexed expression. "Now, Alex," he said as calmly as he could muster. "You know that's not true. Jesse loves you more than anything. And you love him. What'll make him unhappy is if you leave him standing there at the altar and don't marry him. Now, you can't do that to—"

"Shall I start the music?" called Miss Hegarty through the French door.

Annie went to tell her they'd be a few more minutes. She took a peek and saw Jesse and Cal standing at the top of the aisle all ready, as was the minister who looked her way with a raised brow. "Someone ought to go out and say we're running a bit late," Annie said, a small hint of worry showing in her voice.

"Come on, darling," David said. "This is nonsense now. Pull yourself—"

"No!" cried Alex starting to sob again. "I can't. I just can't do it," she said, the tears running down her face.

Tom took David aside. "Best go have a word with Jess," he said. "See what he thinks."

"The groom shouldn't see the bride before the wedding," Sue Ann piped up.

"No dear." Tom patted her shoulder and led David out.

They walked hurriedly down the aisle, past the guests who were murmuring amongst themselves, and on toward a smiling Jesse. The groom had had his hair cut a bit and was wearing a new dress suit and shoes, looking very elegant for a man who spent most of his life in the saddle, in dust and all weathers. Jesse's smile widened as they approached, and he started to reach around in his pockets looking for something.

"How we doin'?" he said with a huge grin. Cal chuckled a bit beside him.

"We have a problem," said Tom barely audibly. "She's refusing to come out. She says—"

"Oh, heck, Tom, I know what she says," Jesse interrupted quite calmly. "It'll be fine...if I ever find..."

"You expected this?" Tom said in disbelief.

"'Course I did. Been expectin' it all along. The only dang surprise is you two didn't see this coming. How long you known her, Tom? How long she been your sister, David? You mean to stand there and tell me you didn't think this would happen? You thought she'd just mosey on down the aisle pleased as punch and ever'thing would be just fine and dandy?"

He stopped to shake his head at Cal who was laughing quietly there beside him, then finally found what he was looking for and pulled it out of his inside pocket. He looked briefly at the folded paper, turned it over and handed it to Tom. "Here, give this to her," he said. "Ever'thing'll be fine. I promise."

David and Tom looked at one another, then turned around and went back to the house. They stood before Alex who was still sniffing, seated on the step. Tom said, "Jesse sent you this," and he handed her the creased and crinkled piece of paper.

Alex sniffed some more as she unfolded it, looked at it, and gurgled a bit. The gurgle became a giggle and the giggle became a laugh and the laughter got loud enough for guests outside the door to hear and start laughing a bit with her. She stood up and tucked into her bodice the old drawing Jesse had done that night at Boyd, the first night they had made love.

She ran her hands down her dress to remove the creases and came down the last few steps to walk slowly toward the front window where her bouquet lay on the table. She glanced out and across to see the corral, the flowers, the ribbons, the torches set out. The extra serving staff they had hired was scurrying about. And in front was Ranger, also beribboned with white flowers—and the old English sidesaddle on his back. "Bloody punchers' humor," Alex murmured to herself. "You just have to love them."

Miss Hegarty put her face around the door again. "Shall I start the music yet?" she asked somewhat timidly.

"Oh, for heavens' sake, yes," replied Alex laughing, giving Tom and David each an arm.

The bridal march played, silencing the guests who stood at last, and Sue Ann and Annie started down the aisle.

In the late afternoon sunshine of that August day, Jesse Makepeace turned to meet his bride.

Author's Note

In writing this book I have tried to recreate the atmosphere, language, mannerisms, etiquette and dress of the Colorado of the 1880s as faithfully as possible. While not all of the books mentioned below are exactly specific to that time and location, they do cover the period of the late 19th and very early 20th centuries and are local to the western states of both the USA and Canada. All of the following memoirs have been indispensable:

Abbott, E.C. "Teddy Blue" and Smith, Helen Huntington: We Pointed Them North: Recollections of a Cowpuncher, University of Oklahoma Press, Norman, 1955;

Bronson, Edgar Beecher: Reminiscences of a Ranchman, General Books, Breinigsville, 2009 (reprint)

Blasingame, Ike: Dakota Cowboy: My Life in the Old Days, University of Nebraska Press, Lincoln, 1958

Hobson Jr., Richmond P.: Grass Beyond the Mountains, McClelland and Stewart, Toronto, 1951; et. seq.

Nothing Too Good for a Cowboy, 1955

The Rancher Takes A Wife, 1961

Russell, Charles M.: Trails Plowed Under: Stories of the Old West, University of Nebraska Press, Lincoln, 1996 (reprint of Doubleday ed., 1927).

I also found useful:

Adams, Andy: The Log of a Cowboy: a Narrative of the Old Trail Days, Feather Trail Press, Lexington, 2009 (reprint from 1903). Although the book was fiction, it was based on the author's personal experience of an 1882 trail drive;

Enss, Chris: How the West was Worn: Bustles and

Buckskins on the Wild Frontier, Twodot, Guilford, 2006

Morison, Samuel Eliot: History of the American People, Oxford University Press, New York, 1965.

I am further indebted to the City of Loveland Museum-Gallery for its many fascinating and informative exhibits.

My description of the terrible winter of 1886-87, which was believed to be a second Ice Age (!), was gleaned from almost all of the above-mentioned as well as the web site: http://www.wyomingtalesandtrails.com/index.html

This site also clearly discusses the formation of the huge cattle companies by British investors, mainly various lesser members of the aristocracy such as Moreton Frewen, who was Winston Churchill's uncle and thereby related to the Duke of Marlborough.

For information on Greeley, I used: www.greeleygov.com./museums/Historyof Greeley.aspx

My apologies to the people of the Loveland/Greeley area for playing around somewhat with their geography for the purposes of fiction. Any other mistakes in the representations of this area and history were purely unintentional and my own.

A word about the author...

Andrea Downing was born in New York but has lived most of her life in the U.K. where she received her master's degree from Keele University. She has co-edited a poetry magazine and worked both in publishing and education.

In 2008 she returned to live in the U.S.A. and visits the West frequently, the area of the country she loves best.

She is a member of Romance Writers of America and Women Writing the West. *Loveland* is her first novel.

http://andreadowning.com
Twitter: @andidowning

Thank you for purchasing
this publication of The Wild Rose Press, Inc.
For other wonderful stories of romance,
please visit our on-line bookstore at
www.thewildrosepress.com.

For questions or more information
contact us at
info@thewildrosepress.com.

The Wild Rose Press, Inc.
www.thewildrosepress.com

To visit with authors of
The Wild Rose Press, Inc.
join our yahoo loop at
http://groups.yahoo.com/group/thewildrosepress/

www.ingramcontent.com/pod-product-compliance
Lightning Source LLC
Chambersburg PA
CBHW070903180626
46817CB00003B/898